One
LAST
SPRING

OTHER BOOKS AND AUDIO BOOKS
BY SIAN ANN BESSEY

Forgotten Notes

Cover of Darkness

Family Is Forever

Kids on a Mission: Escape from Germany

Kids on a Mission: Uprising in Samoa

Kids on a Mission: Ambushed in Africa

Teddy Bear, Blankie, and a Prayer

Deception

Within the Dark Hills

You Came for Me

The Insider

One LAST SPRING

a novel by

Sian Ann Bessey

Covenant Communications, Inc.

Cover image: *Lake Vyrnwy* © JacquiMartin, courtesy istockphoto.com; Figure photography by McKenzie Deakins, www.mckenziedeakins.com.

Cover design copyright © 2015 by Covenant Communications, Inc.

Published by Covenant Communications, Inc.
American Fork, Utah

Printed in the United States of America
First Printing: November 2015

21 20 19 18 17 16   10 9 8 7 6 5 4 3 2

ISBN 978-1-68047-638-5

For my father, Noel Lewis Owen,
who has waited a long time for this story,
and for his great-grandfather Erasmus Owen,
who was the blacksmith in Llanwddyn when the
Vyrnwy Dam was built.

Acknowledgments

SPECIAL THANKS TO EMYR AND Carys Evans of Llansilin and Michael Duggleby of Llanwddyn for all the help they gave me while I was researching the history of the Vyrnwy Dam. The material they shared helped bring this story to life.

Thank you also to my husband, Kent, who makes my writing possible, and to my editor, Samantha Millburn, who makes my writing stronger.

Glossary

BACH—Welsh for "small" or "little"; used as a term of endearment

BACON BUTTY—Bread and butter with slices of cooked bacon

BARA BRITH—Welsh for "speckled bread," a traditional Welsh bread served at teatime and made with dried fruit

CARIAD—Welsh for "love," "darling," or "sweetheart"

COFFERS OF OATMEAL—Oatmeal was a staple for the people of Llanwddyn; every home had a coffer (or large chest) where the oatmeal was kept

COFION CYNNES—Welsh for "warm remembrances/regards"; often used at the close of a letter

CONKER—The fruit of a horse chestnut tree; used to play a game called conkers

CREMPOG—A small, fat pancake

DAU GI BACH—Welsh for "Three Little Dogs," a traditional Welsh children's nursery rhyme

EISTEDDFOD—A Welsh folk festival and competition featuring singing, dancing, reciting poetry, etc.

FORTNIGHT—Two weeks

JAC Y DO—Welsh for "Jackdaw," a member of the crow family; the name of a traditional Welsh children's song

NAVVY—A manual laborer, particularly one employed in a civil engineering project; originally short for "navigators," the men who built the first navigation canals in eighteenth-century Britain

PATTENS—A shoe or clog with a raised sole or set in an iron ring; worn to raise one's feet above wet or muddy ground when walking outdoors

PONT CEDIG—Cedig Bridge

HUW FAWR—*Huw* is the Welsh form of the name "Hugh"; *Fawr* means "big"

TAFFY—An English slang name for someone from Wales

WELSH CAKES—Small griddle cakes made with dried fruit

WINBERRIES—Also known as bilberries; native to Britain, a small, round, dark-purple berry

Prologue

THE VILLAGE OF LLANWDDYN LOOKED much like many of the other small communities nestled in the protective valleys of mid-Wales. Gray river-rock houses with purple slate roofs were common enough in that part of the country. So were the neighboring sheep farms sprinkled across the rolling green hillsides. But to those who lived there, the beauty of the area was inseparably connected to a feeling of belonging—of knowing they were walking the paths generations of family members had walked before. For them, there was nowhere else quite like Llanwddyn. It was their home. And in September 1880, they learned they were to lose it.

Rumors had been flying for almost a year. It had all started with the arrival of two tight-lipped Englishmen who spent three weeks in the village, hauling mysterious boxfuls of equipment up and down the hills, measuring and recording their findings in a black, leather-bound book. Owen Morgan, the blacksmith, who spoke the best English in the village, couldn't get anything out of them about what they were doing or why. All they'd say was that they worked for the Liverpool Corporation and that any questions should be directed to their office. They left Llanwddyn with no one in the village any the wiser.

A few months after the Englishmen left, the Earl of Powys sent his foreman, Jack Gittens, to the village. Virtually everyone in

Llanwddyn was a tenant of the Earl of Powys, and they knew his foreman well. Mr. Gittens had a reputation for being a decent, fair-minded man, and whenever his work brought him to the area, he'd stop in at the Powys Arms so he could catch up on all the comings and goings of the village.

Although he was generally well liked, there was no doubt Mr. Gittens took great pride in his position on the earl's staff and in his superior view of the world from the back of his horse. On that particular day, however, as he rode his horse through the village, he didn't seem to sit quite as tall in the saddle as he usually did. Rhys Jones, the tailor, and William Richards, the sexton, called out friendly greetings as he passed, but he responded with little more than a slight nod of his head. And when he reached Pont Cedig, the bridge at the center of the village, he steered his mare away from the road that led to the Powys Arms and toward the village hall instead.

Once at the village hall, Mr. Gittens got off his horse and drew a folded piece of paper from his jacket pocket. Taking a hammer from his saddlebag, he nailed the piece of paper to the door. Then he mounted his horse and rode back the way he'd come without exchanging a word with anyone. By then, he didn't need to say anything. His grim expression told the villagers all they needed to know. He'd brought bad news.

Within seconds people began gathering in front of the village hall's front door, and it didn't take long for someone to send for Owen Morgan. By the time the blacksmith arrived, a large crowd had assembled. Not many of them could read Welsh; even fewer could read English, so they relied on the blacksmith to tell them what the notice said. Owen read it slowly and deliberately, his face becoming more and more grave.

"What's it all about, Owen?" someone called out.

"Yes!" A general cry of agreement rumbled through the crowd. "What does it say?"

Owen turned around. "As near as I can tell," he said, raising his flat cap a little and wiping his forehead with his sleeve, "the English government has given permission to the Liverpool Corporation to build a dam here in the Vyrnwy valley." He looked out over the people in front of him, his jaw working as he tried to control his emotions. "They're going to flood the village."

There was a moment of stunned silence before everyone started talking at once. As the cries of consternation increased, Reverend Jones crossed the road and made his way up the village hall steps.

"Now, now!" he said, his sonorous preaching voice carrying over the noise of the crowd. "Let's make sure we understand things properly."

The cries became whispers as the villagers watched Reverend Jones quietly consult with Owen Morgan before turning to read the document himself. Minutes ticked by, and as more and more people joined the waiting throng, the tension mounted. At last Reverend Jones cleared his throat loudly, and complete silence fell over the crowd again.

"Thank you for your patience," Reverend Jones said. "This is not easy news to hear or to deliver."

He paused, his eyes flitting from one anxious face to another. "The paper Mr. Gittens hung on the village hall door today is an official notice to the people of Llanwddyn of the passage of the Liverpool Corporation Act.

"It appears that on the sixth of August, royal assent was given to the city of Liverpool to develop a reservoir in the Vyrnwy valley, along with an aqueduct that will pipe the collected water north to the city of Liverpool.

"According to this paper, the building of the dam will necessitate the relocation of the village of Llanwddyn."

"Relocation?" someone shouted incredulously. "How do they think that's going to happen? Some big giant's going to appear from underneath the Berwyn mountains, pick up our houses, and drop them in another valley?"

Reverend Jones shook his head sadly. "All property owners will be compensated. The Liverpool Corporation is to rebuild a new village a mile farther down the valley. Once they've done that, this village"—

he reached out his arm to encompass the small community—"will be razed to the ground."

Several women were now openly weeping. Men muttered together in small clusters, some of them obviously stunned by the news, others looking as though they were ready to pick a fight.

"Reverend Jones," John Ellis, the Welsh Methodist minister, said, having arrived in time to hear the Anglican minister's report. "Very few of our parishioners are property owners. As Mr. Gittens's presence here today attests, they're all tenants of the Earl of Powys. Is there any provision made for them in this despicable act of the English Parliament?"

Mr. Morgan leaned forward and spoke urgently to Reverend Jones. The minister nodded thoughtfully, then turned to face John Ellis. "Your point is well made, Mr. Ellis," he said. "Owen Morgan here has volunteered to go speak with the Earl of Powys. He will discover what is to be done about the matter."

"I'll go with you, Owen." Everyone's eyes turned to Rhys Jones. "You shouldn't have to shoulder the responsibility for the village alone. Two of us will go."

Owen gave the tailor a nod of appreciation. "Thank you, Rhys. I'll be glad of your company."

With a respectful pull on the brim of his flat cap in Reverend Jones's direction, Owen walked down the village hall steps and made his way through his assembled friends and neighbors until he reached Rhys. He clapped his hand on the tailor's shoulder and led him out of the crowd toward Pont Cedig and the road to Powys Castle.

Behind them, a few men argued, their voices becoming more and more animated as they reviewed what little they knew. Most of the villagers, however, slowly made their way to their respective homes, shock and dejection apparent in their slumped shoulders and shaking heads.

Chapter 1

Llanwddyn, March 1884

GWEN HUMPHREYS CLOSED HER SKETCHBOOK and placed it beside her on the large boulder. Pulling up her knees, she smoothed her long brown woolen skirt down to cover her ankles, then wrapped her arms around her legs. The sun was just beginning its descent, and the sky was streaked with shades of pink. Elongating shadows covered the valley below, and the sound of bleating ewes gathering their lambs filled the hillsides. Gwen took a deep breath. The morning rain had moved on a few hours before, but even now the air felt damp. She pulled her shawl up and tightened it around her shoulders. A few more weeks, perhaps, then it would be warm enough to come here without worrying about the cold.

The crack of a snapping twig startled her. Gwen swung around to see her brother, Robert, appear through the trees.

"I thought I might find you here," he said, moving toward her with his long, loping stride.

Gwen lifted her sketchbook and moved a few inches to the left, making room for him to sit beside her. "I'm glad it's only you," she said.

"Only me? Well, that makes me feel important," Robert teased.

"That's not what I meant," Gwen said, frowning.

Robert chuckled. "I know. I pity the poor navvy who stumbles upon your special spot. He may not make it back to the village alive."

"That's not true," Gwen said. She gave him a sidelong glance. "I might discourage a navvy from coming back again though."

Robert rolled his eyes, but Gwen turned away from him to look out over the valley. Beside her, Robert followed her gaze. Just below the village, a gray scar ran from the mountain on one side across the valley to the mountain on the other. Huge blocks of stone stacked six to seven rows deep marked the beginning of the Vyrnwy Dam construction. Five steam cranes, looking like giant grasshoppers from this distance, stood alongside the wall, and black railroad tracks cut through the dirt and rubble and across the green hillside, leading to the quarry on the other side of the mountain.

"Llanwddyn is changing, Robert." Gwen finally broke the silence. She pointed at the view below. "The physical change is obvious enough. But it's more than that. The building of the dam is changing the people too."

Robert nodded his agreement.

"Do you remember when strangers passing through on their way to Bala were always sure to find lodging and a meal in Llanwddyn? The village was known far and wide for its hospitality. Now there's not a spare bed, an empty room, or an unused old barn in the village. Even Bronwen Richards, who never lets anyone forget how much she's set against the building of the dam, is making money putting up the very navvies who are building it."

"You can't blame them too much," Robert said. "The villagers have never had the chance to bring in extra income like this. You know how hard it was for some families to put food on the table before."

"It's just so hard to watch," she whispered. "I hate that our quiet Welsh village is overrun with English and Irish navvies whose language is hard on the ears and as coarse as their behavior. I hate that the way we've lived for generations is suddenly not good enough. We can't sit around a peat fire at night and share traditional stories and old songs like we used to. Now Saturday entertainment means a cockfight or a fistfight—usually involving men who've spent too long drinking in the Powys Arms."

"Take care that you don't judge too harshly, Gwennie," Robert said. "I'll grant that things have changed with the coming of all these workmen from other places, but they're not all bad men. Some of them are here because a few years working on the dam will take them out of penury and help their families. They're so focused on saving every penny they earn that they barely buy enough food to stay alive. They certainly don't waste it on alcohol or bets at the pub."

"Well, I have yet to meet an Englishman or an Irishman like that," Gwen said.

Robert sighed. "That may be, and I'm certainly not going to encourage my sixteen-year-old sister to be overly friendly with the navvies in the village, so you'll have to take my word for it. But regardless of the men's characters, surely you can see that the valley has benefited in other ways from the building of the dam."

"Not that I've noticed," Gwen said, "but I daresay you'll enlighten me."

Robert was quite capable of being as stubborn as his sister. "Very well," he said, coming to his feet and pacing over to a nearby ash tree before turning around to face her. "What about the fact that farmers' wives from all over the county now sell their eggs and butter in Llanwddyn for four times as much money as they would receive in any other village? That's a blessing."

Gwen looked unconvinced, so Robert tried again. "With all the English workmen coming here, the people in the village are being forced to become bilingual. No one's making us give up Welsh, but whether we like it or not, speaking English is going to be more and more important if we want to travel outside these valleys."

He stepped back toward her. "Then there's all the building the Liverpool Corporation is doing down the valley. The special leases that the Earl of Powys wrote for everyone after Owen Morgan and Rhys Jones went to talk to him means that everyone in the village is being compensated. Some are getting new houses. Not to mention the fact that they're building a new chapel."

Gwen looked away. "I like the old one better."

"The old chapel with the leaky roof that drips water all over the pews when it rains?" Robert asked incredulously.

"Yes," Gwen said, turning so her eyes met his again. "That's where Mam and Dad got married, remember? I want to keep that chapel."

Robert shook his head and groaned. Resuming his position on the boulder, he put his arm around his sister's shoulders and pulled her toward him. "How is it," he said, "that two people who look so alike and have the same parents and the same background can be so different?"

Gwen acknowledged the validity of his question. They both had chestnut-colored hair that looked brown on overcast days and shone red in sunshine. She knew his green eyes were identical to her own, and their matching smiles could only belong to siblings. But their personalities could hardly be less similar.

"You probably think I'm being silly and sentimental," she said quietly.

"Perhaps a bit." Robert squeezed her shoulders gently. "And I recognize that stubborn streak too. But although I don't completely understand what you feel for this village, I know that you don't like change. When we moved here to live with Aunty Jane after Mam and Dad died, it took you much longer than me to adjust to our new life. But once you did, you were happy. I adapted quickly, but . . . I don't know; it's almost as though there's something in my blood that makes me restless. Unlike you, I *need* change. I feel trapped by these mountains. I want to travel, to see the world. Have new adventures in faraway places."

"It's not in your blood," Gwen said with a small, sad smile. "You have the same bloodline I have. It must be in your head."

"Or in my heart," Robert responded. Removing his arm from her shoulders, he leaned forward and kicked a small rock lying at the base of the boulder. He watched it bounce away before continuing. "Wherever it's coming from, I can't ignore it anymore, Gwennie. It's time for me to leave Llanwddyn."

For a moment, Gwen could only stare at him. "What do you mean, it's time for you to leave Llanwddyn?"

He turned to face her. "I'm going to sea. It's what I've wanted to do for years. And I've waited long enough. I'm nineteen now, and I've saved enough money to make the journey to Liverpool with some left over to get me by until I find a ship's captain willing to take me on."

Like an iron claw, fear grasped Gwen's chest. "But you've never even seen the sea! What do you really know about living or working on board a ship? How can you possibly—"

Robert reached out and grasped her arms tightly. "Gwennie, have you ever been married to someone who loves you the way Dad loved Mam? Have you ever held your own baby in your arms? Or watched your son take his first step?"

Gwen pulled back, the earnestness in her brother's face completely at odds with his ridiculous questions. "Of course not," she said. "Why are you—?"

"But you've dreamed of those things, haven't you?" Robert challenged her. "You may not have seen them or experienced them yet, but you want to—badly enough that no matter what, the dream never really goes away."

She suddenly understood where Robert was going with this reasoning, and it scared her. Memories of their childhood came flooding back. They'd filled their days with imaginary games of castles and dragons, jungles and tigers, mountains and trolls. And whether she'd been a mystical mermaid, a lost princess, or a magical fairy, Robert had always been a captain: the fearless captain of his own ship, traveling the world and saving others along the way.

He must have seen something—a glimmer of comprehension or remembrance—in her eyes because his grip on her arms lessened. "I'm not fool enough to think this is going to be easy. I have no doubt I'll have to work harder than I've ever worked before. I'll encounter rough characters and people who'll look down on me just because I'm Welsh. I know it may take me awhile to find my sea legs and prove myself, but I also know I can do it." He took a deep breath. "I have to do it."

A single tear rolled down Gwen's cheek, quickly followed by another. "Will you ever come back?" she said.

Robert pulled her into a tight embrace. "Of course, you daft thing. I have to come back to tell you about my ship and seeing real elephants and tasting bananas and the sounds and smells of other lands. Perhaps I'll even bring you something special from a faraway place."

Gwen forced herself to smile. "Have you told anyone else?" she asked.

"Lewis knows," he said, referring to his best friend, Lewis Morgan, "but I haven't told Aunty Jane yet."

Gwen tried not to feel hurt that Lewis had known his plans before she had. He and Lewis had been virtually inseparable since she and Robert had moved to Llanwddyn. In fact, now that she thought about it, Lewis had usually been the first mate in all their imaginary games.

"What does Lewis think about it?"

Robert shrugged. "He's like you. He's content with village life and with working in the smithy with his dad and his brother. He may not understand why I'm going, but he's known it was coming for a long time." He took a deep breath. "Aunty Jane, however, is another story. Even though my bedroom is full of books about seafaring, and a model ship has pride of place on the dresser, I daresay my plans will be a shock to her."

Gwen thought of their aunt, who had taken them in when they'd been orphaned by the measles epidemic that had devastated their village in North Wales. Their father had been the Methodist preacher in the area and had continued to minister to his flock despite the risks inherent in visiting contaminated homes.

Long hours of caring for others had finally taken its toll, and when he and their mother had succumbed to the disease, they'd both been stricken by the deadly pneumonia that was known to sometimes follow. Gwen and Robert had also caught the measles, but they'd not suffered from any side effects or secondary illnesses. Perhaps it was the resilience of youth. Perhaps, as their aunty Jane often told them, they still had a work to perform in this life. Whatever the reason, they had survived and had been forced to move away from all that was familiar, to live with their older, widowed aunt in Llanwddyn. It had been the most difficult thing Gwen had ever done in her ten-year-old life.

Even now, over six years later, she missed her parents every day. Sometimes she ached to feel her mother's arms around her and to hear her father's voice again. Her father's ready laugh and sense of adventure had been a perfect match for her mother's generosity and joyful outlook on life. Aunty Jane had done her duty without complaint, and she'd always treated them fairly, but she had a no-nonsense approach toward everything—from running the village post office to making a meal to parenting. Gwen had no doubt that Robert's desire to go to sea would fall solidly within the nonsense category. Aunty Jane would not be pleased.

"Telling her won't be easy," Gwen said.

Robert looked down at her, and for a fleeting moment, Gwen thought she glimpsed sadness.

"Telling you was harder," he said.

Chapter 2

THE NEXT FEW DAYS WERE very difficult for Gwen. Knowing that Robert would soon be leaving for an undetermined length of time made it hard to not begrudge every moment he was gone working with the sheep on Dai Williams's farm or cutting peat to replenish the dwindling stack in the back shed. The days went too quickly, and she saw too little of him. On the other hand, the dark cloud that hung over her as she contemplated life without him made it hard to focus on the most basic household chores or the simplest schoolwork. Then the days seemed interminable.

The puzzled expression on Aunty Jane's face when Gwen redid the same arithmetic problem three times before getting it right became more of a frown when she later discovered that Gwen had left the milk jug out on the kitchen counter in full view of the cat. As challenging as it was, Gwen knew she had to do better, or her aunt would start questioning her behavior. She was not about to tell Aunty Jane about Robert's plans. That had to come from him.

Gwen was making bread in the kitchen the next Saturday when she heard the sound of Robert's and Aunty Jane's voices coming from the living room. Robert's voice was a persistent rumble, while Aunty Jane's continually increased in intensity and volume. A bang sounded down the hall, and Gwen dropped the dough onto the counter, brushed her floury hands off on her apron, and quickly moved to the kitchen door in time to see Robert bounding up the stairs toward his bedroom two steps at a time. A minute later, he reappeared, this time carrying a large duffel bag. When he reached the bottom step, he looked over and saw her.

"It's time, Gwennie," he said.

She nodded, not sure if words would come without tears.

Robert jerked his head toward the closed living room door. "I didn't expect Aunty Jane to understand, but I didn't want to leave on this bad note either. Will you try to explain to her for me?" He gave a rueful smile. "I don't think I'll ever be a good enough man to be a preacher like Dad. And I truly believe I would go mad if I had to tend sheep the rest of my days."

Again, Gwen nodded.

He lowered his bag to the floor, closed the space between them, and gave her a fierce hug. "I'll write from Liverpool," he said.

"You'd better," she managed.

Robert chuckled softly. "I have connections at the Llanwddyn post office. It will get to you fast."

He pulled away, and Gwen brushed off the traces of flour that had transferred from her apron to his shirt.

"Travel safely," she said as her tears began.

This time it was Robert's turn to nod. "I will." Then he turned on his heel, picked up his bag, and walked out the front door.

Gwen followed him and stood at the doorstep as he walked down the road, his duffel bag over one shoulder. She saw him greet Ioan Llanwddyn, the cripple who often sat on the grass verge beside Pont Cedig, but Robert didn't stop until he reached the smithy. He paused there, and a moment later, Lewis stepped outside. They exchanged a firm handshake and a few words before Robert moved on again. Gwen continued to watch until he reached the fork in the road. At that point, he turned and, seeing her at the doorway, gave a final wave before taking the road to the right that led to Llanfyllin and the train station.

Gwen saw the curtain in the living room window twitch as she reentered the house and shut the door behind her. The last thing she wanted to do at that moment was face Aunty Jane, but somehow she had to go on with everyday life. Not caring about the tears streaming down her face, she walked back into the kitchen and picked up the waiting bread dough. Feelings of abandonment vied with feelings of sorrow, and by the time the dough was in the pans, she suspected it had been pummeled more than any dough had ever been pummeled before.

┄┄┄┄┄┄┄┄┄┄┄┄┄┄┄◆┄┄┄┄┄┄┄┄┄┄┄┄┄┄┄

As Gwen walked up the mountainside a few hours later, she wondered what her aunt was thinking. Soon after Robert's departure, Aunty Jane had left to open the post office and had been there ever since. Gwen had methodically worked her way through her Saturday chores so she could escape the confines of the house for a short time before darkness fell.

Kneading the bread dough and allowing herself to cry had drained Gwen of all emotion. She felt empty and wondered vaguely how long she would experience this hollowness and why loss of any kind was so hard for her to bear. Perhaps, as Robert had suggested, she really was overly silly and sentimental.

She reached the boulder she'd long since claimed as her own and sat down. She held her sketchbook but kept it closed, holding it against her chest as she looked out over the valley. It was illogical, perhaps, this deep love she had for a village and a valley that had been strange to her only six years before. Her only explanation was that she felt a connection to her mother here. This was where her mother had grown up, been married, and was buried. And where her mother's parents had lived before her. Gwen had come to know and love many of the villagers. They too were important to her now.

She openly admitted she didn't like change; once she put down roots, it was very hard to remove them without damage. And it was the same with people. Robert's ease in talking to strangers was completely alien to her, but the people she knew and loved, she loved fiercely, and if they ever left, she felt the loss terribly.

After her parents died, she'd quickly learned that it was the everyday activities that were the hardest to endure without them.

Choosing which color ribbon should go on the end of her braid each morning, running outside to rescue the clothes on the washing line when it began to rain, or going to visit a friend or neighbor in need—these were all things she used to do with her mother, but now she did them alone.

When she'd first moved to Llanwddyn, her feelings of loss had been so raw she'd barely set foot outside her aunt's house, but even at that young age, she'd recognized that her best hope for recovery was to stick to her mother's belief that every day should have at least one meaningful moment. That meaningful moment could be something as simple as expressing gratitude for the sunshine or as time intensive as making a pie and giving it to someone else. Whatever the activity, it meant that no day passed unnoticed or unappreciated.

It had been hard to continue her mother's legacy alone, but as Gwen had looked beyond herself to see the blessings in her life and the small, quiet ways she could reach out to others, her mother had seemed closer. Picking a few flowers to give to a neighbor, watching baby robins fly from their nests, and complimenting the postman on his new hat might seem insignificant to others, but for ten-year-old Gwen, those meaningful moments had helped ease her grief and had formed the foundation of her love for her new home.

With a sigh, Gwen closed her eyes. They stung from her earlier crying. She would add writing to Robert as something she could make into a meaningful moment. Sharing the good things happening in the village would help them both. She turned her face toward the lowering sun and soaked in the last of the warm rays. The sun would rise again tomorrow, she told herself. It would rise on Robert. It would rise on her. And she would make the most of whatever the new day brought.

"Are you all right, Gwennie?"

Gwen jumped; her eyes popped open as her sketchbook fell to the ground. For a fleeting second, she thought it was Robert. Very few people called her anything but Gwen. Only her father,

her brother, and—she looked over at the young man standing in front of her—Lewis. She'd spent little time with Lewis since they'd grown out of their childhood games of make-believe, and she'd forgotten that he'd adopted Robert's name for her then.

"I'm not sure if my heart will ever beat the same," Gwen said, catching her breath.

"Sorry." He looked uncomfortable. "I thought you might . . . I didn't mean to . . ." Embarrassed, he ran his fingers through his dark hair. "Robert told me I might find you here. He asked that I watch out for you—at least for a bit. So I thought I'd better come check and make sure you're all right."

At Lewis's confession, myriad emotions flooded through Gwen. First came irritation that Robert had shared the location of her special place with someone else, but that was quickly followed by gratitude for his concern. Discomfort with her current situation soon mushroomed into perplexity regarding how she was supposed to respond. She really didn't want to admit that she felt as though she'd been abandoned and that she'd spent a good part of the day in tears. It didn't seem like those were emotions a nineteen-year-old young man would readily understand. Somehow she had to feign some level of maturity.

"I'm fine, thank you, Lewis," she said. "It was nice of you to come and ask."

Relief flooded his face. "Well then," he said, "I'll let you be." He stuck his hands deep into his trouser pockets and took a few steps back. "If you don't mind, I'll check with you again before long. I gave my word to Robert, and I'd like to keep it, if it's all the same to you."

Gwen managed a small smile. "I'm not sure I can refuse when you put it like that," she said.

"That's good," Lewis said with an equally hesitant smile. Then, without another word, he turned away and started back down the mountain.

He covered the uneven ground quickly and easily, and Gwen was reminded of how light on his feet he'd been when they were young. Robert, as captain of each imaginary endeavor, would barge into every situation with his wooden sword blazing. Lewis had preferred stealth, catching his enemies unprepared. It was not surprising that he'd caught her unawares just now.

She watched him go until he disappeared between the trees. She hadn't spoken to Lewis for a long time. He and Robert had left school almost three years ago, Lewis to start working in the smithy and Robert to shepherd for Dai Williams. Without an obvious vocation in the offing, Gwen hadn't understood Robert's desire to leave school at sixteen to earn a steady income—until a few days ago.

Now that he no longer attended school with her, virtually the only time she saw Lewis was at chapel on Sundays. His family's pew was not near hers, and even though Robert had often stopped to talk to him after the meetings, she had not. Gwen thought about that. It was a strange situation—to know someone well enough that they shared your childhood memories, yet know them so little that any conversation between you was stilted and awkward.

She sighed and slowly got to her feet. Gathering her shawl a little closer, she bent down and picked up her sketchbook. She hoped, for Lewis's sake, that he did not feel compelled to check on her very often. She wasn't sure how many uncomfortable exchanges she could abide.

Chapter 3

THE WHISPERING BEGAN AS SOON as Gwen and her aunt walked into the chapel the next morning. Gwen didn't know how word had spread. It wasn't as though Robert had never missed a chapel service before. He'd had his share of illnesses and injuries as a boy, and some of them had kept him away from his Sunday meetings. But somehow everyone seemed to know that Robert's absence was more meaningful this time.

Gwen felt everyone's stares boring into her back as she walked down the aisle. Not for the first time, she wished their bench were a little closer to the door. She glanced at her aunt. If possible, Aunty Jane's stiff posture seemed even more rigid than usual. The older lady's lips were set in a thin line, and her pale-blue eyes did not waver from her ultimate goal: the family pew near the front of the chapel. She said nothing until they were safely seated on the bench.

"What possessed me to tell Bronwen Richards about Robert leaving, I'll never know," she muttered more to herself than to Gwen. "That woman has never been able to keep anything to herself. I believe she comes into the post office just so she can be the first one to hear news and spread it."

"I don't understand what the fuss is about," Gwen said softly. "It's not as if Robert's done anything wrong."

Aunty Jane gave the loudest tut acceptable in a chapel and gave Gwen a look that suggested her niece had left her intelligence in bed that morning. "Gwen Humphreys, respectable young men do not run away to sea. It shows a gross lack of common sense, reliability, and decorum."

Gwen stared at her aunt, completely flabbergasted. Only the knowledge that she was in the chapel prevented her from giving an indignant retort. Instead, she counted to ten in Welsh and then did it again in English. It saved her. By the time she'd repeated the numbers backward, the organ prelude music had come to a close, and the Welsh Methodist minister, John Ellis, had taken the podium.

Mr. Ellis launched into a rousing sermon. At least, Gwen assumed it was rousing. The minister's voice certainly ascended to fever pitch, but she didn't actually hear his message. Instead, her aunt's words repeated themselves over and over again in her mind. Was that really what people thought? Even those who knew Robert and had never questioned his character before? Or was her aunt overreacting? Were the buzzing whispers a sign of genuine interest among villagers, or were they voicing their disapproval?

Aunty Jane was obviously upset about Robert's departure. She'd said very little to Gwen since he'd walked out of the house, and what she had said had been terse. Secretly, Gwen had been relieved. It was easier to hide her own pain if she didn't have to talk about it. But she hadn't anticipated her aunt's bitterness or the censure of friends and neighbors.

As the congregation echoed the last amen of the closing prayer and came to its feet, Aunty Jane slipped on her gloves. "I believe we will go straight home today," she said. "There is no one I wish to speak with."

The fact that Gwen's wishes were irrelevant was not lost on Gwen, but she had to concede that leaving quickly was probably for the best. If her aunt lingered after Sunday meetings, Gwen would occasionally talk to Bronwen Richards's daughter, Mabel. They were the same age and in school together, but Mabel's interests tended to lean toward socializing with boys, while Gwen preferred solitude and drawing. Besides, with Mabel's mother undoubtedly hovering nearby, Mabel would be a particularly poor choice today.

Gwen slid out of the pew first and led the way out of the chapel. She purposely avoided making eye contact with anyone all the way to the main doors. When she stepped outside, she realized it had started raining. Breathing a sigh of relief, she turned to make sure her aunt was still behind her. The poor weather would lessen the likelihood of people congregating outside and make their hasty departure seem less obvious.

Just as her aunt appeared at the doors, someone separated themselves from a small group standing beneath the chapel awning. Gwen glanced up and saw Lewis walking toward her. Dread filled her. Not here. Not now. Didn't he understand that her emotions were too close to the surface to have a conversation about how she was feeling in front of everyone exiting the chapel doors?

At the last minute, Lewis must have seen something in her face. He raised his eyebrows in question. Frantically she shook her head, and his steps faltered. He stopped a few feet away and watched as Aunty Jane swept through the doors, took Gwen by the arm, and, with her head lowered against the drizzling rain, marched her through the chapel gate and down the road toward home.

"Well," Aunty Jane said as she shook the rain off her coat in the kitchen a few minutes later. "There aren't many days that I'm thankful for the rain, but this is one of them."

"We can't avoid talking to people forever," Gwen said.

Aunty Jane gave her a stony look. "I am well aware of that, child, but I will do it when I'm good and ready. Not before."

She hung her coat on the coatrack in the corner and began pouring water into the kettle. "Besides, I daresay Robert will be back within the week. He'll only need a few days on his own in Liverpool to realize the mistake he's made. And then, as long as he can talk Dai Williams into rehiring him, we can put all this foolishness behind us and go on as if it never happened."

Gwen considered counting again, but since they were no longer in the chapel, she ignored the idea. "I don't understand Robert's

desire to go to sea any more than you do," she said. "But he's wanted
to do this since he was little, and for years he's saved almost every
penny he's earned for this opportunity, maybe because he knew he
wouldn't get it any other way." She paused briefly to let that sink in.
"I don't think that's the kind of behavior anyone would expect of
someone being reckless or irresponsible. And if you were being as
fair as you pride yourself on being, you wouldn't either."

Her aunt gasped, but Gwen hadn't finished. "I'm no happier
than you are about Robert leaving, but I won't call him foolish for
following his dream. In fact, you're the one who is foolish if you
think he'll be coming back anytime soon!"

Aunty Jane's initial shock at Gwen's outburst was rapidly giving
way to anger. "That will be quite enough, young lady," she ordered.

"Yes," Gwen said. "It will." She walked across the room to
hang her coat up beside her aunt's before moving to the door. "For
what it's worth, Robert was sorry that his decision upset you. He
wanted you to know that."

She opened the kitchen door and let herself out into the hall
before her aunt had a chance to respond. A few moments later,
Gwen heard the clang of the kettle hitting the hob a little too
hard, but by then she was already halfway up the stairs, and she
didn't look back.

Her bedroom was far too small for her to pace efficiently. She
walked back and forth in a tiny triangle between her bed, the
dresser, and the window, but it did little to ease her wound-up
emotions. She and Robert readily acknowledged how much they
owed their aunt for caring for them for so many years, but it was
sometimes hard to reconcile her prickly, proper manner with the
warm, fun-loving personality of her late sister, their mother.

Gwen paused at the window and leaned her head against
the pane. "Oh, Mam," she whispered, "I probably shouldn't have
spoken to Aunty Jane that way, but what she said about Robert was
so . . ." She swallowed the lump in her throat. "Why did you have
to leave? Why did everyone have to leave?"

She watched the raindrops trickle down the glass, and a memory
of her parents surfaced. Her father had been about to visit an ailing

parishioner, and her mother had protested his leaving because of the rain. He'd laughingly told her that no one born and raised in wet Wales should allow a bit of rain to stop them. With a smile, her mother had reluctantly agreed.

Gwen's lips curled into a similar smile at the recollection. The leaden sky did not suggest a break in the weather anytime soon, but she would not stay cooped up indoors all day. With new determination, she walked over to the wardrobe, took out her everyday brown woolen skirt and boots, and quickly changed out of her Sunday best. Grasping her oldest hat in one hand and the doorknob in the other, she opened the bedroom door a crack and listened. The house was silent.

Quickly and quietly, Gwen slipped down the stairs, stopping when she reached the kitchen door. After listening again for a few moments and satisfying herself that her aunt was no longer inside, she entered, hurried over to the coatrack, took down her coat, and put it on. She tied the ribbons of her hat securely under her chin, then let herself out of the house.

Instinctively she turned toward the mountain, but the rain was even heavier now than it had been when she and her aunt had left the chapel, and she knew the path to her boulder would be muddy and the uneven ground slippery and difficult to traverse. Reluctantly she turned around and took the road that led to Pont Cedig instead.

Big puddles were already forming in the street. Gwen walked along the grassy verge when there was one and wove her way around the collecting water when there wasn't. She passed the short row of terraced houses lining the road without seeing anyone else. Because it was Sunday, the village shop, the pub, and other business establishments were all closed. Regardless of the weather, that fact alone kept the navvies away from the village one day a week. On Sundays, the village had the same sleepy feel it had known before the changes brought on by the announcement of the dam. And Gwen was glad.

By the time she'd reached Pont Cedig, the wind had picked up, and the rain was falling diagonally. She pushed down on her hat, making sure it was still securely in place, then she tucked her hands into her coat pockets and stood looking down at the river below. Three ducks were huddled together beneath the bridge, their heads turned under their wings.

"Bit wet, even for ducks, isn't it?"

Gwen swung around as Ioan Llanwddyn slowly made his way across the bridge toward her. She wasn't sure what Ioan's real surname was—she assumed he had one, even though no one in the village ever used it. He was known far and wide as Ioan Llanwddyn, and the name fit because he was a permanent fixture in the village.

She guessed he was in his seventies. His weathered face, lack of teeth, and grizzled, gray hair and eyebrows attested to a long life, which was quite remarkable given the fact that he'd never had full use of his legs. Crippled from birth, Ioan's life had been as difficult as his disposition was cheery.

He didn't have a home of his own, so on most days, he could be found sitting along the side of the road with his legs folded in front of him like a tailor. He always had a kind word for those who passed by, and in turn, the villagers did what they could for him. Apart from regular offers of food and lodging, people went out of their way for Ioan. His britches had a large leather patch sewn onto the seat to keep him warm when he sat on the ground, and several years before, someone had fashioned two wooden pattens with iron rings on the base that enabled him to get around when the road was wet.

He was using the pattens now, springing from one to the other as he navigated the puddles and mud with the aid of his walking sticks.

Gwen waited until he'd almost reached her. "Hello, Ioan." She smiled and received an almost toothless smile in return.

"Missing your brother, I daresay," he said, wheezing a little from his recent exertion.

Gwen nodded. "Yes."

"A good lad, that," Ioan said. "He stopped to say good-bye when he left, you know. I told him then—and I'll tell you now—he'll go far. You mark my words. That brother of yours will make something of himself."

Gwen blinked several times to keep the tears at bay before trusting herself to face the old man again. "Thank you, Ioan. That's very nice of you to say."

"Good heavens, bach. Nice has nothing to do with it," Ioan said. "It's the truth. That's what it is."

"Ioan!"

In unison, Gwen and Ioan turned to see who else was braving the stormy weather. A dark-haired man was hurrying toward them. Ioan swiped at the raindrops covering his face and peered at the oncoming figure.

"Lewis Morgan? Is that you, lad?"

"Yes," Lewis panted as he reached the bridge. "My dad sent me to find you. Said he saw you down the street and wanted to remind you that the cot he made up in the smithy is still there if you need a place to wait out the rain. The furnace is banked for the day, but it's still plenty warm."

"Well now, that's right good of him."

Ioan shuffled forward on his pattens, and for the first time, Lewis noticed Gwen standing behind him.

"Gwennie! What are you doing here?"

"I was out for a walk," she said. "Ioan stopped to talk to me."

"But it's pouring with rain," he said, looking at her as though she'd taken leave of her senses. "You'd best come to the smithy too. It's closer than your house. You can wait there for the rain to pass."

"That's all right," Gwen said, planting her feet firmly against a particularly strong gust of wind. "I won't stay out much longer."

"There's a river of water running off the brim of your hat, and I can only imagine how wet your feet are," Lewis said. "You should get out of the rain before you become ill."

"Really, Lewis," Gwen began, "I'll be—"

"Come along, bach," Ioan said, moving jerkily in the direction of the smithy. "Now's probably not the best time to be stubborn. You and I could both do with a little drying out."

Gwen saw Lewis's lips twitch, something she recognized from their childhood, a sure sign that he was fighting back a smile. "I didn't know you knew Gwennie so well, Ioan," he said.

"Well, that goes to show how unobservant you are, lad," Ioan said. "Young Gwen's been stopping to talk to me and bringing me presents ever since she moved to Llanwddyn." He pulled on a ragged blue scarf that was cinched tightly around his neck. "I have the honor of being one of the only people in Wales wearing a Gwen Humphreys scarf."

Lewis looked at Gwen with wide eyes, and she felt herself blush.

"It was my first try at crocheting. Aunty Jane almost gave up on me because the rows were so wobbly."

"Nonsense," Ioan said with a toothless grin. "This scarf's got personality, just like me." He tucked the ends of the soggy fabric back under the lapels of his ragged jacket. "Now, I don't want my scarf getting any wetter than it already is, so I'm off to the smithy."

A large drop of water fell off the brim of Gwen's hat and trickled down her neck. She suppressed a shudder and raised her skirt a couple of inches to survey her soaking wet, muddy boots. The wind snatched the fabric out of her hand, and in an effort to steady herself, she stepped right into the nearest and deepest puddle.

"Well, that's done it," she said as she felt the water seep into her stockings. "I'm now officially as wet as the ducks."

Lewis chuckled. "It's still not quite as bad as the day you fell into the river trying to catch Robert's fish before it escaped the hook."

The memory of her unforgettable dunking in the Vyrnwy River brought a reluctant smile to Gwen's face. "Robert didn't even bother asking if I was all right. He just wanted to know if I still had the fish."

"And you did too!"

"I knew I'd never hear the end of it if I let it go," she said. She looked at him shyly. "I seem to remember you were the one who helped me out of the water while Robert was busy putting the fish in the bucket."

Lewis smiled and extended his hand to her. "Looks like it was a practice run," he said.

With a groan, Gwen took his hand and stepped out of the puddle. "Thank you," she said. "Again."

"You're welcome," he said with a small laugh. "Now, let's see if we can't catch up with Ioan."

Chapter 4

GWEN FOLLOWED IOAN INTO THE warm, dry smithy and looked around with interest. Two anvils sat immediately in front of her, but behind them, a huge stone fireplace dominated the room. Large leather bellows jutted out of the left side of the fireplace, and hundreds of tools and chains lined the walls and hung suspended from the ceiling. To one side of the fireplace, half a dozen heavy mallets of varying sizes stood upright beside two metal wagon wheel rims, and on the other side, a small pile of horseshoes lay on the smooth flagstone floor next to a wooden barrel half full of water.

Ioan shuffled awkwardly to the far corner of the smithy, where Lewis was already pulling out a pallet covered in a green-and-brown wool blanket. With a muffled groan, Ioan lowered himself onto the makeshift cot, set his pattens and walking sticks to one side of it, and lifted his legs into their customary crossed position in front of him.

Slowly Gwen untied the ribbons beneath her chin and pulled her hat off, shaking it slightly to expel any rain that had not already soaked into the felt. She placed her hat on a nearby wooden table and sat down on a stool beside it. As much as she hated to admit it, it was lovely to be out of the cold, wet weather.

She watched silently as Lewis moved away from Ioan toward the fireplace. He took off his jacket and hung it on a hook on the wall before picking up three blocks of peat and placing them carefully in the fireplace. Using a poker, he positioned the peat over the smoldering ashes, then stepped over to start pumping the bellows.

It was obvious that Lewis had done this chore many times before. His broad shoulders and strong arms made the job look easy, and within seconds, tiny flames were licking the fresh fuel. Giving one last pump, Lewis straightened and ran his hand through his dark hair, pushing back the wet strands that had flopped forward into his face. He glanced her direction and met her eyes. Immediately Gwen looked away, embarrassed at having been caught watching him.

"That should help," Lewis said.

"That's grand, lad." Ioan spoke from the corner. "Thank you for your kindness."

"Will you be needing anything else?" Lewis asked.

Gwen looked over at Ioan in time to see the mischievous twinkle in his eyes.

"Well, that all depends on whether there's any of your mam's bara brith at your house," he said. "The thought of her bara brith certainly stirs up a need."

Gwen lowered her head to hide her smile, but when she heard Lewis chuckle, she looked over at him.

"What about you, Gwennie?" he asked. "Do you need some of my mam's bara brith too?"

Color filled her cheeks. "Oh, I don't want you to go to any trouble for me," she said.

Lewis gave an impatient sigh and walked over to the pallet on the floor. "All right, Ioan. I'll make a deal with you. Your need for my need. I'm willing to go back out in the rain and run home to get you some bara brith if you're willing to help me understand what Gwen's saying."

"What do you mean?" Gwen got off the stool. "Why don't you understand me?"

Lewis ignored her.

Ioan, however, had the same glint in his eyes that he'd had just moments before. "Having a hard time with the way she talks, are you, lad?"

"It's worse than trying to understand the Irish navvies speaking English," Lewis said.

"That's ridiculous!" Gwen strode across the room. "I'm speaking Welsh just like you, just like I always have."

"No, bach," Ioan said with a grin. "You're speaking female. And unless I'm missing the mark, I'm betting Lewis here, who only has one brother and no sisters, can't make head nor tail of it."

Gwen stared at Ioan, and then when she realized he was not going to be any more forthcoming, she transferred her attention to Lewis. "Would you care to explain?"

"Well, it's like this," Lewis began. "If I asked a man if he wanted any of my mam's bara brith, he'd say, 'Yes, please' or 'No, thank you.' When I asked you, you said, 'I don't want you to go to any trouble.' So, is that, 'I don't want you to go to any trouble, but I'd love some,' or is it, 'I don't want you to go to any trouble because I don't want any'?"

"That's it? That one sentence has you all confused?"

Lewis ran a finger under his shirt collar as if to loosen it. "Not just that one," he said. "Earlier today, at the end of church, I came over to ask about you." He looked down. "I heard all the whispering when you and your aunt came into the chapel and knew it had to be difficult."

Gwen hadn't even considered how their neighbors' thoughtless actions would impact Robert's best friend. It had to have been unpleasant for him to sit through chapel today too.

Clearing his throat, Lewis continued. "I saw you shaking your head by the chapel doors, but I didn't know if that meant 'No, I'm fine' or 'No, I'm not all right.'"

"Actually," Gwen said quietly, "it meant 'No, please don't talk to me about how I feel in front of all these people.'"

Lewis threw his arms in the air. "See! I didn't even consider that possibility."

A loud chortling sound drew their attention back to the older man on the floor beside them.

"This is the best entertainment I've had in weeks," Ioan said through his laughter. "Excellent. Both of you. Truly excellent."

"Ioan, if this is your idea of helping, I don't think I'll have to make a trip in the rain to pick up bara brith after all," Lewis said.

"I think I'd better go." Gwen turned around to pick up her hat. She did not want to be the subject of Lewis's consternation or Ioan's mirth anymore. The only time she could remember feeling this humiliated was three years ago when she'd tripped while refilling her inkwell at school and had accidentally poured black ink on Llewelyn Jones's head.

"Wait." Lewis reached out and grabbed her arm. "I didn't mean to upset you. I'm the one who . . ."

Gwen twisted her arm free. "I'll say this as clearly as I can," she said. "You don't need to check on me or talk to me anymore. Please forget about whatever it was that Robert said; I would much prefer that you do nothing. I will be fine."

She pressed her hat onto her head and, without taking the time to tie the ribbons, hurried to the door.

"Good-bye," she said to the two men who were staring at her with equally stunned expressions. Then she slipped outside and closed the door firmly behind her.

The storm still raged, but Gwen didn't care. It matched her mood perfectly. Raising her skirt a few inches, she started to run, and she didn't stop until she reached her aunt's house. She cut around to the back and stood on the doorstep, breathless, mud spattered, and soaking wet. Taking a moment to collect herself, she turned the knob and walked into the kitchen.

"Heavens above, child! Where have you been?"

Aunty Jane's expression mirrored the shock in her voice as she surveyed the muddy puddle collecting at her niece's feet.

"I went for a walk," Gwen said.

Aunty Jane's exasperation was obvious, but after a quick study of Gwen's face, she must have realized Gwen was quite miserable enough without a further tongue lashing. Compressing her lips into their familiar line, Aunty Jane walked over to the linen cupboard, pulled out a large towel, and walked it over to Gwen.

"Take your clothes off here," she said. "We'll have to take care of them tomorrow. And let's hope your old school skirt still fits well enough for you to use it until this one's washed and dried."

Gwen dropped her soggy hat to the floor and used the towel to wipe her hands and face. Then she bent down to untie her bootlaces.

"Thank you," she said as her cold fingers fumbled with the job.

For a moment, her aunt stood silently watching; when she spoke, her voice had softened. "I have some oatmeal on the stove. As soon as you're out of those wet clothes, come sit at the table, and I'll get you some."

⸺⸺⸺⸺⸺⸺◆⸺⸺⸺⸺⸺⸺

An hour later, Gwen's wet clothes were still lying in a pile beside the back door, but she was wearing her warm flannel nightgown and was sitting in front of the fire in the living room. She untied the ribbon at the bottom of her braid and shook her head to loosen her long, chestnut hair. Her unruly curls were still damp, so she ran her fingers through them, rotating her head slightly with the hope that the heat of the fire would help dry her hair before bedtime.

Behind her, Aunty Jane sat in the wooden rocking chair, crocheting by candlelight. Her fingers wove in and around the yarn as she used an ivory hook to develop an intricate pattern for the blanket she was making.

They had spoken very little, but the anger in the air earlier that afternoon had dissipated, and they seemed to have reached an unspoken truce. The peaceful feeling was a balm to Gwen, who still felt battered by the events of the day. She stared into the fire, wondering where Robert was and how he was faring.

"I hope he'll be safe," Aunty Jane said, breaking the silence between them.

Gwen turned to look at her. She didn't need to ask what her aunt was talking about.

"It's not what I would have chosen for him," her aunt continued. "But I realize now that it wasn't my choice to make."

Gwen nodded slowly. "Nor mine," she said softly.

"So now I suppose all we can do is pray for him," Aunty Jane said. "And hope that before too long we hear that he has found a position he's happy with."

"He said he would write," Gwen said.

"That's good."

The crochet hook continued its even rhythm: in, out, around, in, out, around. Gwen waited, but when her aunt remained quiet, she turned and spoke into the fire. "I hope we don't have to wait too long to hear."

"Maybe we should pray for the postmaster in Liverpool too." This time Aunty Jane's voice held a hint of its usual crustiness. "It will take a miracle to read that boy's penmanship. Goodness knows how many Welsh villages he'll send that letter to before it reaches us."

Gwen stifled a smile. Robert's handwriting was quite possibly the worst she'd ever seen. Their aunt had once told him his papers looked like a drunken spider had fallen into an inkwell and walked across the page. Perhaps it would take them both to decipher any letters that made it as far as Llanwddyn. Strangely, the thought lightened her heart. She knew it would take some time before she felt whole again, but even if it were only for a brief moment, Aunty Jane had made them sound like a family once more.

Chapter 5

It rained for almost two weeks. The Rivers Cedig and Vyrnwy swelled dangerously close to overflowing, the streets became muddy walkways, and everyone stayed indoors as much as possible. Gwen stopped cleaning her boots at the end of each day because by the time she arrived at school the next morning, it was as though she'd never touched them. She felt damp to her bones and longed for sunshine to clear away the gray pall that seemed to hang over everyone in the valley.

Unfortunately, the somber skies were a fitting reflection of Gwen's heavy heart. Robert's absence was hard to ignore. She missed his reassuring presence and playful banter in the house, and the kitchen wasn't the same without his work boots at the back door or the telltale trail of crumbs that always marked his extra trips to the pantry.

She made an extra effort to fill the voids her brother had left in her life by focusing on new meaningful moments. Taking time to express appreciation to her aunt for the warm kitchen when she came in out of the rain and taking a loaf of bread to Rosie Evans who'd just had a baby had helped. Guiding old John Roberts across the muddy street because his eyesight was too poor to see the potholes, and showing Catherine Williams's twin boys how to make paper boats that could successfully sail the largest puddles had also been rewarding. But as much as these small acts of kindness lifted Gwen's spirits, she still longed for a letter that would tell her Robert was safe and well.

Every evening Aunty Jane came back from the post office empty-handed. Gwen guessed that her aunt was almost as anxious for word from Robert as she was, but she rarely spoke of him. Sometimes Gwen would catch her gazing at something that belonged to him—his copy of *Moby Dick* in the living room, his old hat on the coatrack, or his favorite mug in the cupboard. On those occasions, Gwen thought she saw emotion in her aunt's eyes, but it was never verbally expressed, and Gwen found herself sharing her own feelings of loneliness with the small portrait of her parents in her room.

Unfortunately, her feelings of being alone only intensified whenever she allowed the memory of her earlier, disastrous outing in the rain to surface. Simply thinking of her interaction with Lewis filled her with mortification, and she did everything she could to avoid running into him again. She walked to and from school as fast as possible, never lingering to watch the duck family at Pont Cedig, and walking particularly briskly past the smithy. She even kept an eye out for Ioan Llanwddyn, but someone in the village must have taken him in during the inclement weather because he was nowhere to be seen.

On the three occasions that her aunt had sent her to the local shop to pick up a few items for dinner, she was grateful to find it almost empty. Emlyn Williams, the shopkeeper, asked about Robert. Gwen found that she preferred his open curiosity to the uncomfortable whispers more common among the villagers. Apart from her teacher and fellow students, whom she interacted with every day at school, the only other people she saw during that time were the ones in chapel on Sunday. There again, the weather had everyone hurrying into the meeting and hurrying back home again afterward. No one lingered. Gwen assumed Lewis was in attendance, but she made a special effort to not look in the direction of his family's pew, so she never saw him.

The rain impacted work at the dam too. By the end of the first week, construction had slowed to a standstill. It was too muddy to work at the dam site, and the navvies working at the quarry one mile to the north were unable to keep the dynamite dry long enough to blast safely. The masons were left to chisel blocks of stone that had already been roughly cut, but even they could not work for long in the downpour. The workmen filtered into the village as the week progressed, looking for something to do. They lingered at the pub and loitered in small groups outside any of the establishments with an overhanging roof.

Gwen tried to remind herself of Robert's reassurance that many of the navvies were good men with families at home, but she still felt uncomfortable walking past them. Her logical side told her she'd managed to disregard the workmen in the village successfully for over three years; time and maturity should only help. Her instincts told her otherwise.

She felt their stares as she passed, sensed their muted conversations, and occasionally heard a catcall that made her squirm. On the few occasions that she opted to walk to or from school with Mabel Richards, the other girl giggled and snuck coy glances at the men, making the journey all the more uncomfortable. It did not take Gwen long to realize Mabel was not interested in arriving at school on time. As far as Mabel was concerned, the more they dawdled, the better.

On Friday, Gwen left school late. She was coming to the end of her schooling in Llanwddyn, and her teacher, Miss Ellis, had encouraged her to take an examination to see if she qualified to continue as a boarding student at the larger school in Llanfyllin. Gwen enjoyed school and loved reading and learning new things, but she wasn't sure how she felt about going away to school. Already she'd had more schooling than many of her peers, and moving on meant facing yet another big change in her life. But Aunty Jane had agreed with Miss Ellis, that it was best to keep her options open.

Only two other students took the examination that day, and they finished before her. Gwen didn't know if that was a good sign or a bad one. Miss Ellis had allowed her to take all the allotted time, and when she finally handed in the papers, she felt both relief and exhaustion. In fact, thinking through the answers she'd given on her test while circumventing the mud puddles on her journey home took so much of her flagging concentration she almost ran into the men on the road before she was even aware of them being there.

"Now then! This is what we've been missing, lads."

"She's a bit of all right, this one! Might have to fight you for her."

The men's voices were loud, their words slurred. And they were speaking English. Gwen looked up in time to see three men slowly circling her. Their gaits were unsteady, and as they drew progressively nearer, they brought with them the distinctive smell of alcohol. She froze.

"What's your name, darlin'?"

A heavyset man with straw-colored hair reached out to touch her. Gwen instinctively stepped back but bumped into another man standing behind her. He grasped her around the waist, and Gwen tore at his hand, desperate to be free of his hold. The third man with small eyes and a hooked nose laughed.

"Doesn't look like she's much taken with either of you knuckleheads," he said. He looked Gwen up and down as though eyeing a piece of meat hanging in a butcher's window. "I think she likes me better."

He slid a rough hand behind her head, his fingers hooking into her hair as he pulled her closer. His reeking breath turned Gwen's stomach; his lecherous smile filled her with panic. Frantically, she tossed her head back, her hair pulling painfully as it caught in his fingers. She gave a small cry, and the man grinned.

"Nicely done, Hurst!" The blond shoved the man with the hooked nose aside with his shoulder and reached for Gwen with his other hand. "You stick with me, darlin'. A few kisses won't hurt at all."

Gwen pulled her arm free of his grasp and spun around. Whatever happened, she would not let her fear of these men paralyze her.

She had to focus on finding some means of escape. The men were standing too close, each one set against her slipping past them. She looked back the way she'd come. The street was deserted. Would anyone hear if she called for help?

Up ahead she heard the distant creak of well-worn hinges, followed by the sound of someone whistling the familiar melody of an old Welsh folk song. The men must have heard it too. All three turned, two of them swaying uncontrollably. A gap opened up between them, barely wide enough to give Gwen a glimpse down the street to where a dark-haired man was opening the doors of the smithy. Despite the distance and the drizzling rain, she knew him. And with that recognition came a sense of safety. The antagonism she'd been harboring over Lewis's recent behavior suddenly seemed insignificant, and without stopping to think, she simply acted. "Lewis! Lewis! Help me!"

Immediately the three men swung around.

"What did she say?" the blond one yelled. "Curse this foul language. What did she say?"

"How are we supposed to know?" The man behind her said. "Ask that bloke. He can probably tell you."

He stuck out a wobbly arm, hitting Gwen across the shoulder as he pointed down the road toward the smithy. The man with the hooked nose swore.

"Peters, you're the biggest idiot I know."

He took a stumbling step away from the other two, and Gwen used this opening between the men to break free. She ran, heedless of the rain, the puddles, the mud, or anyone watching. Her sole focus was on reaching the smithy.

At her cry, Lewis's whistling had stopped abruptly. He had turned and was scanning the street, his gaze immediately falling on the figure running toward him. She saw his posture change the moment he identified her. He left the smithy door behind and hurried to meet her.

"Gwennie! What is it?"

"Those men . . ."

Her viselike grip on his arm and the shake in her voice expressed Gwen's terror far better than words.

"Which men? What happened?"

Lewis's urgency brought the first tears to Gwen's eyes. She pointed behind her.

"Three English navvies. They were drunk, and they . . ."

"Did they hurt you?" Lewis was already scanning the street again, barely suppressing his anger.

"No." Gwen thought of the men's ugly expressions and shuddered. "I think perhaps they would have, but you came out of the smithy, and I ran."

The street was empty once more, but from beyond the row of houses, she heard a faint clatter of footsteps and a distant shout. Under her clenched fingers, she felt Lewis's arm muscles tighten.

"I'll go after them."

"No," she said again. "There are three of them, and they've all been drinking. Who knows what they'd do if you chased after them."

Lewis's expression hardened. "They can't get away with this."

She shook her head. "It will be my word against theirs. And, truth be told, they probably won't remember anything about it tomorrow."

"That doesn't mean they won't try something like this again. And the outcome could be much worse."

Gwen would not allow herself to think that way. Not now. Not while her fear was so real. "Please, Lewis," she begged. "Please just take me home. Aunty Jane and I have been the subject of village gossip for two weeks already. I don't want any more hurtful whispers."

He looked down at her, indecision written across his face. "But if you hadn't run—"

"But I did. And they didn't harm me." She released his arm and took a shaky step back. "I need to go."

Lewis glanced back down the street. All traces of the three navvies were gone. Only the pitter-patter of falling rain broke the silence. With frustration, he ran his hand through his hair.

"Very well," he said. "I don't like it, but we'll do it your way. If there were another man here, it would likely be a different story, but Dad's over at Dai Williams's farm helping with lambing."

Gwen knew her relief showed on her face. "Thank you," she said softly.

He gave a reluctant nod. "Come on, then." He put his hand on her elbow and propelled her forward. "Let's get you home."

They walked in silence until they were within a few yards of Aunty Jane's house, then Lewis's steps slowed.

"I'm sorry about what happened at the smithy a couple weeks back," he said. "It was stupid of me to bring those things up in front of Ioan."

Gwen gave an embarrassed shrug. "Well, you were right about one thing; maybe I do need someone checking on me every once in a while." She looked over at him. "I'm glad you were here today and that you ignored what I told you before."

"You mean the part about me leaving you alone—the part I could understand completely?"

Gwen recognized his teasing tone and managed a small smile. "Yes, that part."

"Ah, so can we establish that that too was a bit stupid?"

"Not stupid," she said defensively. "A bit overstated, maybe."

They'd reached Aunty Jane's front door, so Lewis dropped his hand from her elbow and stuck both hands deep into his pockets. Gwen felt the loss of contact immediately and didn't like the feeling of vulnerability that came with it. She didn't want to be alone. Nervously, she glanced around, but there was no one to be seen—no villagers and no navvies.

"Is there someone you can walk home from school with from now on?" Lewis asked as though sensing her disquiet.

She gave a slow nod. "Mabel Richards is usually at school, but she . . ." Gwen didn't want to discuss Mabel's flirtatious tendencies with Lewis. "She doesn't always leave at the same time I do."

Lewis raised one eyebrow. "Well, can you wait for each other? It's probably best that neither of you be on your own."

Gwen hated that they were having this conversation. Young women's safety had not been an issue in the village before the dam construction began.

"I'll talk to her," she said.

Lewis looked pleased. "Good," he said. He jerked his head toward the house. "You'd best be getting inside."

Gwen nodded and opened the front door. "Thank you for bringing me home, Lewis," she said.

He gave her a small smile. "Just remember those 'overstated' things you mentioned a couple of weeks ago are now null and void," he said. "I'll be around."

Chapter 6

GWEN WASN'T SURE WHAT BUOYED her spirits the most the next morning—the fact that it was Saturday and she didn't have to worry about the walk to and from school or the fact that the sun had finally broken through the gray clouds to reveal a clear, blue sky. They both filled her with gratitude, and she scrambled out of bed feeling much better able to face the world than she had when she'd climbed under the covers the night before.

As usual, Aunty Jane had a long list of chores that needed to be done before Sunday. Gwen glanced over it and refrained from groaning only because personal experience had taught her that complaints tended to add items to the list rather than eliminate them. Mopping the kitchen floor was backbreaking work, but as she was the one who had tracked in most of the offending mud, she supposed it was only fair. Besides which, she'd rather mop the floor than have to hand wash the pile of muddy clothes her aunt had taken care of while Gwen was at school.

She was emptying her second bucket of dirty water outside when she saw Edward Hughes, the postman, walking past the house toward the post office. He wore gray woolen trousers and a navy jacket. A peaked cap covered his thinning hair, and as always, he carried his official postbag across his shoulder.

"Good morning, Mr. Hughes," Gwen said, greeting him with a smile.

Known throughout the area as Ed the Post, the friendly postman had been delivering the mail to Llanwddyn for over seventeen years and was considered an honorary member of the village, even though he actually lived in Llanfyllin. He walked the twelve-mile journey one day, stayed overnight in the village, and returned to Llanfyllin with the outgoing letters the next day. Day in and day out, back and forth, he made the trek, and up until recently, when bridges were built to accommodate the dam construction, he'd had to ford three rivers each way.

Gwen wasn't quite sure why he kept doing it. She'd even asked him once. He'd told her that the long walk kept his legs strong enough to keep up with his two grandsons and gave him plenty of time to work on his singing without a critical audience. It was hard to imagine that Ed the Post had much time or energy for chasing grandsons after his long daily walk, and after seventeen years of singing, Gwen thought he ought to already be proficient or have no hope for further improvement. But she was wise enough to keep her opinions to herself.

"Lovely day at last," Ed the Post said. "About time that rain stopped. Made for a slow walk all week. By the time I got here yesterday, your aunt had already closed the post office. But don't you worry." He gave her a wink. "I slept with the postbag under my pillow for safekeeping. Wouldn't do to lose any letters. Especially one from Liverpool."

Gwen gasped, dropped the empty bucket, and ran over to the postman. "Do you have a letter for me from Liverpool?"

He chuckled. "Why don't you come with me to the post office? It seems to me that the postmistress is someone else who's been looking for a letter from Liverpool for some time now. I daresay she'll be especially anxious to sort today's mail and might just get it done extra fast."

"I'll come right away," Gwen called as she picked up the bucket and ran back to the kitchen. Placing the bucket in the entry and grabbing her shawl off the coatrack, she was back within seconds.

"Well now," he said, "if your aunt's half as efficient as you are, we'll have everyone's letters to them in no time."

"Let's hurry, Mr. Hughes!" Gwen said, grabbing the older man's hand and pulling him toward the post office.

Ed the Post picked up his pace. "I suppose I'd better start praying I've not got your hopes up over one of those arrogant letters from the Liverpool Corporation," he said. "Mind you, I've delivered plenty of those over the last few years, and I've never seen handwriting this poor before."

Gwen laughed. "It has to be Robert. It has to be."

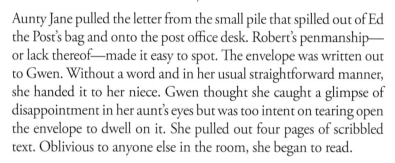

Aunty Jane pulled the letter from the small pile that spilled out of Ed the Post's bag and onto the post office desk. Robert's penmanship—or lack thereof—made it easy to spot. The envelope was written out to Gwen. Without a word and in her usual straightforward manner, she handed it to her niece. Gwen thought she caught a glimpse of disappointment in her aunt's eyes but was too intent on tearing open the envelope to dwell on it. She pulled out four pages of scribbled text. Oblivious to anyone else in the room, she began to read.

Dear Gwennie,

I have so much to tell you, I hardly know where to begin. First, let me reassure you that I am safe and well. The journey to Liverpool was long but relatively uneventful, and I was able to get directions to the docks and secure a small room at a nearby inn without difficulty.

The inn is noisy and dirty—as is Liverpool as a whole. I confess there's not much to recommend the city, and when I see how many people live in squalor and share the same air as the smoking chimney stacks, I'm all the more grateful for my Welsh upbringing. My short stay in this industrial city has helped me understand why so many seek a life at sea, where at least they can breathe fresh air.

For the first few days after my arrival, I spent my time wandering the dockyards, asking for word on any ship that might be hiring. My attempts to join in conversations with other sailors were often frustrated by my poor grasp of the English language. If I'd only known that being Welsh would end up being my biggest asset, I would have been saved from hours of discouragement.

Two days ago, I heard rumor that the captain of the Talookdar was looking for a new cabin boy. I immediately set off to find that sailing ship. Oh, Gwennie, you should see her! She's almost one hundred yards long, with three huge masts, all of them fully square rigged with a small gaff sail on the stern, and she's newly arrived from the dockyard, so her lacquered bows positively gleam.

Somehow I managed to persuade the sailors working on dock to speak to the captain about me. Perhaps I have your prayers to thank for that? Imagine my surprise when I was introduced to Captain Tecwyn Owen and discovered that he's as Welsh as you and me. He told me his mother was born in Pennant near Llanfyllin, so he's familiar with Llanwddyn. I would never dare say this to his face (he's quite an imposing and intimidating man), but I believe that my small connection to his mother was what prompted him to hire me then and there.

And so, my dear Gwennie, I write this from the deck of the Talookdar, where we are readying for our maiden voyage to Calcutta, India. We aim to sail before the end of the week and will be gone for several months. I will send you a letter the moment we reach port, but until then, do not worry about me. Already I have a great love for my ship and deep respect for my captain. I anticipate that many of the crew members will become my friends as my English improves and we work together on the long voyage ahead.

Please share my news with Aunty Jane and with Lewis. I hope that despite her initial displeasure at my decision to go to sea, Aunty Jane has now come to terms with my leaving. I will always be grateful for the way in which she took us in when Mam and Dad died. With your inherent goodness, perhaps you can be a big enough blessing to her for both of us.

Cofion cynnes,
Robert

Gwen raised her eyes from the letter to find Aunty Jane and Ed the Post watching her.

"Well?" There was anxiety in Aunty Jane's voice.

"He's fine," Gwen hurried to reassure her. "He's been hired by a Welsh captain. They sailed for India this week."

"Well, I never!" Ed the Post looked suitably impressed.

"The captain's Welsh?" Aunty Jane said.

"Yes." Gwen felt giddy with relief. "Here." She offered the letter to her aunt. "You can read it."

Surprise lit her aunt's eyes. "You want me to read your letter?"

"Yes," Gwen said with a smile. "I think you should. You need to know how happy he is."

Aunty Jane reached out and took the proffered papers. "Thank you, Gwen," she said with genuine gratitude. "That's very good of you."

Gwen felt a twinge of remorse that Robert had not written to Aunty Jane personally. She suspected their aunt cared for them far more than she would ever admit. She had been married for only three years when her husband had passed away. Never having had children of her own, Gwen guessed that her aunt had known much loneliness in her life. Her parents, her husband, and her sister had all preceded her in death. Perhaps Robert's leaving had reminded her of how often she'd been left behind by those she loved.

Aunty Jane read the letter quickly. When she handed it back, she gave Gwen a nod of acceptance.

"It's as he wanted, and I'm glad for that," she said, "but with all he has ahead, he will need our prayers more than ever."

"India!" Ed the Post said as though he were still trying to talk himself into believing the place really existed. He shook his head. "Well, that gives me something new to think on as I walk back to Llanfyllin, that's for certain."

Ed the Post's words seemed to snap Aunty Jane back to business.

"We need to let you get on your way, Ed," she said, reaching under the counter for the pile of outgoing letters.

"Yes, indeed," the postman replied, taking them from her and shoving them into his postbag. "I should like to get home before dark."

Within minutes he was ready, and with a friendly wave and the jingle of the bell on the post office door, he set off down the street.

Gwen replaced Robert's letter in the envelope and tucked it carefully into her pocket. "I'd best return to mopping the kitchen floor," she said.

Her aunt's thin-lipped frown was back. Picking up a handful of the letters Ed the Post had left on the desk, she started to sort them. "Notwithstanding all this excitement, I expect the cleaning to be done well, Gwen."

With a quiet sigh, Gwen walked toward the post office door. "Yes, Aunty Jane."

Maybe any sensitivity or caring she thought she'd seen in her aunt moments ago had been nothing more than hopeful imagining after all.

Chapter 7

IT WAS LATE AFTERNOON BY the time Gwen finally finished the last of the dusting and was able to escape to the mountain. Despite a day of sunshine, the waterlogged path remained muddy, and she had to catch herself more than once as her boots slipped on the wet grass. Her favorite boulder, however, was dry, so she sat on it to survey the scene before her.

In the valley, the rivers were still running high, their water murky with displaced soil from the riverbanks. The fields were vivid green and dotted with white spring lambs. The trees were in full leaf and the hedgerows thick and lush. Patches of color—the yellow of gorse, the pinkish-white of hawthorn, and the blue of bluebells—stood out amidst the array of greens. She could see a few people walking the main road through the village, and others were on the narrow road that led toward the cluster of buildings put up to house the ever-increasing number of navvies at the dam.

The cranes at the dam remained motionless. Even from her distant vantage point, Gwen could see the large pools of water gathered around the base of the machinery. Three men walked the length of the partially built retaining wall, and a few more stood in a small cluster at the far side of the dam, obviously conferring with one another.

Gwen opened her sketchbook, drew a freshly sharpened pencil out of her pocket, and started to draw. Her eyes moved quickly from the paper to the scene in front of her and back again. It didn't take long before she was completely absorbed and the village, the distant farmhouses, the dam construction—everything that was distinctly Llanwddyn—came to life beneath her fingers.

"I had no idea you were such a talented artist, Gwennie."

With a small shriek, she leapt to her feet. Clutching her sketchbook to her chest, she took a deep, shuddering breath.

"Lewis! You can't keep sneaking up on me like that."

Lewis frowned. "I just walked up the path like anyone else would."

"No." Gwen shook her head vehemently. "Other people make noise. They break twigs, slip on shale, clomp their boots, something that others can hear!"

"Well, I don't especially want to tromp up here like a one-man herd of cows."

Gwen's heart was still racing. "You don't have to tromp."

"What, then? You want me to shout or whistle?"

It was Gwen's turn to frown. "You make it sound like you're calling for a dog." She paused for a moment as a recent memory surfaced. It was Lewis's tuneful whistle that had alerted her to his presence at the smithy when the navvies had her cornered. "What about a tune? Yes, you could whistle a tune. I'd hear that."

Lewis gave an amused shrug. "A tune. All right. Do you have anything particular in mind?"

Gwen tilted her head to one side as she thought. "What about 'Dau Gi Bach'?"

He chuckled. "'Dau Gi Bach' it is."

"Right, then." Gwen smiled, relieved that the children's nursery rhyme was an acceptable solution. "No more giving me heart attacks."

She moved back to take her seat on the boulder. Lewis hovered nearby, suddenly acting uncertain. Gwen pointed to the flattened surface of the large rock.

"Since you're up here, you may as well sit down," she said.

Leaving as much space as possible between them, he took a seat. After a few moments of awkward silence, he pointed to her sketchbook. "Will you show me what you've drawn?"

Somewhat reluctantly, Gwen lowered the sketchbook so it lay open on her knee. "It's the valley," she said.

"I can see that," Lewis said, and she thought she heard a hint of admiration in his voice.

He pointed at the rough outline of the distant buildings she'd added to the hillside. "You've even put in Dai Williams's farmhouse and milking parlor." He gave her an encouraging smile. "This is so accurate you could probably keep track of how many new lambs he has this year."

Gwen shook her head slightly, embarrassed yet unaccountably pleased that he seemed to genuinely like her drawing. "The sheep move around too much. I really don't have any idea how many are out at any given time."

Lewis nodded his understanding, then pointed at her rendering of the partially completed dam. "This is another part of your picture that will be different the next time you look at it."

"I know," she said. "That's why I started drawing the valley; I wanted a record of what it used to be like and how it changes."

She began turning back the pages in her sketchbook. Almost every sheet displayed the same scene, but each picture had subtle differences. Winter scenes showed bare trees and mounding snow. A few pages later, the same barren branches were covered in fat buds, and then they were hidden by blossoms and dense foliage. Dying, curling leaves indicated the return of winter, along with the buildup of ice along the rivers. Sheep and cattle came and went. The sky varied from dark and stormy to cloudless and clear. And even though the old stone buildings that comprised the center of the village remained unchanged, the difference in the construction all around them made each drawing truly unique.

From the steady trickle of men pouring into the valley along the narrow mountain road to the construction of their bunkhouses; from the introduction of the initial rail lines to the arrival of the first mechanical crane; from the digging of the dam's foundations to the appearance of the first blocks of granite. Each milestone in Llanwddyn's rapidly changing history was pictorially recorded in Gwen's sketchbook.

Lewis studied each picture in silence as Gwen slowly flipped from one to the next. When she reached the picture she'd been working on minutes before, she hesitated for only a second before closing the book.

"I daresay that's all the drawing I'll do today," she said quietly.

"Gwennie." Lewis's voice sounded strained. "Those are amazing."

She glanced over at him and was startled by the intensity in his eyes.

"I mean it," he said. "I know we're supposed to ooh and ah over the paintings of the masters in our textbooks at school, but none of them ever really meant anything to me." He pointed at her sketchbook. "Those do. They're important. For you, for me, for all the people in Llanwddyn, not to mention the ones who'll come here years from now and have no idea what it was once like."

Gwen looked back at the village. "I probably shouldn't resent the dam construction the way I do," she said. "But with each change that comes to the valley, I feel like another part of me is lost."

"I don't like the changes either," Lewis told her. "But even though we may not be able to stop the development, we can make sure people don't forget the price the villagers of Llanwddyn paid so Liverpool could have their dam; the loss of our homes, our farmland, and our community as it once was. That's why you mustn't stop drawing. Keep a record of this for your children and for mine."

Slowly Gwen nodded.

"You promise?" Lewis asked.

She nodded again, this time a little more vigorously.

Lewis seemed satisfied. "Is that why you come up here so much? To draw?"

"I always bring my sketchbook but don't always draw. I suppose there are times when I just need to be alone, to be somewhere quiet, where I can think. It's a good place for that. Not many people come up this way."

At her words, the awkwardness between them returned.

"I should leave you be, then," he said, coming to his feet. "I'm sorry if I disturbed you."

"It's all right." Gwen stood up too. "After yesterday . . ." She paused. "I understand why you came. Thank you."

He stuck his hands in his pockets. "Robert would skin me alive if anything bad happened . . ."

Gwen gasped. "Oh, Lewis! How could I have forgotten to tell you? A letter came today from Robert."

Lewis's eyes lit up. "Was it good news?"

Gwen pulled the envelope from her pocket and drew out the four sheets of paper. Already, the creases were looking worn from being unfolded and folded again. She offered them to him. "You can read it," she said. Surprise crossed his face, followed almost immediately by hesitation. Gwen extended her arm farther. "He mentions you."

Lewis took the letter, and when she met his quizzical look with a smile, he began to read.

"Well," he said a few minutes later as he handed the letter back to her. "It seems to me that you and I are in big trouble."

At his words, Gwen experienced a pang of misgiving. "What do you mean?"

"If we thought his stories of sailing ships and foreign lands were bad before, there'll be no stopping him once he's experienced them himself," Lewis said, trying hard to hold back a grin. "He's going to talk our ears off when he gets back."

Gwen laughed. "He will, won't he?"

Lewis rolled his eyes. "It will be awful!"

Chapter 8

OVER THE NEXT SEVERAL WEEKS, Gwen's life seemed to fall into a vague routine. Most days she walked to school with Mabel. If Mabel was running late, Gwen made sure she walked within earshot of other students. The same was true on her return journey, but she also noticed that after the school bell rang, Lewis's brother, Rowland, tended to loiter near the school doors until she left. Rowland and his friends were two years younger than Gwen and never said much to her, but they seemed to have made a habit of walking home behind her.

Despite the reassuring presence of other students nearby, Gwen was always mindful of any strangers on the street. She'd learned the hard way and tensed if she heard English voices, especially if they were coming from the direction of the Powys Arms. The warmer weather kept most of the navvies busy at the dam site or the quarry during daylight hours now, but still she kept her eyes lowered if she passed one and hoped the three men she'd encountered before had been drunk enough to never recognize her or show her unwanted attention again.

There had been quite a few times when she'd been tempted to tell Aunty Jane about the navvies who had accosted her on the street, but she'd been reluctant to mention it, partly because she didn't want to relive the experience through the telling and partly because she really didn't know how her aunt would react. There were days when her aunt treated her with such long-suffering that Gwen wondered if she cared about her at all. On those days, Gwen assumed her aunt would either brush off her account of the encounter as exaggeration or reprimand her for being foolish.

Every once in a while, however, Aunty Jane would say something unexpectedly thoughtful, her expression would soften, and Gwen would experience a glimmer of hope that her aunt did have kind feelings, albeit deeply hidden, for her. During those moments, Gwen considered telling her about the incident that still caused her nightmares. But the moments were fleeting and far between and were usually followed by the assignment of a new chore. The more time that passed, the harder it became to bring the issue up at all, so she remained silent.

She visited the clearing on the mountain often, and occasionally, if she was up there after the smithy closed for the day, Lewis joined her. As promised, he always whistled "Dau Gi Bach" as he neared the boulder, and she no longer jumped like a scared rabbit when he appeared in the clearing. He had also become better at gauging whether or not she wanted to talk, and on her introspective days, he simply sat on the boulder in silence, watching with her as the calm of evening fell upon the valley below.

As the weeks passed, the awkwardness between them all but disappeared, and Gwen found that she looked forward to the time they spent together. Their conversations varied from reminiscing over childhood memories to sharing their concerns for the future of Llanwddyn. Sometimes they spoke of trivial things or daily frustrations, but gradually Gwen found herself beginning to confide in Lewis the way she had always done with her brother, and she realized that in a vital way, he had truly stepped in for Robert.

One day in mid-June, Gwen made a point of waiting until the smithy was closed before heading up the mountain. She didn't take her sketchbook this time, and when she reached the boulder, she didn't sit as she usually did. Instead, she walked over to the nearby oak tree and stood beneath its shady arms.

Despite the lateness of the hour, the summer sun still shone brightly. Gwen took off her bonnet and let the sunlight filtering through the leaves warm her upturned face. Why couldn't life be simple? Why were there so many decisions to make, so many unexpected bends in the road? She shook her head as though the movement would help sort her jumbled thoughts.

The whistled melody of "Dau Gi Bach" reached her, and Gwen moved away from the tree as Lewis entered the clearing.

"Hello," he said, a look of surprise flitting across his face. "Not sitting to draw today?"

"No."

He looked at her quizzically. "Is everything all right?"

Instead of answering him, Gwen pulled a large envelope out of her pocket. "A letter came today," she said.

"From Robert?" he asked.

She shook her head. "No. From the school in Llanfyllin." At his look of confusion, she continued. "Several weeks back, I took the entrance exam to see if I could qualify as a boarding student there."

"I remember," he said. "It was the reason you were walking home late the afternoon you ran into the navvies."

"Yes," Gwen said. She didn't want to go back over the events of that day. "I got the results today."

"And?"

She pulled a piece of paper out of the envelope and handed it to him. For a few moments, Lewis focused his attention on the letter, and when he raised his head again, he seemed momentarily stunned. "You got in—and with a full scholarship!" He glanced back at the letter as though needing confirmation, but then he smiled. "You did it, Gwennie! You can keep on with your schooling and won't even have to worry about paying for room and board."

Gwen nodded and tried to swallow the lump in her throat. But Lewis, it seemed, was coming to know her well.

"You're not happy?" he asked, studying her with concern.

"Of course I am," she said. "Still in shock, perhaps, but thrilled to have done so well." She shifted her feet uncomfortably. "At the moment, moving to Llanfyllin on my own seems a bit overwhelming, that's all."

"Ah," Lewis said knowingly. "It's that fear of change rearing its ugly head again, isn't it?"

She groaned. "It's pathetic, I know. My brother has gone off to sea—to India, of all places—on his own, and I'm worrying about moving twelve miles to Llanfyllin."

"It will be fine. You could probably come home for a weekend every once in a while. Don't worry. Llanwddyn will still be here."

Gwen looked at him with stricken eyes, and Lewis ran his fingers through his hair. "Fine. I admit that wasn't the most brilliant thing to say, but you know what I mean. The building of the dam's not going to change things that fast. And you can come back to stay whenever you're ready." He tried a different tack. "Does your aunt know about the scholarship? What does she have to say about you going to Llanfyllin?"

"She knows," Gwen said. "She was the one who brought me the letter." She gave a ghost of a smile. "That's what happens when your aunt is the postmistress."

Lewis acknowledged the truth of that statement with a small smile of his own. "No clandestine letters in your future."

"None," she said so solemnly that Lewis laughed.

"Tell me what your aunt said."

Gwen sighed. "She told me she was very happy that I'd done so well on the exam. Then she told me what a lucky girl I was to have this opportunity and that she would miss me at the house."

"I see," he said, and the look in his eyes told her that he really did. There had been no discussion between her and Aunty Jane, no expression of real emotion or sharing of feelings. As far as Aunty Jane was concerned, no one ever looked a gift horse in the mouth; Gwen would be leaving for Llanfyllin in September.

"Maybe she's thinking it will be nice to have the house to herself again," Gwen said.

"I don't think that's it. She'll be very lonely with both you and Robert gone. I'm sure she's proud of you and doesn't want to stand in your way."

Gwen looked down at the bonnet swinging gently back and forth in her hands and thought about what this opportunity might mean for her. There would be well-educated teachers in Llanfyllin, new academic subjects to explore, strong students with fresh ideas, students who could become her friends. For the first time since she'd read the letter, she pushed past her fears and allowed herself to explore the possibilities the scholarship presented. And as she did, her excitement began to blossom.

"Except for when I lost my parents and moved to Llanwddyn, it would be the most frightening thing I've ever done," she said, turning her head slightly so she could see Lewis's face. "But it would be a marvelous experience."

Lewis smiled broadly. "See. You're not so different from Robert after all. It sounds like you're describing a journey to India by sailboat."

"Without the seasickness or the elephants," she said.

He laughed. "I certainly hope not. But I tell you what, if you see any animals wilder than Dai Williams's Hereford bull there, I think you'd be completely justified in leaving Llanfyllin and never returning."

"Well, thank you, Lewis. That's good to know," Gwen said, rolling her eyes. "I had no idea you would be so helpful."

"Of course," Lewis said with a grin. " Anytime." He pointed to the path. "Come on, Miss Scholarship, I'll walk you home."

◆

A week later, Gwen's fears about attending school in Llanfyllin had lessened considerably, and her anticipation of the adventures ahead had gradually increased. Aunty Jane had made Gwen's exam results known to a few talkative customers at the post office, and several people had stopped to congratulate Gwen on the scholarship. She was thankful, however, that because of the upcoming St. John's Day festival, her schooling was not the main topic of conversation in the village that week.

The annual festival, always held on the twenty-fourth of June, was originally established to celebrate St. John, the patron saint of the Llanwddyn church, but over the years, it had developed into an all-day event for the entire village. Activities began in the morning, with various competitions kicking things off. Those were followed by a huge football game in the afternoon and a country dance in the evening. The planning committee had worked tirelessly for weeks, and everyone was thrilled when Saturday arrived with cloudless sunshine.

That morning, Gwen and Aunty Jane made their way down the road to the large field beside the church, where the first races of the day were to be held. Children were running around excitedly, their parents talking together in small clusters. Most of the locals had taken time away from their daily work to join the celebration, and Gwen noticed there were a few navvies wandering around the field too.

It had not escaped the villagers that because St. John's Day had fallen on a Saturday, many of the navvies not planning on traveling home for Sunday might make an appearance at the festival. Gwen found the thought unsettling. Saturday was payday at the dam, and too many of the men picked up their wages and headed straight for the Powys Arms. A few inebriated English navvies could easily spoil the traditional festival activities for everyone else.

Gwen and her aunt had barely entered the field when Reverend Jones, who was standing on a wooden box so he could be seen above the crowd, called for the start of the egg-and-spoon race. Moments later, Mabel appeared at Gwen's side.

"Come on, Gwen. You got here just in time." She grabbed Gwen's arm and pulled.

Gwen glanced up at her aunt, who gave her a nod of permission and took the picnic basket from her.

"I'll meet you by the old ash tree when it's time to eat," Aunty Jane said, and as Gwen hurried away, her aunt continued across the field toward a small grove of trees where some of the older members of the community were already seated, watching the festivities from the shade.

Chapter 9

GWEN AND MABEL JOINED ABOUT a dozen other girls who were already lined up at the start of the race, and Mrs. Williams the Shop, the shopkeeper's wife, handed them each a metal spoon and a hard-boiled brown egg. Gwen set the egg on her spoon, steadying her hand as the egg wobbled precariously. She glanced to her right. Mabel had her egg and spoon ready and was watching Mr. Williams the Shop, who stood at the sidelines, a whistle poised at the side of his mouth.

The moment the whistle sounded, Mabel took off with all the other girls close behind. Within seconds, eggs started rolling off spoons, and cries of disappointment mingled with the cheers of the spectators lining the racecourse. Gwen tried to focus on keeping her spoon steady, but when she took her eyes off her egg to gauge the slight slope ahead, she saw Mabel trip on the uneven ground in front of her. Mabel's egg landed in the grass, and within seconds Gwen's egg joined it.

"I can't believe it!" Mabel cried, picking up her egg. Her shoulders slumped as she surveyed all the cracks in the shell. "I've been practicing balancing an egg on a spoon for weeks. I really thought I stood a chance in this race."

A loud cheer sounded, and both girls glanced over at the finish line, where the four competitors who had managed to finish the course without dropping their eggs had just arrived.

"You were ahead the whole time," Gwen said.

Mabel's mouth drooped. "Yes, but that doesn't matter now, does it?"

"Maybe you can try another race?"

Mabel shook her head. "I'm not fast enough in the running races, and I just get tangled up in the sack race."

"What about the three-legged race?" Gwen asked.

"You need a partner for that one," Mabel said, kicking at an offending tuft of grass as she stated the obvious.

"Well, if you don't have one, I'll do it with you."

Mabel raised her head. "You will?"

"Yes." Gwen shrugged. "I know we haven't practiced, but we could give it a go."

Hope returned to Mabel's eyes. "All right," she said, turning toward the starting line. "But we'll have to hurry. I think it might be next."

Less than five minutes later, they were standing at the beginning of the race, with Gwen's right ankle tied to Mabel's left. Gwen had her arm around Mabel's shoulders, and Mabel's arm was securely anchored around Gwen's waist. Their eyes were locked on Mr. Williams the Shop, and as soon as he blew his whistle, they raised their joined legs and leaped across the starting line.

The six-inch discrepancy in their height had Mabel virtually flying across the grass to keep up with Gwen's long strides, but her determination to do well more than made up for her short stature, and they crossed the finish line in second place.

"We did it!" Mabel cried.

Gwen staggered backward on her one free leg as Mabel threw her arms around her.

"Yes." Gwen laughed at her friend's excitement. "You were marvelous."

Mabel beamed, then hurried to untie the rope from around their ankles so she could give the winners her congratulations before running off to share the news of her success with her mother.

Gwen entered the sack race next and, once again, benefited from her long legs. She came in first, and when she joined Aunty

Jane for lunch and showed her the ribbons she'd won, Aunty Jane gave an unsurprised nod.

"Your mam always won the sack race," she said as she handed Gwen a bacon butty.

"Really?" Gwen held her breath. Her aunt rarely spoke of the past, perhaps because it was too painful, but when she did let something slip, Gwen clung to every word.

Aunty Jane nodded again. "She was built just like you, long and lean." She pursed her lips and looked Gwen up and down. "I daresay she was about your height."

"I'm five feet seven inches," Gwen informed her.

"That sounds about right," Aunty Jane said. "I've noticed that you're taller than a lot of the girls in the village, just like your mam was. It seems like she was always taller than me, even though I'm three years older than her." Sadness filled her eyes for a second, but she seemed to steel herself against becoming sentimental. "She knew how to use those long legs though. She could beat most of the boys in a footrace."

Gwen smiled. She liked learning of things she shared with her mother. There had been many times she'd wished she were short and pleasantly plump like Mabel Richards. Perhaps now that she knew she was built like her mother, she wouldn't mind the way she was quite so much. In the past, remembering that her wavy, often unruly mane was the image of her mother's had helped lessen her craving for Mabel's raven, silky hair. Gwen made a mental note to be more thankful for her willowy form.

After lunch, the men's competitions started. Gwen was glad to see that Lewis and his brother, Rowland, were on the winning side of the tug-of-war, and she was quite sure that most of the villagers were secretly elated that one of their own—Huw Fawr, a local farmer whose strength and stature were legendary—beat out all the navvies, including the burliest quarryman, in tossing the traditional seventy-five-pound stone the farthest.

The competitions concluded with a giant football game, the English and Irish navvies joining the local Welshmen until there were over a hundred men chasing the ball around the field. Even though men exchanged angry words several times when the tackling got rough, the game concluded without a single punch being thrown, and the villagers breathed a collective sigh of relief that despite the inclusion of a few pub-frequenting navvies, they'd averted an all-out brawl.

At the end of the football game, everyone dispersed to their homes to put young children to bed or to prepare for the dance. Aunty Jane was too set in her nonconformist ways to deign to attend any kind of dance, even one that included youth as young as thirteen and fourteen, but given the fact that their minister, John Ellis, had not specifically preached against going, she was allowing Gwen to attend for the first time. Gwen had been filled with excited anticipation for weeks, but now that the time had come, she found herself standing in front of the small mirror in her bedroom, overcome by anxiety.

After changing into her Sunday-best dress, she'd taken her hair out of the long braid she usually wore and, in an effort to appear a little older, had pulled her hair up into a loose bun. To her chagrin, however, her bun didn't look anything like the tidy chignons she'd seen on other young women in the village. The unfortunate combination of her desperately lacking hairdressing skills and her thick, wild curls had proven to be her undoing. Wispy tendrils were already falling out of the many hairpins she'd tucked around her bun, but a glance at the small clock on the dresser told her she had no time to redo it.

Taking a deep breath, Gwen placed her hand on her stomach to calm the butterflies inside. She'd always planned on attending her first dance with Robert beside her. She'd been depending on him to guide her through any unknown protocols and to be her partner or moral support should it seem as though she was destined to be a wallflower for the night. But as much as she wished it were different, his reassuring presence was not going to be there, and Gwen knew she had to face this new experience alone.

She squared her shoulders and gave her reflection an encouraging smile. She could do this. It would help prepare her for all the things she would have to face on her own in Llanfyllin. This was part of growing up, and she was ready.

A knock sounded on her bedroom door. "Gwen?"

She opened the door.

"Mabel is here for you," Aunty Jane said.

Gwen couldn't help smiling at the fact that the same Mabel who was consistently late for school had arrived early to accompany her to the dance.

"I'm ready," Gwen said.

Aunty Jane gave her a scrutinizing look. "You hair is already falling out of your bun," she said.

Gwen gave a defeated sigh. "I know. I couldn't seem to get it quite right."

Her aunt walked around her. She brushed out a couple of small wrinkles in Gwen's dark-blue dress and studied her hair with a frown. "I daresay it will stay together for a couple of hours. It's too late now, but next time, ask for my help."

Gwen glanced at her aunt's graying hair that was, as always, scraped back into a tight bun at the base of her head. It was not exactly the look she had been trying for, but she had to concede it was tidy.

"Yes, Aunty Jane," she said quietly.

"I hope you will have a nice time," Aunty Jane said, facing Gwen once again and clasping her hands in front of her. "Remember, no excess frivolity. I expect you to behave like a well-mannered young lady."

"Yes, Aunty Jane." What little self-confidence Gwen had had in her appearance was now gone, and her enthusiasm for attending the dance at all was diminishing rapidly, but she put on a brave face and forced a smile. "I'd better not keep Mabel waiting any longer."

"Very well, then," Aunty Jane said. "Off you go."

Gwen swallowed her disappointment. Perhaps her aunt didn't realize how nervous she was. Perhaps she really thought Gwen was completely confident when it came to interacting with young men or her skills on the dance floor. Neither could be further from the truth. But it seemed a little late to admit to those things now. No matter how much she wished it otherwise, she would be setting out for her first dance without an encouraging word or reassuring embrace from anyone.

⸙

They held the St. John's Day dance in the village hall. Someone had decorated with tall vases full of gladiolus flowers, which helped cheer up the drab, functional room. Wooden chairs had been placed against the wall, leaving the center of the room completely clear. In one corner, there was a table with an enormous steaming tea urn and a pitcher of water surrounded on either side with rows and rows of cups. On the small wooden stage, Rhys Jones, the tailor, was tuning his fiddle and Huw Fawr, still glowing from his victory in the stone toss, was discussing the order of the dances with him. Gwen could hear Huw's deep voice all the way across the room, which was why he was the most requested country-dance caller in the county.

Men and women dressed in their Sunday best were flowing into the hall. The sounds of talking and laughter filled the air. Gwen stood at the door and looked around. Even though familiar faces surrounded her, she felt completely out of place and very alone.

Beside her, Mabel was busily scanning the room too. "Come on, Gwen," she said happily. "I see some of the boys from school."

Without a backward glance, Mabel hurried across the floor toward the table in the corner. Gwen was quite sure that standing by herself at the door was preferable to maintaining stilted conversation with a group of young men, but as people filtered into the hall behind her, she realized she was going to be forced to move out of the way. Reluctantly, she trailed after Mabel.

She was halfway across the hall when she heard her name being called. "Gwen! Gwen Humphreys!"

Turning to her right, she saw Ioan Llanwddyn sitting cross-legged on the edge of the stage. The elderly man beckoned to her. Gwen wasn't anxious to revisit her last humiliating encounter with Ioan, but talking to him seemed less intimidating than facing the crowd of young men now buzzing around Mabel. She stepped closer.

"I haven't seen you for a long time," he said. "But I did hear you got word from your brother."

"Yes." Gwen smiled, remembering the kind things Ioan had said about Robert. "He found work on a ship captained by a Welshman. They sailed for India several weeks ago."

"Well now, that's grand!" Ioan said. "Won't he have some stories to tell!"

Gwen laughed. "I daresay he'll be more than happy to share them all with you too."

Ioan gave his characteristic toothless grin. "And I'll be mighty glad to hear them."

"Are you ready over there, Ioan?" Huw called over to him.

"Just say the word," Ioan called back.

"What are you going to do?" Gwen asked, curiosity getting the better of her.

Ioan lifted one of his walking sticks. "Ah, well now, I may not be much of a dancer, but there's plenty of rhythm in me. Young Huw Fawr, over there, rather likes to have a bit of help with keeping everyone where they need to be."

"What do you do?"

The twinkle was back in Ioan's eye. "Just you watch," he said.

On the stage, Rhys played a long, piercing note on his fiddle, and Huw stepped up to the edge of the stage. "Take your partners, ladies and gentlemen," he called. "It's time to dance the Jac y Do!"

The lull in people's chatter when Huw spoke was suddenly replaced by a flurry of activity as several men led women into the center of the room and lined up facing their partners. At a nod from Huw, Ioan raised his walking stick and tapped it against the stage floor in a smooth, regular beat. With the nodding of his head, Rhys picked up the beat and began to fiddle, and Huw's voice followed immediately after, calling out the first dance steps.

Fascinated, Gwen watched the couples step together, step apart, and follow the lead through arched arms. The fiddle music swelled, and she caught herself humming along to the familiar tune and tapping her foot in time with Ioan's rhythmic beat until the last note sounded and everyone on the dance floor turned to face the stage and clap.

"That was wonderful," Gwen said, smiling broadly.

"Not too bad for a farmer, a tailor, and a cripple, eh?" Ioan said with an answering grin.

"Can I stay here and watch?"

Ioan chuckled. "You can stay here until some young man comes and sweeps you onto the floor. I don't reckon you'll be here long, mind."

"I'd rather watch."

"What you'd rather do may not play into it," Ioan said sagely, but he didn't have time to elaborate because Huw was already calling for the next dance.

Chapter 10

GWEN WATCHED TWO MORE DANCES before Rowland approached her.

"Hello, Gwen," he said, running his finger under his collar just as she'd seen his older brother do when he was anxious about something.

She gave him a tentative smile, hoping it would help put him at ease. "Hello, Rowland," she replied.

"I was wondering . . ." he began. "Uh . . . would you be my partner in the next dance?"

Gwen didn't look at Ioan. She knew all too well that he'd have mischief written all over his face.

"I'd be glad to," she said quickly, even though she was already worrying over whether she'd remember any of the steps she'd learned years before in school.

Rowland's look of relief made her smile. Perhaps she'd found someone even more unsure of himself than she was. He offered her his arm, and as Huw called for the next set of dancers to take the floor, he led her to the end of the line of couples.

The music began, and Gwen directed all her attention to following Huw's instructions. At first she struggled to keep up, but after repeating some of the steps a few times, her memory of the dance began coming back, and she started to relax and enjoy the experience. By the time Rhys played the final note, she was smiling.

"Thank you, Rowland," Gwen said as she took his arm again.

"I told Lewis I thought you'd be a good dancer," he said. "And I was right."

Gwen felt her cheeks color. "That's very nice of you to say," she said, "even if it's not entirely true." Feeling suddenly uncomfortable again, she changed the subject. "Is Lewis coming to the dance?"

"Oh, yes, he'll be here," Rowland said, steering her to the side of the room where Mabel was standing. "Mam insisted we bathe after the football game, and he had to wait his turn."

Rowland must have suddenly realized what he'd said because his ears turned red, and Gwen had to work hard to prevent a giggle that she knew would make him feel even worse.

"You must have beaten him home, I suppose," Gwen managed at last.

"That's right," Rowland mumbled.

They had reached Mabel, and Gwen relinquished Rowland's arm. Rowland formally thanked Gwen for the dance and hurried away before Gwen could say another word.

"Dear me," Mabel said. "What did you do to scare Rowland so badly?"

Gwen watched him disappear with a sinking heart. She hoped she hadn't done anything to embarrass him further. "Nothing," she said.

"He doesn't usually—" Mabel stopped midsentence. "Oh, my," she continued, her tone changing completely. "Rowland's brother, Lewis, is here." She dug her fingers into Gwen's arm. "Isn't he the most handsome man you've ever seen?"

Stunned by the dreamy look that had suddenly entered Mabel's eyes, Gwen glanced across the room to see Lewis stopping to greet someone by the door. His thick hair glistened as though still damp, and even though his face was partially obscured by someone else, Gwen could tell he was smiling by the way his blue eyes lit up. He stood a little taller than most of the other men in the room, and his Sunday suit coat did little to hide the broad shoulders he'd developed over the last few years.

A disturbance at the hall's entrance interrupted Gwen's study of Lewis. Even above the sound of the fiddle, Ioan's beating stick, and the dancers' feet, she recognized the sound of English voices. She watched with dismay as five navvies pushed their way past the villagers standing near the door to stand at the outskirts of the dance floor. From across the room, they silently watched the dancers for a few moments before separating to slowly circle the room.

At first the dancers blocked Gwen's view of the men's progress, but as the dance came to an end, she got her first good look at the navvy closest to her. And for a couple of seconds, time stood still. It was one of the men who had stopped her on the road from school.

"Mabel, I'm really sorry, but I've got to go," she said.

"Why?" Mabel looked at her in confusion. "Are you not feeling well?"

Gwen pressed a hand to her cheek, confident that all color was gone from her face. "I . . . I suddenly feel faint. I have to . . ." Frantically she swept the room, searching for a quick means of escape—any way that she could reach the door without going directly past the man who was quickly bearing down on her.

Gwen saw Lewis lean forward to say something to a neighbor, and then, as though he suddenly sensed something was wrong, he straightened and turned to look right at her. She didn't know what he saw in her face, but for a split second, he tensed, then in long fluid strides, he was crossing the dance floor. Gwen took an instinctive step toward him but was stopped by a hand on her arm.

"Don't rush off, young lady," the Englishman said. "I've just walked all the way over here to ask you to dance."

Gwen drew on every ounce of courage she possessed to turn and face the man from her nightmares. "I'm afraid I can't," she said in English, praying he would not feel her trembling beneath his hand.

"And just why is that?" he said, moving closer.

"Because she already promised this dance to me." Lewis stepped up to her and offered her his arm.

Gwen slid her hand around his elbow, her fingers clutching his arm as though she was drowning and he'd just thrown her a rope.

"Now, just a minute," the Englishman growled, still not releasing Gwen's other arm. "What happened to 'first come, first served'?"

"Exactly my point," Lewis said. "This dance was promised to me first." He used his head to gesture toward the other side of the room. "There are plenty of other young ladies here who are still waiting for a partner."

When the navvy still made no move to relinquish his hold on Gwen, Lewis leaned forward and said in a low voice, "I think your chances of being forced to leave this dance before you're ready will rise significantly if you cause a scene, don't you?"

For a moment, the navvy didn't say a word, but the malicious look in his eyes was undeniable. Lewis met his glare without flinching, and finally, with a curse directed at everything Welsh, and Lewis in particular, the navvy dropped Gwen's arm as though it had suddenly scalded him.

Lewis didn't hesitate. He immediately led Gwen right onto the dance floor.

"Lewis, I can't," Gwen said. She was sure he could feel her shaking through his suit-coat sleeve. "My legs . . . they're too wobbly . . . I just don't think . . ."

Lewis placed his hand over hers. "I know it will be hard." He spoke softly. "But I also know you can do it. Apart from the fact that that English thug will be watching our every move for the next little bit, Mabel's eyes were as big as saucers throughout that encounter. If I walked you right out of here—which I know you'd prefer—she'd make sure the whole village was talking about it by the end of the dance."

Gwen turned slightly and instantly confirmed that Lewis's concerns were justified. Not only were Mabel's eyes the biggest Gwen had ever seen, but they had also obviously not strayed from

Lewis since he had first appeared at Gwen's side. Gwen did not bother looking for the navvy; she sensed his eyes upon her and knew he was close.

Lewis positioned Gwen beside Mrs. Williams the Shop, and with an encouraging nod, he moved to stand across from her.

Mrs. Williams the Shop beamed at her. "I always say it's too bad we don't hold these dances more often," she said. "So nice for all you young people to socialize like this."

Gwen managed to respond with a weak smile before Ioan's stick sounded and the fiddle began.

Somehow she made it through the entire dance. It passed in a blur, but the important thing was that she was still upright when the music stopped.

As everyone around them clapped, Lewis stepped forward and took her arm again. "Come on," he said gently. "I think this would be a good time to make our escape."

Doing her best to match Lewis's long strides, Gwen was almost running to keep up with him as he maneuvered through the milling crowds to the village hall door. They hurried down the steps, and with a quick glance over his shoulder, presumably to reassure himself that no one was paying them too much attention, Lewis continued his swift pace until they passed the bend in the road. As they approached Pont Cedig, he finally slowed his steps.

"Are you all right?" he asked, the calm expression he'd been wearing for the last fifteen minutes now replaced by one of genuine concern.

"That was the man who stopped me on the road," Gwen said, unable to suppress a shudder.

"I guessed as much."

There was a steely tone to Lewis's words that Gwen had never heard before, and as she glanced at his face, she realized his relatively cordial interaction with the navvy may have taken more self-control than she'd imagined. She squeezed his arm.

"Thank you for coming when you did." She looked down. "You seem to be getting into the habit of rescuing me."

He grimaced. "I may not be there next time. And that thought scares me to death." He looked over at her. "You know, it would help a lot if you weren't so pretty."

Gwen stopped midstride. "What did you say?"

Color crept into Lewis's face, and he cleared his throat uncomfortably. "It's just that I'm quite sure every navvy in the village has noticed you. That idiot at the dance won't be the only one wanting to get to know you better."

Gwen had a vague memory of her mother once telling her that she was pretty, but since her mother's passing, no one had ever complimented her on her appearance—certainly not her aunt or her brother. Thoughts of Aunty Jane reminded her of their last interaction, and Gwen's free hand immediately flew to the bun at the back of her head. To her dismay, it had not held up well during her dancing.

"How can you say such a thing?" she said, embarrassed that so many people had seen her in such disarray. "My hair . . . It's . . ."

"I like your curls, Gwennie," he said. "And I daresay I'm not alone."

Gwen stared at him, sure that if she looked hard enough she'd see the teasing glint in his eyes. But all she saw was sincerity. She swallowed hard. Something small and bright and warm burned deep inside. She wasn't sure what it was, but it was doing a remarkable job of dispelling the cloud of fear she'd been under only minutes before. Afraid that if she said anything the feeling would disappear, she simply slid her arm more securely around Lewis's and started walking again.

They made the remainder of the walk to Gwen's home in silence. Lewis stopped just outside the gate that led to the back garden, and Gwen withdrew her hand from his arm.

"Will you go back to the dance?" she asked.

"For the sake of keeping up appearances, I probably should," he said. "If anyone asks, I'll tell them you were feeling poorly and I walked you home. I don't think anyone could object to that."

"I told Mabel I wasn't feeling well," Gwen said.

"Ah, so I won't have to perjure myself twice in one night."

"Twice?" she asked.

"Yes," he said, his lips twitching as he held back a smile. "The first one was a certain falsehood about you having promised me a dance."

"Oh, that." Gwen felt like squirming but forced herself to hold still. "Well, it could have been true. I'd just danced with Rowland, so I could have very easily told you I would be your partner next."

Lewis's eyebrows shot up. "Rowland asked you to dance? That little scamp!"

Gwen smiled. "He did. And he was a perfect gentleman."

"I'm glad to hear it," Lewis said, although he didn't sound like he was.

"I think the only person who may question the promised dance is Mabel," Gwen said. "She'll wonder why I never said anything to her about it."

Lewis sighed. "Perhaps I should go back to ask Mabel to dance."

Remembering Mabel's reaction to Lewis's entrance into the village hall, Gwen had a pretty good idea of how her friend would respond to such an invitation. "That would make her very happy," Gwen said, wondering why she felt quite the opposite.

"Well, I'd best get back there, then," Lewis said. He took a step away from the gate.

"Good night, Lewis," she said. "And thank you."

"Anytime," he said. Then he turned on his heel and strode away.

Chapter 11

IF GWEN HAD BEEN WORRIED about Mabel's questions when they met to walk to school on Monday, she needn't have been. From the moment Gwen stepped out of her door to the moment Miss Ellis called for quiet in the schoolroom, Mabel talked of nothing but her experience at the dance with Lewis. He'd danced with her twice; he'd brought her a cup of tea; he'd stayed beside her and talked about every little thing. The list of Lewis's virtues was never ending, and by the time Gwen had endured a second installment all the way home, she was quite sure she never wanted to hear Lewis Morgan's name again.

She stomped into the kitchen, feeling particularly grumpy. Leaving her muddy boots at the door and hanging her shawl on the coatrack, she marched over to the kitchen table and dropped her satchel on the floor beside her chair. Then she sat down heavily and rooted through her satchel until she found her arithmetic textbook and her workbook.

Pulling them out, she set the books on the table in front of her and glared at them. She normally excelled in arithmetic, but today, for some reason, she hadn't been able to concentrate, and that had led to an unusually long homework assignment. Gwen frowned. She may as well get the problems behind her before she

made supper. Having them hanging over her head all evening
would simply make her more miserable.

Gwen made it through three-quarters of the problems before
raising her head long enough to glance around the room. When
she did, her eyes fell upon a yellowed envelope standing upright
against the china plates on the Welsh dresser. Even from a distance,
she could see the sloppy penmanship and the unusual pink-
colored stamp. Her breath caught in her throat, and she stood,
pushing back her chair with a clatter.

"Robert," she whispered before hurrying across the room to
retrieve the letter. She picked up the envelope and studied it. The
paper was very thin and crinkled when she touched it. The pink stamp
in the upper right corner bore the word *India*, and the envelope was
written out to *Miss Gwen Humphreys*. With trembling hands, Gwen
opened it and withdrew three sheets of fine paper. She walked back
over to her chair, set the papers on the table, smoothed them out
gently, and began to read.

> *Dear Gwennie,*
>
> *It has been barely three months since the SS* Talookdar *set sail
> from Liverpool, and already we have arrived in India. We made port
> in Calcutta early yesterday morning amidst great cheering from the
> crew. The ship has withstood strong currents and violent storms, but
> we were spared becoming becalmed as we navigated the Cape of Good
> Hope, and according to the captain, we traveled here faster than ever
> before.*
>
> *It is marvelous to see brown earth and green trees again, although
> I confess, now that I've finally found my sea legs, walking on land is
> quite strange. I walked along the dock this morning and found that I
> could not do it without swaying from side to side. No wonder sailors
> are known for their odd gait!*
>
> *I'm pleased to report that my ship has truly become my home away
> from home. I know my way around the vessel, even in the dark of
> night, and I feel as though I'm becoming a more competent cabin boy.
> Captain Owen has been patient with me—as have most of the other
> men. There are always a few who like to cause trouble, but my ability*

to speak to the captain in a language that only he understands has been a great blessing.

My closest friend on the ship is Monk. His real name is Jimmy Abbott, but everyone calls him Monk. It doesn't make much sense, seeing as he's a Methodist and has probably never met a Catholic abbot in his life, but he doesn't seem to mind. Almost every crewmember has a nickname. They call me Taffy. Not very imaginative, but since I'm the only Welshman on board, other than the captain (and no one would dare call him anything but Captain), it was an obvious choice.

Monk is from Manchester and is only a couple of years older than I am. Until recently, he was a cabin boy on a different ship, so even though he doesn't know exactly how Captain Owen likes things done, he's taught me a lot, and he's saved me from making an idiot of myself more than once!

I can see a little of Calcutta from the top deck, and it's unlike anything I've seen before. The heat and the flies and the smell of strange spices are overwhelming—even here on the water. The Indian people working on the dock are dark haired, dark eyed, and dark skinned, and when they speak to each other, it's impossible for me to understand a word. Believe it or not, however, I think the elephants know exactly what they are saying.

Yes, Gwennie, I've seen my first real elephant! It was the most incredible thing. It was the height of two men combined and as broad as a barn, and it lumbered down the dock with an Indian sitting astride its neck. The man had nothing more than a short stick and his voice to guide the massive beast, but I watched it roll its trunk around a wooden crate, pick the crate up, and carry it the length of the dock. If I hadn't seen it myself, I wouldn't have believed it. Monk tells me they use elephants here the way we would use a wagon and a team of horses. I hope I will see many more of them before we set sail again.

I've heard that we could be in Calcutta for up to a fortnight. The ships don't usually dock for so long, but because we arrived earlier than expected, we will have to wait for all of our return cargo to arrive. Perhaps I will be here long enough to see more exotic animals before we put to sea again.

I think of you every day and pray that all is well. Tell Lewis that after three months of hardtack biscuits, I've concluded that my memories of his mam's bara brith are the worst form of torture. I hope he never takes her cooking for granted! Give my best wishes to Aunty Jane.

    Cofion Cynnes,
    Robert

Gwen finished the letter and released a long breath. He was safe and well and happy. With a thankful heart, she picked up the pages and read them one more time. Then she tucked the pieces of paper back into the envelope, hurried over to the door, and pulled on her boots. It took only a couple of minutes to tie the laces, but she didn't waste any more time reaching for her shawl. Instead, she ran out through the back door and up the street toward the smithy.

She was halfway there when she remembered that only an hour before she'd determined that she'd had enough of Lewis for the day, the week, and quite possibly the entire month. What was she thinking? After all, it was quite possible that after the fiasco at Saturday's dance he'd had enough of her too. According to Mabel's account, he'd certainly had a much more enjoyable time when he'd returned to the village hall than he'd had with her.

Gwen's steps slowed, and she came to a stop on Pont Cedig, indecision gnawing at her. Did she really want to rush into the smithy carrying Robert's letter? Would Lewis be pleased or irritated that she hadn't waited until he was off work to share it with him? Maybe she should walk up the mountain and wait for him to join her there whenever he was free.

She chewed on her lip, considering her choices. She didn't want to sit on her boulder and wait for Lewis; he may not show up for days. And no matter what had happened on Saturday between Mabel and him, he was still Robert's best friend. Gwen tightened her hold on the envelope in her hand. For Robert's sake, she would do it now. It would be all right. She would simply show Lewis the letter and leave.

The ringing sound of metal hitting metal reached her several yards before she arrived at the smithy. The large door was ajar, so Gwen grasped the heavy latch and pulled it toward her, creating a gap large enough for her to enter. She slipped inside, then paused, waiting for her eyes to adjust to the change in light. Straight ahead, bright orange flames hungrily reached up from the furnace, creating a tangible wall of heat around the two men working in the center of the room.

With his back to the door, Owen Morgan was placing a long metal bar into the fire. Right behind him, Lewis was standing at the anvil, holding a pair of long metal pinchers and an enormous hammer. Gwen watched as Lewis used the pinchers to adjust the position of a red-hot horseshoe on the anvil, then with a mighty swing, he slammed the hammer onto the horseshoe. Sparks flew, and Gwen covered her ears as the deafening sound reverberated throughout the small room.

A leather apron covered the front of Lewis's trousers and button-down shirt. His sleeves were rolled up, and the top two buttons at his neck were undone. From across the room, Gwen could see the sweat glistening on his skin, and as she lowered her hands from her ears, he raised his arm to wipe his forehead with his sleeve. Using the pinchers, he lifted the horseshoe and rotated it, studying it carefully.

"I think it's getting close, Dad," he said, holding the horseshoe up for his father's inspection.

Owen turned to look, and as he did, he spotted Gwen standing at the doorway.

"Hello, Gwen!" he said with surprise. "When did you slip in here?"

Lewis swung around, barely maintaining his hold on the horseshoe.

"Just now, Mr. Morgan," Gwen said, doing her best to focus on Lewis's father rather than Lewis. "I'm very sorry to disturb you. It's only that a letter came from Robert today, and I thought Lewis would want to know."

"Did you now?" Owen said.

With a clatter of metal, Lewis placed the pinchers and horseshoe on the anvil, grabbed a nearby rag, and hurriedly ran it across his face, neck, and arms.

Gwen was rapidly regretting her decision to enter the smithy. It had been a very bad idea after all. Why had she ever thought the matter so urgent? It had taken Robert's letter weeks to reach her. Mr. Morgan was probably wondering why a few hours more would make any difference.

"One more time in the fire, and I think that shoe'll be finished, Dad," Lewis said. "I'll have it ready before Mr. Gittens gets back."

"Very well," Owen said. "Mind you don't take long though."

Lewis untied his heavy apron and hung it across the back of a wooden chair before walking over to join Gwen.

Feeling foolish, Gwen handed him the letter. "I'm sorry," she said quietly. "I should have waited."

"Did I look like I was enjoying myself?" he asked with a hint of amusement. "That was the seventh horseshoe I've made today. I'm going to owe any feeling I have left in my right arm to you."

He pointed at the window a few feet away. "Let's go over there so I can read it in better light."

They moved toward the window, and Lewis withdrew the three sheets of paper from the envelope.

"Is it good news?" he asked.

At Gwen's nod, he smiled and started to read.

When she heard Lewis chuckle, Gwen knew he'd reached the end of the letter.

"First Ioan Llanwddyn, now Robert. What is it about your mam's bara brith that has people dreaming about it?" she said.

Lewis grinned. "I don't know. She wins ribbons at the county show whenever she enters, and I have yet to taste any better." He handed the letter back to her. "Robert's doing well—and I don't think going without a little bara brith will hurt him any."

Behind them, a light knock sounded on the smithy doors, and a second later, Mabel walked in.

"Good afternoon, Mr. Morgan," she said, walking into the room but only seeing Owen in front of the furnace. "I was wondering if Lewis is here."

Gwen glanced from Lewis to his father and wasn't sure which of them looked more astounded. Mabel smiled prettily as though walking into a smithy and asking for the blacksmith's son was an everyday occurrence.

Owen, who probably couldn't believe this was happening twice in a fifteen-minute period, ran a weathered hand across his face. "Well, yes," he began.

"Wonderful!" Mabel said. "I made some bara brith today, and I thought he might like to try some."

For the first time, Gwen noticed the metal plate covered with a white cloth in Mabel's hands. Gwen looked at Lewis and saw him swallow hard. Poor Mabel! She would have to tell her that the way to Lewis's heart was not through any bara brith but his mother's. But she couldn't do that today. Instead, she would simply leave as quickly as possible.

Clutching Robert's letter, Gwen stepped away from the window and toward the door. Mabel turned around.

"Gwen!" she said in astonishment.

"Hello, Mabel," Gwen said. "I just came to give Lewis a message from Robert." She turned quickly. "Good-bye, Mr. Morgan. It was nice to see you again." Then, before anyone could respond, she slipped out through the door and hurried back the way she had come.

Chapter 12

MABEL DID NOT BRING UP the subject of Lewis with Gwen again. School ended for the summer, and without their daily walks to and from the schoolhouse, they rarely saw each other. Gwen spent most of her time working at the post office, but she found being inside when the sun was shining to be almost more than she could bear. Whenever she could, she'd head for the mountain.

She hiked well-worn paths she'd known for years, sometimes encountering changes she hadn't anticipated: streams and rivers that had been diverted to facilitate the dam construction and new footbridges that made travel easier. Every once in a while, she discovered areas where vegetation had been cut back, but she also found places where the Liverpool Corporation had started planting trees to prevent soil erosion.

Of all the evenings she spent on the mountain, however, her favorites were the ones when Lewis joined her at the boulder in the clearing. During all their conversations, he never once mentioned Mabel, but over the weeks, Gwen gleaned quite a lot of information from Rowland. The fact that Gwen had been willing to dance with him on St. John's Day must have lowered some imaginary barrier in the young man's mind because he'd gone from never speaking a word to her to seeking her out after chapel services and stopping by the post office on his way to or from his favorite fishing hole.

Gwen had not gone back to the smithy since the day she'd arrived minutes ahead of Mabel, but according to Rowland, Mabel had not been similarly deterred. She stopped by about once a week, usually bearing a gift from her kitchen. By Rowland's reckoning, the bara brith had been a complete failure, as had been the Welsh cakes. Mabel's gooseberry jam had been so tart their dog had refused to eat it. Her scones and baked apple had been marginally better, but the only offering Lewis had really enjoyed was the crempogs.

As the day that Gwen was to leave for school drew closer, her mixture of apprehension and excitement mounted. Her aunt had made arrangements for her to stay with a Mrs. Pritchard, who owned a house on Llanfyllin's High Street and regularly let rooms to boarding students. Ed the Post, who knew everyone in town, had voiced his approval. He told Aunty Jane that Mrs. Pritchard was known as a fair-minded woman who kept a clean, well-ordered home. Gwen secretly wished his description of Mrs. Pritchard had included kindhearted, but she was glad to know of his support nonetheless.

Mabel and her mother visited her at the post office on the eve of her departure to wish her well. Gwen was a little sad that Mabel seemed quite happy to see her go. Although their differing interests and personalities had prevented them from being close friends, they'd become even more distant since the St. John's Day dance. And Gwen was sorry for that.

Rowland also stopped to see her. He was on his way home from picking winberries on the mountain, and he must have forded at least one river because the lower ten inches of his trouser legs were so wet they dripped water all over the post office floor. Aunty Jane shooed him back outside so quickly he only had time to say good-bye and wave at her through the window.

When she walked up the mountain that evening, Gwen focused on trying to memorize every sight, sound, and smell. This was one of the things she would miss the most, and she dreaded the changes that would occur while she was gone. Her valley—and her view of the valley from this spot—would not be the same when she returned.

She started another drawing but eventually gave up. The concentration she needed to do the picture justice was missing. Her thoughts and emotions were too turbulent. This time she just needed to sit.

She heard Lewis's whistle moments before he appeared in the clearing.

"Hello," she said.

"Hello," he replied, giving her a small smile before taking a seat beside her on the boulder.

They sat quietly for a little while, gazing out at the view before them. From somewhere nearby, they heard a piercing whistle followed by the bark of dogs and bleating of sheep.

"It sounds like Dai Williams is bringing in his sheep," Gwen said. She looked down. "He offered to drive me to Llanfyllin in his cart in the morning."

Lewis nodded. "That was good of him."

"Yes. Yes, it was."

Silence descended again, but this time it wasn't peaceful. Gwen squirmed uncomfortably. This wasn't normal. And this evening, right before she left behind all that was familiar, she desperately needed normal. She glanced at Lewis, concerned to see something that looked like pain in his expression. Hesitantly, she reached out and touched his hand. "Thank you, Lewis, for being such a good friend to me after Robert left. I'm glad he told you about this place. I'm going to miss coming here and sharing it with you."

Lewis curled his fingers around her hand. His touch was warm and comforting, and she didn't want him to let go.

"I'll miss you too," he said, his voice sounding a little strained. "Will you write and tell me how you like school?"

"Yes," she said.

He rose to his feet, and since he was still holding her hand, she stood too.

"Look after yourself," he said with a faint smile. "Llanfyllin's a bit far away for me to launch a rescue attempt."

"I'll do my best to stay out of trouble," she promised.

He gave her fingers a quick squeeze before releasing them and stepping away.

Gwen wanted to cry, but no tears would come. Instead, a hollow emptiness filled her. "Wait, Lewis!" She covered the short space between them in two steps and threw her arms around him. For a split second, he stiffened, then he released a deep breath and pulled her closer. He rested his cheek on the top of her head, and for a moment, they stood there, not saying a word. Then, at last, he pulled away.

"Good-bye, Gwennie," he said.

"Good-bye," she whispered.

Then he turned and disappeared down the path without looking back.

◆

Gwen finished her bowl of oatmeal just as the clip-clop of a horse's hooves sounded on the street outside. It was daybreak, and peach-colored rays of sunlight were touching the sky above the mountains. Birds were warming up their voices to welcome the new day and barely paused their song when Dai Williams walked up to the house and knocked on the door. Aunty Jane opened the door and moved aside so he could enter the hall.

"The trunk's over there, Dai," she said, pointing to the small brown trunk behind him.

"Very good," he said. "I'll put it in the back of the cart right away."

He picked it up effortlessly and took it outside. Taking her hat and shawl off the coatrack, Gwen wrapped her shawl around her shoulders and moved to the door.

"I'll write as soon as I'm settled," Gwen said, tying the ribbons of her hat beneath her chin.

"I'd appreciate that," Aunty Jane said.

Gwen glanced outside. Dai had finished loading her trunk and was moving to wait at the front of the cart. It was time to go, but still she hesitated.

"I'll miss you, Aunty Jane," she said, surprised by how much she meant it.

Aunty Jane's expression softened. She lifted a small cloth bag off the hall table and handed it to her. "A little bit of home to take with you," she said.

Gwen took the bag and gave her aunt a questioning look.

Aunty Jane nodded. "You can open it."

Peeking inside, Gwen saw a jar of strawberry jam and one of the loaves of bread her aunt had made the night before. It was the most thoughtful, sentimental gift Aunty Jane had ever given her, and the gesture brought a lump to Gwen's throat. "Thank you," she said.

"You're welcome." Aunty Jane put a hand on Gwen's shoulder and turned her slightly so she was facing the open door. "Off you go, now. It wouldn't do to keep Dai waiting too long."

Gwen stepped out of the house. "Good-bye," she said.

"Good-bye, bach," Aunty Jane replied. "Work hard, and I have no doubt you'll do very well."

Still carrying the cloth bag, Gwen joined Dai at the cart. He helped her onto the seat before climbing up himself. Then, with a click of the reins, the horse moved forward, and the cart rolled slowly through the sleepy village to join the road that led to Llanfyllin.

The journey took the best part of three hours, but Gwen didn't mind. From her seat at the front of the cart, she had a wonderful view, and she soaked in the beauty around her. The steep mountains and rolling hills were awash with color. Verdant green grass contrasted with the browning bracken of late August. The purple heather blanketing the ground was punctuated with bright patches of yellow gorse, and meandering white sheep dotted every hillside. Stone walls bordered the fields and the narrow road, and every once in a while, the cart rolled past a farmhouse built of the same gray river rock.

As the morning wore on, the sun became brighter and the temperature increased. Gwen took off her shawl. After a moment's hesitation, she took off her hat too. Her nose and cheeks would likely be covered in tiny freckles by the time she reached Mrs. Pritchard's home, but that was a small price to pay for experiencing the warm sun and soft breeze on her face.

Dai didn't say much as they traveled, which suited Gwen just fine. The restful scenery did more to calm her nervousness than conversation ever could have done. But as they crested the last hill, Dai glanced up at the sky before directing his gaze toward the town below. "I'm afraid our pink sunrise this morning means rain by the end of the day," he said. "I'll drop you off at your lodgings, make a stop at the saddlers to pick up a harness I left there to be repaired, and be on my way as quickly as I can."

"Thank you, Mr. Williams," Gwen said. "I really appreciate the ride."

"Happy to do it," he said.

Minutes later they pulled up in front of a redbrick house with a black door and a shiny brass door knocker. At least half the brickwork was covered in ivy, and a telltale trail of smoke floated out of the chimney pot, indicating that someone was home.

Dai helped Gwen down from the cart and went to unload her trunk while she approached the door. Gwen took a deep breath, then raised the knocker and tapped it a couple of times. Almost immediately, she heard footsteps coming from the other side of the door. A short, white-haired lady wearing a long gray dress opened the door and studied Gwen curiously.

"Hello," Gwen said. "I'm looking for Mrs. Pritchard."

"Well, you've found her," she said. "And I'm guessing you are Gwen Humphreys. I got your aunt's letter two days ago, telling me to expect you today." She peered around Gwen to see Dai carrying her trunk toward the door. "Just one trunk, is it?"

"Yes," Gwen said.

"Very good. We'll take it straight up to your room," she said. "You'll have plenty of time to get settled because supper won't be until six. Every day's the same, so it's easy to remember: breakfast at eight, supper at six."

Gwen gave a hesitant smile. "That sounds fine."

With an approving nod, Mrs. Pritchard moved aside so Dai could enter the house. Then she led the way up the narrow wooden staircase and into a small bedroom on the right side of the landing.

Chapter 13

By the beginning of November, Gwen felt as though she was finally adjusting to her new situation. She still had moments of homesickness, but they didn't last as long and were not as severe as they'd been during the first few weeks of living in Llanfyllin. It had been hard to transition into a new environment and a new school all at once. She was now living in a bustling country town—bigger and noisier than anywhere she'd been before.

Unlike Llanwddyn, where it was the birds and an occasional rooster that welcomed the morning, here it was the sound of tradesmen opening their businesses and farmers with their horses and carts that woke her each day. It was challenging to get to know people by name because there were so many more names to learn.

Mrs. Pritchard was everything Ed the Post had promised, and although she didn't express much warmth or affection, Gwen was thankful to be staying with such an equitable woman. Her meals were not always the best tasting, but they were warm, filling, and always served on time, and Gwen's bedroom, although spartanly furnished, was a welcome refuge when she needed one.

At first Gwen had felt somewhat isolated at school. Most of the other students knew at least one other person in class, either because they'd been going to school there for years or because they were attending with friends from their own villages. There were no other students from Llanwddyn, and Gwen had been forced to reach out to strangers. In the process, though, she had found friends.

She had sat next to Rosamond Owen on the first day of her English, French, and Latin classes and had already benefited immeasurably. Rosamond had a gift for languages and had helped Gwen with pronunciation and memorization; Gwen now felt that she could keep up with the class. Alice Jones excelled in needlework and field hockey, two seemingly unrelated subjects but both areas in which Gwen needed a little extra coaching. Alice was patient and kind and had even gone as far as to repeatedly invite Gwen to play on her hockey team despite the fact that she was still learning the rules.

Most of the students at school came from homes where Welsh was spoken, but unlike Gwen and Rosamond, Alice's first language was English. She understood Welsh fairly well, but when they were together, the girls usually spoke in English, which meant Gwen's English vocabulary increased rapidly, along with her confidence in communicating in that language.

To her surprise, she also discovered that her love for arithmetic put her at the top of the class in algebra and geometry. Rosamond and Alice had started coming to her when they were stuck on particularly challenging math problems, and Gwen was glad to have found a way that she could reciprocate their kindness to her. As time went on, their warm, laughter-filled, girlish friendship filled a void that had been empty for too long.

It was not quite powerful enough to take the place of another unique friendship, however. And there were times, particularly during the quiet of night, that Gwen found her thoughts drifting to Lewis. When they did, she experienced the same empty ache she'd felt when he'd said good-bye on the mountain. She wondered if Mabel was still making regular visits to the smithy. The thought irritated Gwen more than it should, but she had no way of putting her mind at rest because even though she'd written to both of them, she'd received no letters from Mabel and had only heard back from Lewis once.

She tried not to let Lewis's lack of communication hurt too much. After all, they had not always enjoyed a close friendship. But she was disappointed. She'd kept her promise and had written to him soon after school had started to tell him about her lodgings with Mrs. Pritchard, the subjects she was studying, and some of the people she'd met at school and in the town. He'd written back a short note telling her he was glad she was settling in well and that there had been no big changes in Llanwddyn during the couple of weeks she'd been gone.

In her second letter, she'd told him about Rosamond and Alice and about how she'd recently studied the various trade routes between England and India in her geography class. She'd waited a couple of weeks, and when no reply had come, she'd written to him again. This time she'd told him of her love of geometry and her dislike of Latin. She'd described the speckled, rock-hard slab that Mrs. Pritchard called bara brith and regularly served for supper. And she told him how much she missed visiting the mountain and, in particular, the boulder in the clearing. But again she'd received no response.

Gwen also wrote to her aunt. Aunty Jane wrote short letters back, but her news was usually limited to the weather, the state of her garden, and the subject of the minister's most recent sermon. Occasionally Aunty Jane would pass along news about someone in the village, but she never once mentioned Lewis or Mabel, and Gwen could not bring herself to ask about them.

The only surprise Gwen received in the mail during that time was a small package that arrived on her seventeenth birthday. Gwen had already determined that since Robert was undoubtedly hundreds of miles out at sea, Lewis didn't know her birthday, and Aunty Jane did not approve of frivolity of any kind, it was unlikely that the sixteenth of November would be any different than any other school day. So the brown paper package waiting beside her bowl of oatmeal at the breakfast table that morning was completely unexpected—as were her tears when she opened it to reveal a crocheted green scarf with matching mittens.

Gwen blinked the moisture away and picked up the card from inside the box. *Happy Birthday, Gwen. Love, Aunty Jane.* She wrapped the scarf around her neck and picked up the mittens, touched by her aunt's thoughtfulness. It was not hard to picture Aunty Jane sitting in the rocking chair by the fire each evening, her crochet hook flying as she worked on this gift. As soon as she finished her breakfast, Gwen ran back up to her room to write a thank you note before school started.

Rosamond and Alice noticed Gwen's new scarf and mittens as soon as they saw her, and when they asked about them, Gwen admitted they were a birthday gift. The girls then insisted that they stop at the local shop at the end of the day, where they pooled their money to buy Gwen a few pieces of treacle toffee. By the time she went to bed that night, Gwen determined that it had been the best day she'd experienced since she'd moved to Llanfyllin.

Her happiness that day, however, paled in comparison to her joy two weeks later. She was sitting in her French class enduring the torturous ritual of conjugating irregular verbs when the headmaster walked in. Immediately, all the students stopped what they were doing and rose to their feet.

"I apologize for interrupting." The headmaster directed his remarks to the French teacher. "I need to excuse Gwen Humphreys from the remainder of class today."

The French teacher gave a nod of assent. "Gather your books, Gwen," she said.

Rosamond turned to look at Gwen, her eyebrows raised, but Gwen could offer no explanation. Trying to ignore all the curious looks from her classmates, she hurriedly gathered her books and dropped them into her satchel before leaving her desk and joining the headmaster at the door. Nervous butterflies danced in her stomach as she faced the imposing man. What could this mean? Had she done something wrong?

The headmaster opened the door and allowed Gwen to precede him into the hall.

"You have a visitor, Gwen," he said. "He's waiting for you in my office. I understand you have not seen him in some time, so I am excusing you from your classes for the remainder of the day."

Stunned, Gwen could only stare at him. "A visitor, sir?"

"Yes." He pointed down the hall. "Come along."

She was halfway there when a young man stepped out of the headmaster's office. He wore gray flannel trousers and a black sweater. His chestnut hair could just be seen beneath his peaked hat, and when he smiled, his green eyes sparkled.

"Gwennie!" he said.

Gwen felt as though her heart would pound out of her chest. "Robert!" She prayed this was not a dream. "Robert! You're home!"

"Almost," he said with a grin. He held out his arms, and without sparing the headmaster or decorum another thought, Gwen ran into them.

After a tight hug, she pulled back and studied her brother. "You've seen a lot of sun," she said.

Robert laughed. "Almost every day until we came into English waters. I don't think my face will ever be rid of all these freckles."

The headmaster stepped up behind Gwen and offered Robert his hand.

"Thank you, sir. I'll make sure she's back in school tomorrow," Robert said.

"Excellent." The headmaster gave Gwen a stern look. "I will inform your other teachers of your absence this afternoon, but I expect you to catch up the missed work."

"Yes, sir. Thank you." Gwen wanted to laugh and cry at the same time. Robert was back, and she was to spend the rest of the day with him.

The headmaster gave them both a final nod of dismissal, then entered his office, and Robert, with his own duffel bag over one shoulder and Gwen's satchel over the other, led the way to the school doors.

Gwen stopped long enough to retrieve and put on her coat. She pulled her new mittens out of her coat pockets and handed Robert her scarf.

"Here," she said. "You don't have a coat on."

Robert didn't argue. "It's beastly cold here," he said as they walked into the blowing, drizzling rain.

"It's the end of November," Gwen reminded him.

"Yes, and it's sunny and warm in India," Robert said.

Gwen linked her arm through his. "Are you going to tell me all about it? India, your ship, the crew, everything?"

Robert laughed. "Of course. Just find us somewhere warm and dry to sit, and I'll talk as long as you want."

Gwen led her brother to Mrs. Pritchard's house. After having been introduced to Robert and reassured that Gwen had the headmaster's permission to be away from school, Mrs. Pritchard offered them the sitting room and went off to the kitchen to make them a cup of tea. Robert sat as close to the fireplace as he could.

"Probably not the best time of year to come back," he said.

"Probably not," Gwen agreed with a smile. "But I'm so glad you did. Now tell me all about your adventures. Did you see a monkey?"

He grinned. "They were everywhere! There was a market not far from the dock, and the place was crawling with monkeys. They ran through the tables, swung from the awnings, and leaped from the rooftops.

"The Indians hated the cheeky blighters. One minute a merchant would be bartering with a customer over the price of his fruits and vegetables, and the next minute a monkey would jump onto his table, steal the biggest banana, and be back up on a rooftop before anyone could do anything about it. The merchant would yell and shake his fist at the monkey, and the monkey would screech back at him, then sit in full view of the poor bloke while it ate the stolen fruit."

Gwen wasn't sure whether to be fascinated or terrified at the thought of monkeys running wild through a marketplace. "Did they ever hurt people?"

Robert shrugged. "I daresay they'd bite if they felt threatened. And Monk had a fistful of hair pulled out by one of them."

Gwen felt her eyes widen, but Robert was chuckling at the memory.

"What happened?" she asked.

"Every few days, Monk would head down to the market and buy a whole bunch of bananas for the crew to share. He'd carry them back to the ship on his head, just like the natives do. One day, he must have chosen the same bunch that one of the monkeys had had its eye on, because the monkey wasn't having it. He jumped onto Monk's shoulder and tried pulling the bananas off one by one."

"The monkey was on his shoulder?" Gwen gasped. Terror was definitely winning over fascination.

"Yes," Robert said. "But it didn't stay long once Monk started yelling. It gave up on the bananas and settled for a chunk of Monk's hair instead." He laughed. "The rest of the crew teased Monk for days. They said the monkey must have known his nickname and thought it was time he looked more like the bald monks at the monasteries."

Gwen shook her head at Robert's shipmates' antics. "What about you?" she asked. "Did you like bananas?"

"Yes," he said. "But I liked mangos even more."

"What's a mango?" she asked, repeating the strange-sounding word.

"It's a fruit," Robert told her. "It's about the same size and shape as a large pear, but the inside's orange, and it tastes incredibly sweet."

A light tap on the sitting room door announced Mrs. Pritchard's arrival with the tea tray. The older lady placed the tray on the small table beside Gwen's chair, made sure they both had everything they needed, then returned to her work in the kitchen again. Robert waited only until Gwen had poured the tea and handed him his cup before picking up his narrative again.

"The animals in that part of the world are so different from the ones here in Wales. Enormous birds with bright red, blue, and yellow feathers, cows with horns on their heads and humps on their backs, elephants of every size." He leaned forward in his seat, his eyes shining with excitement. "I even saw dolphins. When we were still in the warmer waters of the Indian Ocean, a school of dolphins swam alongside us for an entire day."

Robert's enthusiasm was contagious, and for the next few hours, Gwen listened with rapt attention as he recounted one adventure after another. He told her more about his short time in India, then about his ship and his shipmates, including Captain Owen and Monk and a host of other men whose names all blurred together. It was obvious that while there were some crewmembers he'd avoided, he had also made some good friends. He described his experience on board ship, his mistakes, his victories, and his slow road to improvement as cabin boy.

Gwen was quite sure he'd purposely omitted some of his more difficult experiences, especially when he glossed over their time trapped by rough seas and sail-ripping wind, but it was easy to see that despite her own heartache over his departure from the village, her brother had been right. Going away to sea had given him a joy for life he'd not had before.

"We arrived in Liverpool early last week," Robert told her. "I truly think the *Talookdar* may be the fastest ship on the seas. Once again, we made port earlier than expected."

"How long will you be home?" she asked, already dreading the answer.

"I'm expected back on board in three days," he said.

"Three days!"

Robert nodded. "When we first arrived, we had cargo to unload and repairs to take care of—sails that needed mending, ropes that needed to be replaced, parts of the ship that needed fresh lacquer. It took time. We're due to sail again at the end of the week.

"Your letters were waiting for me in Liverpool, and I read them as soon as we got into port. I wanted to see you here in Llanfyllin to make sure you were well and as happy as can be expected while attending school."

Despite herself, Gwen laughed at the grimace on her brother's face. "Oh, Robert, we are so different! You thrive on adventures into the unknown, and I love poring through books at school. So don't worry; I'm happy here. Mrs. Pritchard has been good to me. I've made new friends, and I'm managing quite well in my classes."

Relief filled Robert's face. "I'm glad," he said. He reached out and took her hand. "I need to travel to Llanwddyn to see Aunty Jane. I wish I had longer to be with you, but I feel that I must go there."

Gwen nodded. "Lots of people in the village will want to see you—Lewis, Ioan Llanwddyn, the minister, Dai Williams. But especially Aunty Jane."

"Has she forgiven me for leaving the way I did?" Robert asked.

"Yes, I think she has," Gwen told him. "She'll be happy to see you."

Robert came to his feet. "Then I'd best be on my way," he said. "It's a long walk to Llanwddyn."

Gwen glanced out the window. The days were shortening, and already dusk was close. "But it will be dark soon," she said.

"I'm not afraid of the dark," Robert said with a smile. "And I know that road well. If I'm lucky, someone will pass by in a cart and take pity on me. I don't have the luxury of extra time. If I'm to visit Llanwddyn, I need to go tonight."

Gwen rose and picked up her scarf and mittens. "Take these," she said.

"But what will you . . . ?"

"You can drop them off on your way back," she said quickly.

Robert considered that for a moment. "Thank you," he said.

He took the scarf and mittens and pulled her into a tight embrace. Then, before she could say anything that could slow him, he pulled away and walked to the door. "Look after yourself," he said.

"You too," she whispered.

He smiled. "Always."

And then he was gone. Gwen ran to the window and watched him walk up the High Street until she couldn't see him anymore.

◆

Two days later, when Gwen arrived back at Mrs. Pritchard's house after school, there was a small brown package waiting for her. Inside she found her scarf, mittens, and half a dozen Welsh cakes wrapped in wax paper. A note written in Robert's virtually illegible pen said, *The Welsh cakes are from Aunty Jane. She also gave me some. You were right; she has forgiven me. I will always be grateful for the good people in my life, especially you. Cofion cynnes. Robert.*

That evening, Gwen couldn't help but feel disappointed that she'd missed seeing Robert on his way to the train station, but when she opened her bedroom curtains the next morning, she was glad he hadn't waited any longer to return to his ship. The first snow of the season had arrived. Large flakes, like gently falling goose feathers, were softly spiraling from the sky, and a sparkling white blanket already covered the ground.

Chapter 14

WITHIN A FORTNIGHT, THE SNOW'S novelty had begun to wane. The cold, damp conditions made it hard to keep the school warm, and by the time Gwen walked to school each morning, her boots, hat, and coat were already wet. Her feet were constantly cold. She tried to warm them by the fire in Mrs. Pritchard's sitting room each evening, but if she faced the fire, her back became cold, and if she turned around, her nose turned pink. The most obvious solution was to slowly rotate, but that just made her dizzy.

Mrs. Pritchard provided a warm brick wrapped in flannel that she placed in Gwen's bed each night. That and the feather eiderdown were the things Gwen looked forward to the most at the end of the day, even if it did make getting out of bed in the morning all the more difficult.

Unfortunately there didn't seem to be any end in sight for the wintery weather. According to Mrs. Pritchard, the locals had been predicting a hard winter. The almanac and the animals had all pointed to it. The sheep farmers had talked about how unusually thick the wool was this year, as though the sheep had been preparing for colder-than-normal temperatures. The wild winberry crop on the mountains and the blackberry crop in the hedgerows had been particularly good, and farmers' wives claimed that that meant more for the wild animals to hoard. How much truth there was to these things, Gwen didn't know, but as the end of the school term drew closer, she began to worry that her long-anticipated return to Llanwddyn might be in jeopardy.

She'd heard that Ed the Post was still making the journey back and forth but was now doing it on skis. Two days before school was supposed to close for the Christmas holiday, Gwen and Alice saw him on the High Street.

"Mr. Hughes!" Gwen called.

Ed the Post turned and saw her across the road.

"Hello, Gwen," he said, waving in greeting.

She hurried across the road with Alice close behind her. "I've heard the road to Llanwddyn is bad," she said without preamble. "Are people still getting through?"

Ed the Post raised his cap a little and scratched his head. "I daresay a good horse could still make it, but I'm afraid the snow on the pass is too deep for a cart already," he said. "I've managed on my skis, but another six inches of this white stuff and there'll be no going anywhere over that mountain for a bit."

Gwen bit her lip and looked up at the cloud-laden sky. Two days. She needed the snow to hold off for two more days.

"Thinking of Christmas, are you?" he asked.

"Yes," she said. "I've been looking forward to going home."

Ed nodded understandingly. "I'm sure your aunt's anxious to see you too." He gazed up at the sky just as Gwen had moments before. "I don't know, bach. It might be wise to have a backup, just in case. It smells like another storm to me."

Alice stepped closer and slid her arm through Gwen's. "If she doesn't make it to Llanwddyn, she's coming home with me," she announced.

Gwen turned to her friend, her expression a mixture of surprise and appreciation. "But, Alice . . ."

"There are no buts about it," Alice said. "There's already nine of us at home; one more won't make any difference. Mam will be thrilled to have someone to spoil, even if my dad makes up for it by having you get up early to help with the milking."

Ed the Post looked relieved. "I'm sure Dai will come if he can, Gwen. But it's good to know you'll be taken care of if the pass is closed."

A gust of wind rattled a nearby window, and once again, Ed surveyed the skies. "I'd like to think I'll make it to Llanwddyn tomorrow," he said, "but I have to confess, I'm beginning to have my doubts."

$$\blacklozenge$$

Ed the Post was right. Later that night a blizzard moved into the valley. Howling wind and swirling snow prevented anyone from leaving their homes until midafternoon the next day, and when the storm finally moved on, Llanfyllin was a sea of white. Snowdrifts reached above the windowsills, and roads were indistinguishable from open fields. As people slowly emerged into the winter wonderland, the only sound that could be heard above the excited cries of playing children was the steady scrape of shovels.

It did not take long for word to spread that the headmaster had been forced to close the school and would not reopen it until after the Christmas holidays. The students were thrilled, but it was difficult for Gwen to share their enthusiasm for the biggest snowstorm the area had seen in twenty years. Swallowing her disappointment at not being able to go home, she accepted Alice's offer and traveled with her by horse-drawn sleigh to her family's nearby farm.

They had barely pulled up in front of the large redbrick farmhouse when the front door flew open and five children of varying ages poured out.

"They're here, Mam!" the tallest boy yelled over his shoulder as the youngest girl made a beeline for Alice.

"Hello, Elsie," Alice said, picking up the little girl. "What are you doing out here without a coat?" She turned. "This is my friend, Gwen."

Elsie buried her face in Alice's shoulder but peeked out long enough to give Gwen a shy smile.

"Hello, Elsie," Gwen said. "You look just like Alice. Has anyone ever told you that?"

Elsie's head nodded up and down.

"Come on, Alice!" One of the boys shouted from the door. He was bouncing up and down with excitement. "You need to see the Christmas tree Dad cut down this afternoon."

"Hurry!" the other children called in chorus.

"Did I mention that we don't have quiet, peaceful Christmases?" Alice asked, her expression apologetic. "And we'll all completely understand if you run off to the bedroom with your hands over your ears to escape the noise."

Gwen shook her head good-naturedly. "Don't worry about me. I'm excited to see the Christmas tree too."

Alice grinned and handed Gwen her bag from the bottom of the sleigh. "Let's take our things in, then."

Gwen followed Alice along the snowy path to the front door. Alice's siblings backed into the hall to allow them room to enter, and from the other end of the hall, a door opened, and a short, slightly plump woman bustled in, wiping her hands on her apron. She gave her attention to the girl standing nearest the door.

"Lizzy, Dad and Ben will be in from the milking any minute. It's time to set the table. And maybe Elsie would like to help you."

Elsie wiggled out of Alice's arms and disappeared after Lizzy.

"I'm glad you got home safely," Mrs. Jones said as she came over to give Alice a kiss on the cheek. Then she turned to Gwen. "And this must be Gwen." She put her arms around Gwen and gave her a quick squeeze. "Welcome to Glanypwll Farm."

"Thank you," Gwen said. "It was very kind of you to let me come."

"It's our pleasure, bach," Mrs. Jones said. "I always say Christmas is meant for sharing. It will be a treat to have you here." She moved toward the stairs. "Give your bag to David. He can carry it up for you, and I'll show you where you'll be sleeping."

The nearest boy reached for the bag, and Gwen handed it to him. "Thank you, David."

"Welcome," he said, his smile exposing the gap where his two front teeth should have been.

"Come on." Alice linked her arm with Gwen's. "You're sharing a room with me and Lizzy, and as soon as we've shown you where it is, we'll go into the parlor to see the Christmas tree."

"Yeah!" David cried as he raced ahead of them with her bag.

Gwen moved toward the stairs and blinked back the tears that threatened. Perhaps she'd have to miss John Ellis's Christmas sermon in her own Welsh chapel, and she may not taste her aunt's delicious mince pies this year, but she had a feeling that being with these good people would make being away from home bearable after all.

◆

A week after school resumed following Christmas, Ed the Post left Llanfyllin in his third attempt since the holiday to ski into the Vyrnwy valley. The previous times he'd tried, he'd returned hours later, having been unable to cross the huge snowdrifts still covering the pass. This time he didn't come back. Gwen prayed that he was safe and that his continued absence meant he'd successfully made it to the isolated village.

Even though Alice's family had done a marvelous job of making her feel welcome for Christmas, her thoughts had never been far from her loved ones in Llanwddyn. She hoped Aunty Jane had not been too unhappy spending Christmas alone. And more than that, she hoped her aunt had all the provisions she needed to survive comfortably until the pass cleared and supplies could reach the villagers.

She'd thought a lot about Lewis too. She wondered if he was at all disappointed that she'd been unable to return home. His lack of communication still troubled her. It seemed so unlike him to sever all ties after he'd made repeated efforts to reach out to her after Robert left. Each time she pondered it, the same niggling worry surfaced: perhaps it was Mabel who consumed his thoughts and attention now.

When a second day passed with no sign of Ed the Post, however, Gwen's overriding concern was for the welfare of the postman who had risked so much to reach her family and friends. Darkness had already fallen, but she still sat beside the window in Mrs. Pritchard's sitting room, watching the road. She'd just about given up hope of seeing the postman when she noticed a bright speck of light in the distance. She continued to watch until the light increased enough that she could make out the silhouette of a man around the glow of a lantern.

By the time she reached the front door, the vague silhouette had materialized into a man with skis on his feet and a bulging bag across his shoulder.

"Mr. Hughes!" Gwen shouted.

The man holding the lamp veered toward her, the swishing of his wooden skis against the hardpacked snow echoing eerily in the night.

Gwen held up her candle, its feeble light giving him direction. "I'm so glad you're safe!"

Breathing heavily, Ed the Post came to a stop and leaned on his ski poles. "I was very glad to see the lights of Llanfyllin, I must say."

"Do you want to come in?" Gwen said.

He shook his head. "No. I must be getting home. The wife will be anxious." He pulled back the flap on his bag and reached inside. "But I'm glad you stopped me. I have something for you."

"A letter?" Gwen asked hopefully.

"Well, I think there's one of those in here somewhere too," he said with a smile. "But I can't give you that. It has to go through the post office first. No, this is more of a personal delivery."

Puzzled, Gwen watched as Ed the Post pulled out a long, thin package wrapped in brown paper and tied with string.

"Here you go," he said, handing it to Gwen.

"What is it?" she asked.

Ed the Post laughed. "I'm afraid I didn't ask." Then, perhaps sensing her confusion, he continued. "I'd just started back to Llanfyllin and was crossing Pont Cedig when Owen Morgan's son called out to me."

"Which son?" Gwen asked, her heartbeat suddenly quickening.

"The eldest, I think," Ed the Post said.

"Lewis?"

"That's the one."

Gwen tightened her grip on the package. Why was she so thirsty for news of him?

"He gave me that and asked if I'd get it to you. Said he'd planned on giving it to you himself, but when you didn't make it back for Christmas . . . Well, I could tell he was right anxious to have it reach you soon, and I didn't have the heart to tell him no." Ed the Post looked a little uncomfortable. "Having said that, I'm not sure that I should be carrying parcels that haven't gone through the post office, so it might be best if you didn't say anything to your aunt."

"It was very good of you to bring it," she said. "And I won't say a word."

Ed the Post gave a relieved nod. "Well, there we are. It wouldn't do to upset the Llanwddyn postmistress, after all."

Gwen gave a small laugh. She wasn't sure what Aunty Jane did to intimidate fully grown men, but she did it well.

"How is Aunty Jane?" she asked.

"Just the same as always," he said. "I asked her how everyone in the village is managing. She said most people are relying on their coffers of oatmeal, and the local farms are keeping them in milk and eggs. They'll be right glad to have the pass open again though."

Gwen was relieved to know the villagers were safe but knew that by now she would be very tired of having oatmeal for breakfast, lunch, and dinner. "How much longer will it be before fresh supplies can get through?"

Ed the Post shrugged. "If we get a little melting and the storms hold off, it's possible a cart could do it in a week or two," he said, moving stiffly as he straightened up. "It's a long, hard journey at the moment though."

"Thank you for doing it, Mr. Hughes," Gwen said. "I've been very eager for news."

"You're welcome, bach. Now get inside before you catch your death of cold out here. And I'd best be on my way before all my joints seize up and I can't even make it as far as the local post office."

Still clutching her package, Gwen stepped back, and with a grunt of effort, Ed the Post pushed off on his skis. She watched only long enough to see him turn toward the town center before she slipped back into the house.

Chapter 15

GWEN'S FINGERS WERE NUMB WITH cold, and she could barely keep the candle upright as she hurried up the stairs to her bedroom. Placing the candle on the chest of drawers, she moved closer to the fireplace. The glowing embers were only strong enough to take the edge off the chill in the room, but Gwen prodded them with the poker, and a few small flames rose to lick the last of the coal. She held her hands out to warm them and stared at the package on the floor beside her. What would Lewis want to give her?

She took a blanket off her bed and wrapped it around her shoulders. Then, kneeling down in front of the small fire, she started pulling at the string around the parcel. Her hands had gone from numb to shaking, but she persevered, and within a few moments she had it untied. She opened the brown paper and gasped. Sitting on her knee was a perfect wild rose made entirely of iron. The stem was about ten inches long and a quarter-inch wide. Four leaves and multiple thorns had been formed along the stem, culminating with an exquisite rose blossom at the top.

Gwen searched the brown paper for a note, but there was none. Carefully she lifted the rose and turned it between her fingers, examining it from every angle. It was beautiful. The attention to detail took her breath away. There were lines in the leaves and ripples in the petals. The fact that the stem was not perfectly straight made it all the more realistic. She'd never seen anything like it, and she could only imagine how long it had taken to make something so intricate.

Why would Lewis give her a gift like this when he'd only sent her one letter in the five months she'd been gone? It made no sense. She placed her hand on her stomach. The warm feeling she'd experienced walking home with Lewis after the St. John's Day dance had returned. Confused, she searched the packaging again, but there was no accompanying note. Without Ed the Post's account and the fact that only a skilled blacksmith could create something so beautiful, she would not even have known who had sent it.

Slowly she got to her feet and placed the metal rose on her chest of drawers, where she'd be able to see it from her bed. Then she changed into her nightgown and blew out the candle. In her nightly prayer, she expressed particular gratitude for Ed the Post's return, for the safety of her family and friends in Llanwddyn, and for Lewis's gift. Then she crawled into bed with a smile on her face; perhaps she hadn't been completely forgotten after all.

◆

Gwen wrote Lewis another letter, thanking him for his gift. But he never replied. Even when the pass opened two weeks later and Ed the Post was able to make more regular trips to and from the village, she heard nothing. She didn't understand, and there were times when she actually wondered if the postman had delivered the rose to the wrong person by mistake. Occasionally, however, when she held his gift and studied the intricate work, she could imagine Lewis working on it at the smithy, and on those days, he seemed closer.

As the new school term progressed, Gwen's teachers began demanding more of their students. With completing homework and studying for examinations always in the forefront of Gwen's mind, there didn't seem to be much time for anything else. She'd improved enough in field hockey to play on the school team with Alice, and Rosamond had persuaded her to enter a choral recitation competition with her. Practice sessions for the upcoming school eisteddfod were time-consuming and made her already busy schedule even more challenging.

February brought a warm spell, and much of the snow melted, leaving a sloppy wet mess on the roads. Gwen kept hoping Aunty Jane would send word that Dai was coming to town so she could travel home with him, even if she was only able to stay for a day or two. But the only time she saw the farmer from Llanwddyn was on a Wednesday morning toward the end of February when he'd been on his way to market. With disappointment, Gwen had waved as he'd driven by and had continued on to school, knowing there would be no trip home for her that weekend.

For that reason, she was completely unprepared to find Dai waiting for her at the headmaster's office only six days later. She'd been summoned there from her geometry class. Her teacher had read the note another student had handed to him and had promptly excused Gwen from class, telling her to take all her books with her. And now, as she stood in the headmaster's office, carrying her satchel, she felt almost as nervous as Dai looked.

"Please take a seat, Gwen," the headmaster said.

Gwen dropped into the closest chair but did not relax.

"I assume you know Dai Williams," the headmaster continued, taking his own seat behind the large desk as Dai sat near Gwen.

"Yes, sir."

"I'm afraid he's come bearing some bad news." The headmaster looked over at Dai. "Would you be good enough to give Gwen the details, Mr. Williams?"

Dai fiddled with the brim of the hat he was holding. "I'm afraid it's your aunty Jane," he said.

For a split second, the room seemed to tilt. As it straightened again, Gwen clenched her hands together to stop them from trembling and focused on keeping her breathing even.

When he realized everyone was expecting him to continue, Dai cleared his throat. "She had a fall sometime last night, but no one knew it until Ed the Post showed up at the post office to find no one there. He and Owen checked the house and found her in the kitchen." Dai looked down as though he couldn't quite bring himself to meet Gwen's eyes. "Owen thinks it's a case of apoplexy."

"Is she . . . ?" The words wouldn't come.

Dai shook his head. "She's still with us, bach, but she hasn't come 'round yet. Owen had his wife, Mair, come over, and between them, they managed to make your aunt comfortable in her own bed. Ed the Post left straightaway to get the doctor from Llanfyllin, then Owen sent his boy Rowland over to the farm to ask if I'd come into town for you."

Gwen immediately stood, and the men followed. "I'll come with you now," she said.

The headmaster came around from the other side of the desk and put his hand on Gwen's shoulder. "I'm very sorry, Gwen. We will do all we can to help you with your schooling, but as you may be gone for some time, make sure you gather all your belongings."

Gwen nodded numbly.

He gave her shoulder a reassuring squeeze before releasing it. "Be assured that everyone here at Llanfyllin school will be praying that your aunt makes a full recovery very soon."

"Thank you, sir," Gwen managed.

The headmaster turned to Dai. "I'll let you be on your way," he said. "Thank you for coming for Gwen as quickly as you did."

The men shook hands, and then, as if in a fog, Gwen was walking through the school hall, gathering her coat and hat, and following Dai out to his waiting cart.

They didn't speak until Dai pulled up outside Mrs. Pritchard's house. "I'll come explain to your landlady what's happened while you collect your things," he said.

"Thank you," Gwen said, scrambling down from the cart before Dai reached her. "It won't take me long."

She entered the house and ran up the stairs without seeing Mrs. Pritchard. Pulling her trunk out from its position at the end of her bed, she opened the lid and started dumping things into it. Her clothes, her books, her hairbrush—there was no folding or organizing. Gwen simply emptied everything from the drawers and the wardrobe. Finally, when she was sure she hadn't missed anything else, she took Lewis's rose and placed it carefully on the top of her clothes and closed the lid.

Dai carried the trunk down the stairs and loaded it into the cart. Mrs. Pritchard, who had obviously been updated on Aunty Jane's condition, stopped Gwen in the hall. "Your room will be here waiting for you whenever you're ready," she said, surprising Gwen by giving her a big hug.

"Thank you, Mrs. Pritchard," Gwen said. "You've been very kind."

"Pshh. It was nothing," the older lady said. "You take care of yourself now."

Gwen nodded.

"Are we ready?" Dai asked from the door.

"Yes." Gwen hurried to the cart and let Dai help her up. He handed her a blanket before climbing up beside her. With a final wave to Mrs. Pritchard, Gwen braced herself against the seat, and the cart jolted forward.

Gwen's thoughts went around and around with the cart's wheels. What would she find when she returned home? Surely her aunt was strong enough to recover. But how would apoplexy affect her aunt's future? She prayed the doctor would reach Aunty Jane in time and would know how to help her. If not . . . what would she do if Aunty Jane died? She had no idea where Robert was, and she had no other family.

Gwen took a steadying breath. She would not think that way. She couldn't. She would go home and do all in her power to help her aunt heal completely. And that included prayer. Bowing her head and closing her eyes, Gwen shut out the bumpy road, the brilliant white landscape, and the man sitting tensely beside her, and she prayed.

She lost track of time. It was hard to identify the usual landmarks along the way, as most of them were still buried in snow. Only the lowering of the sun and the lengthening of the horse's and cart's shadows on the snowdrifts indicated how long they'd been traveling. Dai pulled another blanket out from under the wooden seat.

"It's going to get much colder once the sun sets," he said, handing it to her.

Numbly, Gwen unfolded the blanket and stretched it out so it covered both her legs and Dai's. He gave her a small smile of appreciation.

"How much longer, do you think?" she asked.

He pointed to a farmhouse on the hillside. "That's Huw Fawr's farm," he said. "We're getting close."

Gwen turned to look. From this distance, the stone structure was barely recognizable. She could see only half the slate roof beneath a huge snowdrift. The chimneys were noticeably absent of smoke, and the windows were shuttered. The nearby barns were simply enormous mounds of snow, and there was no sign of tracks in the farmyard or the lane leading up to it.

"It doesn't look like anyone's there," Gwen said. "D'you think Huw and his mam are all right?"

"As well as can be expected, I imagine," Dai said, his expression grave. "They moved away a week before the storm hit. To somewhere near Welshpool, I think."

"They moved?" Gwen's voice reflected her shock. Huw Fawr had been born and brought up in that farmhouse—as had his father and grandfather before him. He'd never married but had managed the house and the farm quite well with the help of his widowed mother.

"That's right," Dai continued. "Apparently Huw's cousin has a farm down there and was looking for a new foreman. His cousin heard what was happening here with the dam going up, so he offered the position to Huw. We all know how hard it's going to be to find work once they start flooding the valley, so Huw decided to take the job while it was available." Dai shook his head. "Had to have been a bitter thing though. Going from farming your own land to working for your cousin."

Gwen's chest ached for Huw Fawr's loss. "It must have been hard for his mother too."

Dai nodded. "She didn't let on how difficult it was, but you can't uproot after so many years without it hurting."

Beneath the blanket, Gwen chaffed her hands together, thinking of the many people whose lives would be forever changed by the construction of the dam.

"What will you do when the time comes to leave, Mr. Williams?" she asked.

For a few moments, the only sounds were the jingle of the harness, the creak of the wheels against the hardpacked snow, and the panting of the horse as it started up another incline. But when Dai finally spoke, his voice was filled with sadness, and his weatherworn face looked unexpectedly vulnerable. "I don't know, bach," he said with a sigh. "Like too many others, I've been putting off the decision. But the village has lost four or five families in the last six months, and it's only going to get worse."

Gwen didn't want to ask which other families had left. In a community as small as Llanwddyn, she would know every single one of them, and their departure would leave a hole impossible to fill.

"I'm glad your aunt will still have work at the post office, even if it's in a new spot down the valley," Dai said.

"Yes," Gwen said, the word sounding hollow even to her own ears.

They both knew there was a very real possibility that Aunty Jane may never be well enough to work again or may not survive the apoplexy at all. Anxiety gnawed at Gwen, making her stomach churn. Was she strong enough to face what lay ahead, no matter what the future held?

"Oh, please, please, let her be all right," Gwen whispered a little while later as they finally rolled into the village.

Dai gave her a sympathetic look and clicked his tongue at the horse, urging the tired animal to move just a little faster. They crossed Pont Cedig. It was late enough that the shops and the smithy were closed. Even the houses looked closed, with little or no light escaping the tightly drawn curtains. They passed the post office and saw another horse and cart standing outside Aunty Jane's house.

"I daresay that's the doctor now," Dai said, pulling on the reins and bringing his horse to a stop right behind the other cart.

"Thank you, Mr. Williams," Gwen said, tearing the blankets off her legs and scrambling down as quickly as she could. "Really. I can't thank you enough." Then she ran for the house, pausing only long enough to unlatch the back door before rushing up the stairs to her aunt's bedroom.

Chapter 16

WHEN SHE REACHED THE LANDING, Gwen paused to catch her breath. Male voices were coming from her aunt's bedroom, and she noticed that the door was ajar. With some trepidation, she continued forward, and after giving a light tap on the door, she pushed it open. Immediately, the two men inside fell silent, turning to face her as she walked in. A woman rose from a chair at Aunty Jane's bedside and moved toward her.

"Gwen!" she said softly. "I'm so glad you're home."

Lewis may have inherited his stature from his father, but his dark hair and startlingly blue eyes were the spitting image of his mother's. And when Mair Morgan put her arms around Gwen, Gwen clung to her. Until that moment, she hadn't realized how much she'd needed physical and emotional support.

"How is she?" Gwen asked, pulling back a little.

Mair gave a gentle smile and took Gwen by the hand, leading her to the bed. "She's resting peacefully."

Gwen looked down at her aunt. Lying under the covers of her bed, with her gray hair spread across the pillow, Aunty Jane looked smaller and frailer than Gwen had ever seen her. Gwen reached out to touch her aunt's hand. Its warmth was reassuring.

"Has she woken yet?"

Mair nodded. "She opened her eyes for the first time about an hour ago. The doctor was here, and he can tell you about it."

The man standing next to Owen stepped forward and shook her hand. "Miss Humphreys," he said. "I'm Dr. Edwards."

Dr. Edwards looked as though he was in his midthirties. He wore a rather shabby black suit and shoes that had obviously seen a lot of wear. His brown hair was parted carefully down the middle, and his serious gray eyes studied her through dark-rimmed, round spectacles.

"Thank you for coming, Dr. Edwards," Gwen said. "Do you know what's wrong with my aunt?"

The doctor cleared his throat. "I believe your aunt has suffered a stroke," he said, and when Gwen looked at him blankly, he explained further. "You may be familiar with the term *apoplexy*. For years, medical science has been trying to understand what causes that sudden, violent attack that usually ends in death. We now believe it's caused by either too much or too little blood reaching the brain. The severity of this brain attack, as it's sometimes called, determines the seriousness of the symptoms."

Gwen glanced at Lewis's parents. Were they following this? Other than her family's exposure to the measles, she'd had very little experience with medical issues. Dr. Edward's explanation sounded credible—in a farfetched sort of way—but she didn't know what this meant for her aunt. "How bad was my aunt's brain attack?" she asked.

Dr. Edwards sighed. "At this point, I'm afraid I can't tell you," he said. "The fact that she awoke, even for a short time, is very encouraging, but until we can talk to her, we won't know much more than that."

Gwen experienced a wave of panic. "But surely you can tell me something! Will she recover?"

"Recover from her current condition, yes," Dr. Edwards said. "I believe that is probable. But I have to be honest. It's far less likely that she'll be just as she was before the stroke hit."

"What do you mean?"

"Some patients experience paralysis or difficulty with the most basic physical movement. Speech and memory can also be affected. We won't know your aunt's condition until she's able to respond to my questions."

"Your aunt's a strong woman, Gwen." Owen spoke for the first time. "She'll fight back from this."

Mair nodded her agreement and squeezed Gwen's hand that she still held. "Of course she will, bach."

There was a faint moan from the bed, and everyone's attention suddenly became riveted on Aunty Jane. Dr. Edwards moved closer.

"Mrs. Jones, can you hear me?" He patted her hand.

Aunty Jane's eyes fluttered open. For a second, she stared, unseeing, at the doctor, then a look of panic filled her eyes and she gave a small cry. Gwen stepped up beside him.

"It's all right, Aunty Jane. You had a fall," she said, willing her voice to remain steady. "This is Dr. Edwards. He's here to help you."

Aunty Jane's eyes flickered between Gwen and the doctor, but still she said nothing.

"Can you understand what we're saying, Mrs. Jones?" Dr. Edwards asked.

Slowly Aunty Jane moved her head up and down.

"Excellent." The doctor seemed genuinely pleased. "I'm going to test the feeling in your arms and legs," he explained. "I don't want you to be alarmed. It will take only a moment."

Aunty Jane continued to lie completely still as the doctor took a pin out of his jacket pocket. He touched the pin to Aunty Jane's right hand. "Can you feel that?" he asked.

She gave a small, mute nod, and the doctor moved to the end of the bed, pulled the bed clothes up, and touched the pin to her right foot.

"What about that?"

Gwen knew Aunty Jane was not herself when her only response to a man's exposing and touching her feet was another slight nod. She clenched her hands. *Please, God*, she prayed silently, *please bless my aunt.*

Dr. Edwards moved over to the other side of the bed. This time when he touched the pin to Aunty Jane's left foot, she lay quietly, unresponsive. The doctor tried again. "Nothing?" he asked.

Aunty Jane watched as he moved up to her left hand and touched the pin to her middle finger. She blinked several times, her expression puzzled.

"Can you move your fingers?" Dr. Edwards asked.

Slowly two of the fingers on her aunt's right hand moved.

"How about your feet?"

The blanket covering Aunty Jane's right foot twitched a fraction of an inch, but the left foot remained still.

Dr. Edwards moved to stand beside Gwen. "Do you know who this is, Mrs. Jones?" he asked, pushing Gwen a little closer to her aunt.

Aunty Jane stared at her, and Gwen watched her aunt's mouth move as though she were formulating silent words. A tear rolled down Gwen's cheek, quickly followed by another. A look of distress crossed her aunt's face.

"G . . . G . . . Gw . . . e . . . en." Her voice was soft, and her articulation painfully slow, but there was no mistaking the name.

"That's right." The doctor said with satisfaction. "Well done, indeed."

Aunty Jane's eyes had not left Gwen's face. Gwen wiped the tears away with her hand and gave as brave a smile as she could muster.

"You'll be feeling better in no time, Aunty Jane," she said.

"G . . . Gwen." This time Aunty Jane's voice was stronger. Gwen knelt down beside the bed and reached for her aunt's lifeless hand. "I'm here," she said.

Her aunt's eyelids fluttered again before slowly closing. Gwen laid her forehead against the bedcovers, feeling as though her heart was going to break.

"Well, that was very encouraging," Dr. Edwards said.

"Encouraging?" Gwen could hardly believe her ears.

"Indeed." The doctor was smiling. "Your aunt has feeling on at least one side of her body, recognized you, and was able to say your name. Believe me, Miss Humphreys, that is very encouraging."

"You mark my words, Gwen," Owen said. "She'll beat this."

"I tend to agree with Mr. Morgan," Dr. Edwards said, still directing his comments to Gwen. "The fact that she tried your name again with noticeable improvement is a very good sign."

"A little time, bach." Mair spoke behind her. "That's what it will take. That and some heartfelt prayers."

Gwen got to her feet, brushed the dust off her skirt, and dug deep for some measure of courage. "What do I need to do, doctor?"

Giving her an approving look, Dr. Edwards reached into his black medical bag and pulled out a small bottle of liquid.

"I'll leave you with some medicine and instructions for your aunt's immediate care," he said. "Then I'll come back next week to check on her."

Mair put her arm around Gwen. "And you won't have to do it alone either. Bronwen Richards has already stopped by, offering to help. With the two of us willing to take a shift, there's no reason for you to wear yourself to the bone. We'll help you all we can."

Gwen fought back her tears. "Thank you," she said.

"You're welcome," Mair said. Then, with a knowing look, she added, "And when the doctor has finished talking to you, I want you downstairs in the kitchen. Making sure you don't wear yourself out includes reminding you to eat. I daresay you haven't eaten anything since Dai picked you up in Llanfyllin, have you?"

It seemed incredible that meeting Dai in the headmaster's office had happened earlier that very day; it felt like a hundred years ago. "No," Gwen admitted. "No, I haven't, but to be honest, I'm not sure that I can manage anything at the moment."

"I'll not take no for an answer, Gwen Humphreys," Mair warned. She started for the bedroom door. "I'll have a cup of tea and some toast ready for you as soon as you've finished here." Then she turned and faced Dr. Edwards. "You too, doctor. You'll need something before you leave."

As Mair walked out the door, Owen gave a low chuckle. "There's no point arguing, Gwen," he said. "The boys and I learned that long ago."

The thought of tall, broad-shouldered Lewis being bossed around by his pretty, petite mother produced Gwen's first smile since she'd walked out of her geometry class. Overwhelmingly thankful for the good people of Llanwddyn, who treated her like family even though she'd been gone from them for months, Gwen directed her attention to the doctor and on memorizing everything he told her.

Chapter 17

FOR THE NEXT TEN DAYS, Gwen didn't leave the house. Mair and Bronwen alternated days, coming to sit with Aunty Jane for a few hours each morning so Gwen could catch up on some sleep. Just as she'd promised, Mair made sure Gwen ate at least once every day, leaving her something for supper in the kitchen whenever she came over.

One day Gwen discovered two fat slices of bara brith wrapped in wax paper sitting on the kitchen table. It truly was the best bara brith she'd ever tasted, but she couldn't eat it without thinking of Lewis, and for some reason, that left her feeling sad. Despite his lack of contact while she was in Llanfyllin, she'd hoped that now that she was back home, he would come by the house to see her. But he hadn't come, and neither Mair nor Bronwen had spoken of him.

Dr. Edwards made two official visits to the house and seemed gratified by Aunty Jane's progress. Her aunt was now awake for several hours each day, and her speech, although still laboriously slow, was becoming easier to understand. The fact that Aunty Jane's mental faculties seemed virtually undamaged was a huge relief to everyone—except perhaps Aunty Jane herself. With her sharp mind, she found it extremely frustrating that she had to struggle so much to form words and that both her left leg and left arm were too weak to be of much use to her.

The doctor expressed confidence that all these symptoms would improve with time, but Aunty Jane was not the most patient person, and Gwen was rapidly learning that she wasn't either. Occasionally, when Gwen was downstairs in the kitchen, she would hear a loud clang from her aunt's bedroom above. Nine times out of ten it was her aunt taking out her frustrations by using her stronger right arm to hurl an inanimate object, such as a hairbrush or book, against the wall. There were times when Gwen wished she could hurl something too, but then she would remember how close she'd come to losing her aunt, and it put the more temporary aggravations in perspective.

The days and nights all blurred into one great whole. Gwen lost track of what day of the week it was, and her sleep came in small snatches. She checked on her aunt throughout the night and tried to rest when one of the other ladies was in the house. Her entire focus was on her aunt's recuperation, and she'd given almost no thought to anything else. And so it came as rather a shock when Owen came over almost a fortnight after she'd arrived back in Llanwddyn and asked if he could speak with her.

Gwen hadn't entered the more formal sitting room since she'd arrived back, and she didn't think it worth the effort to light a fire in that drafty room, so she invited him into the kitchen, where she made a cup of tea and they sat down on opposite sides of the old wooden table.

"Mair says you've been marvelous with your aunt," Owen said.

Gwen gave a tired smile. "I don't think I could have done it without her and Mrs. Richards."

Owen nodded his agreement. "They're good women." He stared into his teacup for a moment. Then, looking as though he was about to grasp a stinging nettle, he said, "I hate to bring this up when you've had so much on your plate, but it's like this, Gwen. The village has been without a post office going on two weeks now. Don't get me wrong; we managed fine without regular post when the pass was closed, but with your aunt laid up like she is, people are wondering if we should bring in another postmaster." He looked at her as though trying to gauge her reaction. "I didn't think we should do anything until I knew your feelings on the matter."

Gwen looked at him in horror. There'd been no functioning post office for two weeks!

"Oh, Mr. Morgan, I didn't even think . . . how could I have forgotten about something so important?" She put an unsteady hand to her head. "What should I do?"

"Well now," he said, his voice steady and kind. "It seems to me there are a few choices. We can contact someone at the General Post Office and ask them to send us a new, permanent postmaster, or we can explain what's happened and see if they can't send a temporary postmaster until your aunt's on her feet again.

"I know you spent a good deal of time at the post office before going off to school, so the other possibility is that you take it on until your aunt's feeling up to it. The benefit to that is that we wouldn't have to wait for anyone else to get here, and your aunt could maybe ease back into it by working with you for a while."

It was a good thing Gwen already had her hand on her head because it was starting to spin. Was she capable of managing the post office on her own for an undetermined length of time? Owen was right; she knew how virtually everything was done, but being in charge of something so important was different from merely helping. She felt as though she'd failed the village for almost a fortnight already, and she wasn't sure she could live with herself if she did nothing and her friends and neighbors had to wait even longer for postal service.

"I'll be there tomorrow morning, first thing," she said, sounding far more confident than she felt.

A look of concern crossed Owen's face. "I don't want you to feel pressured, bach," he said. "Why don't you sleep on it and let me know after you've had time to think it through?"

"No." Gwen shook her head. "Everyone's been patient enough. I may not be as efficient as my aunt, but I can make a start. There must be a terrible backlog of letters already."

"Ed the Post is due here tomorrow. I'm sure he'll do all he can
to help. And Mair said to tell you she'll come and stay at the house
for as long as you need."

Gwen was already starting to think through how she could
make this work. "Do you think it would be all right if the post
office was only open in the morning for the first week or so? That
way I won't be gone from home quite as long and won't impose
on Mrs. Morgan or Mrs. Richards quite so much."

"I think that's a splendid idea," Owen said.

Relief washed over Gwen. And something else. Something
that felt remarkably like excitement. For the first time in what felt
like forever, she would be doing something productive, something
that got her out of the house and interacting with other people,
and something that hinted at a return to normalcy.

"Will you get word out for me, Mr. Morgan?" she asked. "The
post office will be open first thing tomorrow until noon. And tell
your wife how much I appreciate her willingness to help with
Aunty Jane while I'm gone."

"I'd be happy to," he said, coming to his feet. "Thank you for
taking this on so readily."

Owen picked up his hat from the kitchen table and put it
on, then followed Gwen to the front door.

"Lewis was sorry to have missed you on Sunday," he said.

Gwen stumbled to a halt. "On Sunday?"

"Yes. He didn't know about your aunt." Owen looked a little
uncomfortable. "We hadn't been able to get a letter to him, see."

"A letter to him?" The spinning sensation was starting again.
"Why would you need to get a letter to him?"

It was Owen's turn to look confused. "Why, because he's in
Pen-y-Bont Fawr, of course."

"I . . . I didn't know." Gwen's thoughts were racing. What
was Lewis doing in the village of Pen-y-Bont Fawr? How long
had he been there? And why had no one told her?

"Well, I never!" Owen said. "I thought for sure someone would
have said something to you. He's been gone the best part of a month
now."

"But he was here on Sunday?" Gwen was still trying to come to grips with this new information.

"That's right. He's staying with my brother, Griffith, and his family. Griff's the blacksmith in Pen-y-Bont Fawr." He gave a good-humored shrug. "I suppose that's all we Morgans know."

"Anyway, right after Christmas, Griff fell on ice and broke his arm. He doesn't have any boys and needed someone to help him keep the smithy going. It made sense for Lewis to go. He's been apprenticing with me long enough to be a good help to Griff, and with Rowland turning sixteen this week, he can take Lewis's place here."

"So he'll be gone for a while, then," Gwen said.

"It looks that way. Not that I'm glad Griff broke his arm, mind, but it has worked out quite nicely. Griff needed the help, and I needed to start training Rowland."

Gwen wasn't sure she agreed. In fact, the more she thought about it, the worse she felt. No wonder Lewis hadn't been to see her; he wasn't even here anymore.

"Will he come back for another visit soon?" she asked.

"That I can't tell you, bach. He's working at the smithy six days a week, pretty well on his own until Griff's arm heals, and as you know, it's a good three-hour walk over the hills from Pen-y-Bont Fawr. With the short winter days and the miserable weather we've had recently, it makes it hard to go very far.

"He did the journey last Saturday night to be here for his brother's birthday. But he arrived in the early hours of the morning and only had time for Sunday services and dinner with the family before he had to head back. He did stop by here after chapel when we told him you were home, but he said no one answered the door."

"I must have been upstairs with Aunty Jane and didn't hear him knock," Gwen said.

"That was probably it," Owen said. "Never mind. I daresay he'll try again next time he's here."

Whenever that was. Gwen was so disappointed she wanted to cry. Oblivious to the impact his news had had on Gwen, Owen wished her a pleasant evening and set off down the road toward his own home.

Gwen stood at the doorway and watched him go. She knew every bump in the road, every chink in the gray stone wall, and every depression in the grass verge along his route. The colors of the doors and the patterns on the curtains hanging at the windows of the short row of houses between here and Pont Cedig would always be indelibly imprinted in her mind.

There had been nights when she'd lain in bed in Llanfyllin visualizing this familiar scene, aching to be back. Now, for the first time since she'd returned, she had a chance to stop and soak it in, but the sense of deep contentment she'd always associated with this memory was missing, and Gwen had to admit that much of her longing for home had been tied to her desire to be with Lewis again. She sighed. It appeared that she had yet another change to make. Lewis was gone, and even though it felt as though something vital was missing, she would have to adjust to life in the village without him.

Chapter 18

REOPENING THE POST OFFICE PROVED to be a blessing for everyone. Ed the Post was happy to resume his regular trek between Llanfyllin and Llanwddyn. For the first week, he stayed in the village a few extra hours each day, helping Gwen catch up with the stacks of letters that had accumulated during the two weeks her aunt had been ill, but it was not long before Gwen felt they had things well under control. She was pleasantly surprised by how much she was able to accomplish on her own.

The villagers were grateful to have their postal service restored and stopped by often for updates on Aunty Jane's recuperation. It was good for Gwen to interact with friends and neighbors again and to become reimmersed in the happenings of the village.

It didn't take long to catch up on the ongoing development of the dam. Most of the villagers were more than happy to grumble about one thing or another. Three more cranes had been delivered, bringing the total up to eight—and considerably increasing the noise at the site. The village policeman had had to break up four disorderly fights between navvies who had spent too long at the pub, and three pompous Englishmen from Liverpool had spent a few days surveying the dam before declaring Llanwddyn too wet and cold for them to stay any longer.

The winter weather had done little to slow the progress of the construction, however. Only two things had stopped the work for more than a couple of days. The first had been when supplies had been cut off by the blizzard that closed the pass to Llanfyllin, and the second was when one of the locomotives steaming up and down the valley hauling stone derailed. Three men had been injured, and it had taken several days to repair the train and the track.

Perhaps the most startling news was the Liverpool Corporation had started exhuming and reinterring bodies from the existing graveyard near the chapel to a new graveyard two miles down the valley. They were estimating that it would take three to four years to complete the job and had promised that family members would be notified before loved ones were moved. Despite that reassurance, Gwen resolved to go check on her parents' graves before the week was over.

She also hoped it wouldn't be too long before she was able to view the changes to the dam from her boulder on the mountain. From that vantage point, she knew she'd easily spot the progress that had been made while she'd been gone. For the time being, though, she spent every morning at the post office, then hurried home to spend the afternoon with her aunt before making supper and tumbling into bed exhausted.

Gwen had written a letter to the headmaster in Llanfyllin, updating him on her aunt's condition and explaining that it was unlikely that she would be returning to school in the foreseeable future. It was a difficult letter to write because as hard as it had been to move away from home, attending school in Llanfyllin had introduced her to new school subjects and friends. She promised herself she would keep up her studies at home and maintain contact with Alice and Rosamond.

It had been surprisingly hard to reconnect with her Llanwddyn friends. Having Lewis gone was a huge blow, and now that Rowland was working in his stead at the smithy, he had less free time than he'd had before. His working hours were even longer than hers, so she rarely saw him. Mabel visited her at the post office once or twice a week. Her mother kept her updated on Aunty Jane's condition, so she obviously didn't think it was necessary to ask any questions of Gwen. Instead, she used every minute of her time to talk about a new dress she'd ordered, her latest delicious creation in the kitchen, or, worst of all, how much she missed Lewis and how much time they'd spent together before he'd left.

Gwen had lost track of how many times Lewis had walked Mabel home from chapel meetings or how many times he'd stopped to talk to her when he finished his work at the smithy. She also wasn't sure if Lewis's favorite treat was now Mabel's crempogs or Mabel's blackberry crumble; Mabel didn't seem sure either. Gwen tried really hard to be happy for her, but despite her best efforts, she always seemed to go home grumpier on the days Mabel visited her.

On one of those days, the March sun was making a valiant effort to warm the wet earth, and as Gwen walked home, she felt a desperate need to escape to the mountain. It had been almost six weeks since she'd returned to Llanwddyn, and she had yet to visit her boulder. Her aunt had improved enough to leave her bed for a few hours each day and was happy to sit in her armchair by the fire as long as someone was there to help her move to and from her bedroom. In fact, she seemed quite eager to regain her independence. Gwen's decision to forgo requesting a replacement postmaster had proved motivational for Aunty Jane. If the people of the village were expecting her to return to her position, then she needed to work toward doing so.

Mair and Bronwen now limited their time with Aunty Jane to checking on her once each morning, and Gwen had extended the post office's closing time from noon to three o'clock. So, when she entered the house that afternoon to find Aunty Jane dozing peacefully in her chair with an open book on her knee, Gwen didn't bother to wake her. She wrote a brief note explaining her absence and put it within the open pages of her aunt's book. Then she ran upstairs and grabbed her sketchbook, her oldest boots, and her warmest shawl, then headed out the door again.

The path was muddy, and moisture from the rain earlier that day still clung to some of the branches and leaves. Gwen tried to avoid brushing up against the bushes, but her shawl was soon damp from the drips falling from tree limbs. Spring flowers cowered under protective bushes: white snowdrops, purple crocuses, and even a few early daffodils. Somewhere up ahead, a blackbird's song filled the air, and Gwen paused in her upward trek to listen.

She was out of breath by the time she reached the boulder, but it was wonderful to stand in the clearing and look out over her beloved valley again. She could see the new cranes standing sentinel above the semiconstructed dam. The wall itself had grown by several feet in places, the enormous rectangular stones looking like perfectly cut building blocks. Piles of shale littered the area, and the muddy puddles were so large she could see the water from where she stood. A few buildings stood off to one side of the construction, new since she was last here, and there were men walking between them.

Gwen sat on the large rock and studied the valley and the village below. Sheep were grazing in the fields, all traces of the snow now gone. The rivers were running high, and the trees were covered in the bright green of new leaves. She opened her sketchbook and turned to a fresh page, ready to record the view as it was today.

She drew for some time, absorbed in her work, but when the blackbird took up his song again, she stopped, instinctively turning to look at the area where the path reached the clearing. It was a bird, not Lewis. She lowered her pencil and gazed at her drawing. This was about the time Lewis usually arrived. He'd stand above her, studying her picture before remarking on some of the details: the gnarled tree beside the River Cedig, the huddle of sheep up against the shepherd's hut on the mountain, the men standing at the feet of the nearest crane at the dam.

She bowed her head, the ache in her chest suddenly too much to bear, and for the first time since she'd learned that Lewis was no longer in Llanwddyn, Gwen allowed herself to cry. She cried for the loss of his companionship, for the fact that he wasn't there to share his concern for her safety and his faith in her abilities.

Remembering his stumbling attempts to understand her made her wish she'd told him how much she wanted him to stay in contact. She wished he knew how much she missed him. And then, because she allowed self-pity to finally have its moment, she cried because Mabel had taken her place in his life while no one had taken his place in hers.

Her tears were cathartic but exhausting, and she sat for a few moments with her swollen eyes closed, resting and letting the peaceful sounds of the valley wash over her. Then, when the hoot of a barn owl replaced the trill of the blackbird, she knew it was time to leave, and she slowly made her way home.

◆

Two days later, Aunty Jane announced she was going to the post office. Even though she'd not left the house since her stroke, she'd been practicing walking in between rooms and was becoming more confident in her ability to make her own way. Her left side was still weak, but with the aid of a cane, she could make it from one end of the hall to the other without stopping, and although her steps were labored and a little unsteady, her balance was improving.

Aunty Jane's speech had also become clearer over the last few weeks. Even if it took longer for her to express herself than it had in the past, it wasn't hard to understand her. With a touch of guilt, Gwen recognized that she'd unexpectedly benefited from her aunt's difficulty. There were fewer sharp words or brisk reprimands directed toward Gwen than there'd ever been before. Whether this was due to some level of gratitude on her aunt's part or simply because it was too much effort, Gwen wasn't sure, but whatever the reason, she was thankful to be spared further scolding.

Gwen woke an hour earlier than usual that day so she could help her aunt get ready. After buttoning her aunt's gray dress, she began brushing her hair. As she pinned Aunty Jane's hair into a small bun at the base of her head, she remembered Aunty Jane's poor assessment of her hairstyling skills on St. John's Day, and she tried extra hard to make the bun smooth and tight. Rosamond had given Gwen some good pointers on hairstyling when they were preparing for their choral recitation at school. She hadn't had complete success with Gwen's thick mane, which was why Gwen still preferred to wear it in a long braid, but the tricks she'd used seemed to help with Aunty Jane's hair.

After breakfast, they set off together. The sky was clear, and the air held a hint of frost. Gwen tightened her shawl around her shoulders, but Aunty Jane stood at the garden gate and sniffed appreciatively.

"It's good to be out in the fresh air again," she said. "I can smell the tree blossoms."

"Some of the crocuses are out," Gwen told her, pointing to a cluster of yellow and purple beside the wall.

"I've always liked spring," Aunty Jane said. She looked down the road toward the post office. "Except for all the mud, of course."

Gwen stifled a smile. Their route, although short, would be an exercise in circumventing puddles. She knew it, and it seemed her aunt had just been forcibly reminded of it.

"Do you want my arm?" she asked.

In a movement that Gwen recognized all too well, Aunty Jane stiffened her shoulders and faced her destination. "No," she said. "I'll manage."

Gwen let Aunty Jane take the lead. They walked slowly, with Gwen staying at her aunt's elbow in case she lost her balance or needed to rest. Neither of those happened, however, and when they finally arrived at the post office, Gwen opened the door for her aunt to enter.

Aunty Jane was just taking a seat on the other side of the counter when Ed the Post walked in.

"Well, bless my soul, that's a sight for sore eyes!" he said, giving Aunty Jane a big smile.

"Hello, Ed," Aunty Jane said. "How are you?"

"All the better for seeing you here today," he said cheerfully. He slid his postbag off his shoulder. "Are you going to be the one to help me with today's delivery?"

"I believe I am," she said.

"Right, then," Ed said. "Let's see if you remember how."

Aunty Jane gave an insulted humph, and Ed managed a surreptitious wink at Gwen. With a smile, Gwen headed for the fireplace to coax the banked fire back to life.

Ed stayed until the mail was sorted, but that initial busyness proved to be only the beginning. For over two hours afterward, a steady stream of villagers came and went, some of them lingering for a long time so they could chat with each other and Aunty Jane. When tiredness began to take its toll and it became difficult for Aunty Jane to formulate her sentences, she simply listened to those around her and nodded her head at appropriate times. Despite Gwen's repeated suggestions that she return home to rest, she would not leave until the last visitor had gone.

It was obvious Ed the Post had done an impressive job of spreading the word that Jane Jones was at the post office, and it was heartening to see so many friends and neighbors genuinely happy to have her back. Even Aunty Jane's crusty exterior fell prey to such kindness, and later that night, when Gwen helped her aunt into bed, she couldn't help but notice that the contentment evident on Aunty Jane's face far outshone her exhaustion. It seemed that returning to the post office had been the best possible medicine.

Chapter 19

OVER THE NEXT FEW WEEKS, as Aunty Jane spent more and more time at the post office, Gwen was able to spend less. She still went every morning to help with the mail sorting, but if her aunt was functioning well, she sometimes excused herself after a few hours to return home to study her school textbooks or, if the weather was good, to go hiking. It wasn't long before her sketchbook was full of pictures she'd drawn while on the mountains, but the view from her boulder remained her favorite.

One afternoon, Gwen was sitting on the boulder, engrossed in her sketch, when a long shadow suddenly crossed her page. Looking up, she discovered a man had entered the clearing and was standing less than two yards from her. With a small yelp of surprise, Gwen leapt to her feet, dropping her sketchbook to the ground.

"I'm very sorry," he said. "I didn't mean to startle you. I didn't know anyone was here."

English. He spoke English. Gwen's already-racing heart started to pound even harder. She was all alone on the mountain with an Englishman she'd never met before. Instinctively, her eyes darted to the path. Could she make a run for it? Then she remembered her sketchbook. She swung around in time to see the man reaching down to pick it up. Frozen, she watched as he brushed the dead leaves off the page before pausing to study it. He looked out over the valley, then back at the drawing.

"This is amazing!" he said.

Gwen stood silent, poised for flight.

"Do you speak English?" he asked.

"A little," she whispered.

The man smiled, and Gwen felt herself relax a fraction. It was a genuine smile—not mean or lascivious like some of the navvies she'd encountered before. For the first time, she noticed his clothes. He didn't dress like a navvy. They usually wore old smocks and worn corduroy trousers held up with a piece of string or a strap. This man was wearing a brown wool suit. His shoes, although muddy at the moment, did not look shabby in the least. He appeared to be in his late twenties or early thirties, his light-brown hair was well groomed, and his dark-brown eyes showed no hint of the fog so common in the eyes of the navvies leaving the pub.

He moved toward her. Despite her hopeful assessment, she took a step back, and immediately he stopped.

"I should introduce myself," he said. "My name's Thomas Henley. I'm an engineer working for the Liverpool Corporation."

"You're an engineer?" Gwen hadn't intended to say another word, but she couldn't help herself. For as long as she could remember, she'd loved drawing, and her time in Llanfyllin had taught her that she had an aptitude for geometry. She'd often wondered what it would be like to design a real building, to be responsible for blending precision with beauty. And here was a man who did just that.

"Yes," he said slowly. "Do you know what that is?"

Gwen nodded. She knew she was about to reveal that she spoke considerably better English than she'd first implied. "What do you design?"

"Dams," he said. "Not much of surprise, I suppose, seeing as I'm here in Llanwddyn."

Gwen worked hard to hide her wince at his mangled pronunciation of the village name.

"I've worked on a few other things, but dams seem to have become my specialty," he added, looking down at the picture he was holding. "When we first survey an area, I usually draw some rough sketches to show the lay of the land, but believe me, they're nowhere near as good as this."

An unexpected breeze caught a few of the pages in the sketchbook, and for the first time, he realized there were more pictures beneath the one he'd already seen.

"Would you mind if I look at your other drawings?" he asked.

Gwen wasn't sure what to say. What she really wanted was to have him hand over her sketchbook so she could leave, and she didn't know which response would give her that outcome the fastest.

He seemed to take her silence as assent because he started slowly flipping through the pages, pausing every once in a while to study some of the details more carefully. Finally he raised his head and looked directly at her.

"Can I buy some of these?"

"You . . . you want to buy my drawings?" Gwen couldn't hide her astonishment.

"Yes. Your attention to detail is amazing. It's an incredible record of the work we've done here."

His reference to the record she was keeping struck a chord. For a split second, she was transported back to the year before when Lewis had first seen her sketches in this very clearing and had begged her to keep drawing, to preserve a record of how the valley once was.

"I . . . um . . . I'm not sure I want to sell any of them," Gwen said.

"Think about it," Thomas suggested. He pointed at the dam in the distance. "You see the building that's closest to the crane?"

Gwen glanced back at the familiar scene. "Yes."

"That's my office. If you decide you're willing to sell, you can find me there."

"Very well." Gwen had absolutely no intention of ever going anywhere near so many navvies, but she did not feel she needed to share that with Thomas Henley. She held out her hand, and he handed her the sketchbook.

"Will you tell me your name?" he asked.

"Gwen," she said.

"Well, Gwen, it was a pleasure to meet you, and I hope I will see you again."

She gave him a tiny nod of acknowledgment before tucking her sketchbook under her arm and escaping down the path as quickly as she could.

He wanted to buy my sketches! Gwen's bewilderment mingled with delight as she hurried down the narrow trail. If only Lewis were here, she'd go straight to the smithy to tell him what had happened. What would he think of it? Other than Robert, Lewis was the only other person who'd ever seen her sketches. She knew he appreciated them, but would he encourage her to sell them or hold on to them?

As her thoughts tumbled over each other, her steps slowed. Lewis had not bothered to exchange a word with her in months and months, so why did she even think he'd care? An all-too-familiar ache filled her. Clutching her sketchbook a little closer, she desperately tried to redirect her thoughts. Perhaps she would make pancakes for supper. If she was fast, she could surprise her aunt by having them ready when she returned from the post office. Without even glancing in the direction of the smithy, Gwen ran down the road toward home.

❖

The next Sunday, John Ellis was in fine form. There'd been another drunken brawl in the village, this time at the Cynon Huts, the navvies' housing north of the dam, and it had fueled a rousing sermon. For at least thirty minutes, Mr. Ellis expounded on the ills of strong drink and filthy lucre. He reminded his flock of their commitment to abstinence from alcohol and urged them to be free from the love of money. Gwen couldn't help but think that the minister was preaching to the wrong people since no member of his flock had set foot inside the Powys Arms and very few villagers had enough money to do more than subsist. But his message did help firm her resolve to not sell any of her drawings to Thomas Henley.

When the last amen was said, Gwen stood and offered her arm to Aunty Jane. Her aunt still relied heavily on her cane, but she was now strong enough to work half days at the post office and attend her Sunday meetings. Her speech had continued to improve, and there had even been a few times when Gwen had witnessed the return of her aunt's sharp tongue.

"I'd like a word with the minister today, Gwen," Aunty Jane said as Gwen led her slowly down the chapel aisle toward the door at the back.

Gwen waited for the Williams family to exit their pew ahead of them. As usual, the minister was standing at the arched doorway, greeting his congregation as they left the chapel. When they reached him, he shook Aunty Jane's hand warmly.

"Mrs. Jones, how lovely to see you here today," he said. "You're looking remarkably well."

"Thank you, Mr. Ellis," Aunty Jane said, moving her weight to her cane so she could lean a little closer to him. "I appreciated your sermon. In fact, I wanted to mention that the scripture you quoted in 1 Timothy has long been a favorite of mine. I'd be very interested to hear your interpretation of God's ability to 'quicken all things.'"

"Why, of course," the minister said. "It's certainly worthy of our consideration."

At her aunt's gratified expression, Gwen suppressed a groan. She'd waited through similar doctrinal discussions before; they were never short. Concerned that a few people still needed to exit the chapel, she checked that Aunty Jane's footing was secure, then slipped her arm free and moved to stand just outside the chapel door. Half a dozen people slipped past her, wishing her a cheerful good morning before moving on to talk with others who were standing outside in the spring sunshine.

"Hello, Gwennie."

Gwen swung around, her heart hammering. "Lewis!"

For a terrifyingly long moment, she could not put a single coherent sentence together. Only two thoughts rattled through her head: he'd caught her unawares again, and why had she not remembered how handsome he was?

He smiled. "It's so good to see you."

"And you," she said, willing her brain and her mouth to finally connect. "When did you get back?"

"Late last night," he said. "I've been wanting to come for weeks, but one thing or another kept preventing . . ." He stopped and started again. "I heard that Mr. Williams the Shop was making a trip to Pen-y-Bont Fawr this weekend, so I thought if I walked home after work on Saturday, I could maybe get a ride back."

"And have you talked to him?"

"Yes." With a frustrated sigh, he raked his fingers through his dark hair. "He's leaving in an hour . . . much earlier than I'd hoped."

Gwen was sure her disappointment showed. "Well, I'm very glad you . . ."

"Lewis!" Mabel's voice reached them seconds before she arrived at Lewis's side. Sidling up to him with a coy smile, she slid her arm through his. "I'm so sorry to have kept you waiting. Mrs. Evans simply wouldn't stop talking." She tore her eyes off Lewis and gave Gwen a brief glance. "Oh, hello, Gwen."

"Hello, Mabel." Gwen clasped her hands together, hoping the action would prevent her from giving in to her overwhelming desire to reach out and pry Mabel's fingers off Lewis's arm one by one.

Thankfully, she didn't have to endure the discomfort for long. Lewis took matters into his own hands, gently disengaging Mabel's arm and taking a small step to the side. "I'm sorry, Mabel," he said. "I was just explaining to Gwen that Mr. Williams the Shop is giving me a ride back to Pen-y-Bont Fawr within the hour. I'm afraid I can't stay."

Mabel gave a petulant frown. "But you haven't been here for weeks. When will you be back again?"

"Soon, I hope." Lewis looked as let down as the girl at his side; Gwen's heart sank. He really did want to spend time with Mabel.

"Have you heard from Robert, Gwennie?"

"No," she said. "It's going on six months since he was here, so I hope I'll hear soon. He should have arrived back in India by now."

"It was good to see him in November. He stopped by the smithy to talk for a bit, but it was Ioan Llanwddyn who heard all his stories." His deep blue eyes shone with humor. "I really think Robert came as close to talking Ioan's ear off as anyone has ever come."

Gwen laughed. "We both knew what to expect. Perhaps we should have warned Ioan."

Smiling, Lewis shook his head. "It was good for them both."

"Goodness me," Mabel said. "Everyone knows that once Ioan starts talking, there's no stopping him. Most people avoid him for that very reason. It's about time someone gave him a taste of his own medicine."

Gwen stared at Mabel, all trace of amusement gone. Why would she say something so catty? And why would Lewis want to spend time with someone who did?

Behind her, she heard the rustle of fabric and the distinctive tap of a cane.

"Good morning, Mrs. Jones," Lewis said.

Gwen had never heard him sound so formal. She turned around in time to see her aunt give Lewis a curt nod.

"Lewis."

"I was sorry to hear of your illness," he said.

"Thank you," she said. "As you can see, I'm much improved."

"I'm very glad," he said.

Aunty Jane turned to Gwen. "I'm ready to leave now, Gwen," she said.

Gwen was quite sure it wouldn't matter how old she was or how independent she became; Aunty Jane would always treat her with some measure of condescension. She lived in hope that at some point her aunt would refrain from doing so in front of others.

With resignation, she took her Aunty Jane's arm. "Good-bye, Mabel," she said. "Good-bye, Lewis. It was very nice to see you again."

"Good-bye, Gwen," Mabel and Lewis said together.

Out of the corner of her eye, she saw Mabel's pitying look, but Lewis took a step forward as though he would say something more. Aunty Jane, however, was not going to have it. Making sure Gwen's arm was securely around her own, she started walking, and Gwen was forced to follow.

Chapter 20

LEWIS'S UNEXPECTED BRIEF APPEARANCE DID nothing for Gwen's peace of mind. She found herself thinking of him far more than she wanted to, puzzling over why he'd sent her a gift at Christmastime and treated her with such friendliness on Sunday yet ignored her for the months in between. She tried not to think about his relationship with Mabel. She didn't know how far it had progressed—she didn't want to know. It simply made her miserable.

To her irritation, it was difficult to concentrate on her school studies, and she usually ended up abandoning her textbooks in favor of drawing outdoors. So it wasn't a big surprise that a few days later, Thomas Henley found her sketching on the mountain again. This time, however, Gwen heard him coming. The snapping of twigs and gentle swoosh of branches springing back into place alerted her to the presence of someone on the path, and she was already on her feet when he entered the clearing.

"Wait, Gwen," he said as she started to move toward the path. "You don't need to leave. Please stay and finish your drawing."

She shook her head. "I'm not going to sketch anymore today."

"Then may I see what you've done?"

Gwen hesitated. "I don't want to sell it," she said.

He chuckled. It was a pleasant sound. "Fair enough. But I'd still like to see it."

Reluctantly, Gwen turned her book around so her sketch faced Thomas. It was a picture of the dam, but this time, instead of drawing the overall scene, she'd narrowed her focus to the stones that made up the base of the retaining wall itself. Thomas stepped closer and examined the picture.

"Have you ever seen the stones up close?" he asked.

Gwen shook her head. "I've seen them going down the mountain from the quarry on the locomotives," she said.

"It's hard to get a feel for how big they are unless you're standing right beside them," he said. "Most of them weigh ten to twelve tons, and the masons at the quarry sometimes work on one stone for a full month just to get the shape and size exactly right. They follow the plans given them by the draughtsman and make sure each stone is numbered with a ticket so it's placed into the wall exactly where it's meant to go."

He looked at her picture and pointed to the pile of logs Gwen had sketched in the corner. "You know," he said, "if you were to sit on those railroad ties, you'd be less than twenty yards from the dam and have an unobstructed view. It would give you a whole new perspective and enable you to sketch details you can't see from this distance."

"That's probably true," Gwen said. "But as no one from the village is allowed that close to the construction site, I'll content myself with the view from here."

Thomas thought about that for a moment. "If I accompanied you there, you could do it."

For a split second, Gwen considered it. To be able to draw not only the enormous rock wall but also the ongoing activity at the dam from close quarters would be a new and exciting challenge. Then reality set in, and she remembered who else would be there. "The workmen," she said. She stopped, not wanting to divulge her fear of the navvies to someone she hardly knew. "It wouldn't be right, me being there with all the men."

Thomas frowned. "They wouldn't be anywhere near you. Most of the construction is happening on the other side of the dam at the moment. And even if it weren't, if the men are at the site, they're working. You're not in any danger of them socializing."

Gwen felt the blush on her cheeks. "It's good to know you have such control over all those navvies," she said. "Maybe if you could extend that to overseeing how much alcohol they consume, none of the girls in the village would need to worry about them anymore." She swung on her heel and started for the path.

"Wait! Gwen!" His hand reached out and grabbed her arm.

"Don't touch me!"

Thomas dropped her arm and stepped back as though he'd been burned. "Gwen, I'm so sorry. I had no idea. Have any of the workmen bothered you?"

"Bothered me?" she said, barely controlling her emotions. She pointed toward the dam site. "That may be the most obvious scar that's been inflicted on this valley since the Liverpool Corporation arrived, but believe me, it's not the only one. The damage done to my village by men who've come here with loose morals and foul mouths is just as permanent and equally unwelcome."

She'd shocked the man into silence. Ruefully, she realized this wasn't the first time her sudden outbursts had had a similar effect; Lewis and Ioan Llanwddyn had shown similarly stunned expressions at the smithy. And now, just as had happened then, she had nothing more to say. Before Thomas could gather his wits, she ran out of the clearing and hurried down the path as quickly as the uneven terrain would allow.

It was Gwen's turn to look stunned the next morning when Thomas Henley walked into the post office.

"Hello, Gwen," he said.

Gwen almost dropped the pile of letters she was sorting. Aunty Jane slowly lowered her pen onto the ledger book in front of her and gave Gwen a curious look before turning her steely gaze to the stranger.

"Good morning, Mr. Henley," Gwen said.

"Thomas," he corrected her.

"Thomas," she said, acknowledging his olive branch with an accepting nod. "How can I help you?"

"I've thought a lot about what you said yesterday, and I'd like a chance to show you the dam as I see it—not a scar that ruins a beautiful valley but a magnificent piece of architecture that may actually come to enhance this area. With your artistic eye, I don't think it will be hard for you to visualize the end result once you've seen the blueprints and renderings we have in the office."

He lowered his voice a little. "I'd also like the opportunity to prove to you that not all the Englishmen who invaded your village are the cads you've had the misfortune of meeting up until now."

Aunty Jane cleared her throat. "Gwen, as you already seem to be acquainted, would you introduce me to this gentleman?"

Only when Aunty Jane spoke to her in Welsh did Gwen remember that her aunt's English was nowhere near as good as her own. With guilty relief, she realized it was unlikely Aunty Jane had understood much of what Thomas had said, which meant she might be able to avoid an awkward explanation.

"Aunty Jane," she said in Welsh. "This is Thomas Henley. He's an engineer at the dam. I spoke to him briefly yesterday, and he's come in to ask if you'd let me go to the construction site. He thinks I'd be interested in seeing the blueprints of the dam."

Aunty Jane raised her eyebrows. "An engineer, is it?" She looked over at Thomas again. "He doesn't dress like a navvy, but you never can tell with these Englishmen."

"Is something wrong?" Thomas asked in English.

Gwen switched languages again, hoping she could maintain them both without too much confusion.

"No. Nothing's wrong. My aunt was curious to know who you were, is all."

"This is your aunt?" he asked.

Gwen nodded. "Yes. Mr. Thomas Henley, this is Mrs. Jane Jones, the village postmistress and my guardian."

Thomas reached over the counter and shook Aunty Jane's hand. "It's nice to meet you, Mrs. Jones," he said.

"Thank you," Aunty Jane said in English before turning to speak to Gwen in Welsh. "They've been working on that dam going on five years. If he's the engineer, ask him why we haven't seen him here before?"

Gwen couldn't deny Aunty Jane's point was a valid one.

"My aunt's English is limited," Gwen told Thomas, "but she'd like me to ask why she hasn't seen you in the village before."

"I actually haven't been here very long," he said. "I'm a junior engineer working under Mr. George Wainwright. Mr. Wainwright was on-site up until three weeks ago—perhaps she's met him—but he started experiencing some health issues and asked that I take his place until he has them resolved."

Gwen relayed this information and saw the skepticism in her aunt's face begin to diminish.

"Well, at least he's honest," Aunty Jane said. "I'll give him that. I know Mr. Wainwright. He's come in to post things a few times. I always thought he looked a bit sickly, so I'm not surprised he's taken ill."

For her part, Gwen was feeling the pinpricks of shame over her outburst the day before. If Thomas had only been here three weeks, it was no wonder he had little knowledge of the navvies' tendencies to carouse away their earnings every Saturday afternoon.

"Will you tell her why I came in today?" Thomas asked. "Ask if I may have permission to escort you to the dam site." He paused. "Or perhaps I should ask you first? Will you come?"

Gwen hesitated. It would seem pigheaded to tell him no when he'd gone out of his way to find her after she'd been so rude to him. She knew he wanted her to see the dam from his perspective, but her reservations about the navvies remained. "If I go with you, I need to know that I can leave anytime I wish," she said.

"You have my word," Thomas said, and the sincerity on his face convinced her that he was telling the truth.

"Mr. Henley would like your permission to show me around the dam," Gwen told her aunt.

"Without a chaperone?" Her aunt's eyebrows rose alarmingly high.

Trying to hide her discomfort, Gwen translated Aunty Jane's query.

"I'd love to escort your aunt too," he said. "She's welcome to come with us."

It appeared that the surprises were not over. Upon hearing Thomas's offer, Gwen watched Aunty Jane's entire expression transform. Her habitual frown melted into a pleasant smile. "That's very thoughtful," her aunt said. "And I would be delighted to go, but it's too far for me to walk in my current condition, and someone must stay here to run the post office." She gave a nod as though she'd come to a decision. "You may go with him, Gwen, but I trust you will maintain a respectable distance while you are together."

Gwen hoped that her astonishment did not show. She'd never known her aunt to capitulate so easily or so happily. "My aunt will stay here, but I will go with you," Gwen told Thomas.

He gave a pleased smile and leaned over the counter to shake Aunty Jane's hand again. "I will return Gwen to you soon," he said.

Aunty Jane nodded. "I want to hear all about it afterward, Gwen," she said.

"Yes, Aunty Jane." Gwen put on her shawl and waited until Thomas walked ahead of her to open the door. "Thank you for letting me go," she said. "I won't be long."

As soon as the door closed behind them, Gwen turned to Thomas. "I don't know how you did that."

"Did what?" he asked.

"Won my aunt over so quickly," she said. "I've rarely seen her respond the way she did with you."

Thomas smiled. "She reminds me of my mother." He gave a small shrug. "I've noticed that Mother rarely leaves home to go out in the evenings with me or my sister, but she likes to be invited nonetheless. I've come to the conclusion that no one wants to feel that they've been overlooked, no matter how elderly or infirm they may be."

Gwen studied him thoughtfully. Thomas may have believed he was sharing a lesson he'd learned through experience, but she felt sure he'd actually given her a glimpse of his generous nature. "Thank you," she said, warmed by his kindness. "I'll remember that."

Chapter 21

THE SKY WAS OVERCAST, THREATENING rain as Gwen and Thomas walked through the village. Mrs. Williams the Shop gave them an inquiring look through the shop window as they passed, and Ioan Llanwddyn raised his hand in greeting from his spot on the ground beside Pont Cedig. But no one stopped to talk with them, and Thomas made use of the time to ask her questions about the village and the people who lived there.

The time passed quickly, and when she could hear the sound of men's shouts over the roar of the cranes and the squeal of metal wheels on metal tracks, Gwen knew they were getting close. Feeling a little like Daniel walking into the lions' den, she instinctively slowed her pace.

Thomas noticed and gave her an encouraging smile. "It will be fine," he said. "I'll take you to the office first and show you the designs. That way when we go on-site you'll have a better understanding of the big picture."

"All right," Gwen said, trying not to flinch as an enormous thud shook the earth.

Thomas didn't seem to notice that the ground beneath their feet had shaken. He led the way along a well-worn path, seemingly oblivious to the noise and dust in the air around them. He'd been right; no one was working nearby. To her right, a pile of dirt and rubble exposed the bedrock that lay far beneath them. Men, like ants, moved around on the enormous mound of earth, navigating the large rocks and the wooden scaffolding, focusing their attention on the stone wall that towered above their heads. Rickety railroad tracks led all the way to the cranes that stood over the waiting railroad cars.

Fascinated by the sight, Gwen's footsteps faltered.

Beside her, she heard Thomas chuckle. "Come along," he said. "I promise to show you everything, but we should start at the beginning."

He walked a few more yards and opened the door of a nearby building, stepping back so she could precede him inside. Rolls and rolls of paper covered every surface area in the small room. An assortment of mysterious objects that she assumed were engineering tools fought for space with rulers, protractors, pencils, pens, and ink. At first glance, it looked like complete chaos, but Thomas did not seem the least deterred. He stepped up to one of the tables and unrolled a large sheet of paper.

"Here it is," he said. "Our ultimate goal. It will be the first masonry dam in Britain and will form the largest reservoir in Europe."

Gwen moved closer and gazed down at a sketch of the completed Vyrnwy Dam. The design in front of her was grander than anything she could have imagined. Thomas pointed to a series of arches that ran along the upper edge of the retaining wall.

"This will be the first dam ever to carry the overflow water over its crest instead of through a channel cut into the hillside," he said. "Any excess water in the reservoir will run down the face of the angled retaining wall into the river below."

Gwen nodded her understanding. "And the road will be built on top of the archways."

"That's right," Thomas said. "Some of the old roads have already been graded and modified to accommodate all the equipment we had to bring in, but when all is said and done, there will be eleven miles of new road around the reservoir."

"What's this?" Gwen pointed at a tall tower standing in the water at the edge of the lake.

"That's the straining tower," he said. "The water from the reservoir will go through the straining tower before entering a sixty-eight mile aqueduct that will take it to Liverpool."

"It doesn't look very Welsh," Gwen said, studying the round tower with its conical copper roof more carefully.

Thomas laughed. "I agree. I had nothing to do with the straining tower design, but someone told me it's supposed to look like one of the castles on the Rhine in Germany. It's attractive but perhaps a little out of keeping with its surroundings."

"A bit," Gwen said. "It looks like it belongs in my book of fairy tales."

"It does look sort of magical," Thomas said.

Gwen rolled her eyes. "I don't think I'd go quite that far."

With a grin, Thomas moved over to the next table and began unrolling some of the blueprints. "Come and see how the outlet chambers work," he said.

◆

When they stepped outside half an hour later, Gwen understood why Thomas had insisted she see the paperwork first. Now that she knew the direction each part of the project was to take, she could tell which sections were near completion and which were just beginning to take shape. She viewed the massive retaining wall as a giant jigsaw puzzle, with enormous blocks of stone making up the bulk of it but with steps, ledges, arches, tunnels, and decorative masonry strategically placed to add form and function. Even the ugly wooden scaffolding was easier to forgive now that she could see its specific purpose.

She followed Thomas around some enormous boulders toward the closest crane. It looked as though two men were inside the control box, and four or five were standing at its base, where more boulders lay in seemingly haphazard formations beside the railroad tracks.

As Gwen and Thomas drew nearer, one of the men broke away from the others and walked to meet them. His worn clothes, hat, and shoes were covered in fine powder, and when he tried brushing his hands off on his trousers, he sent a small puff of dust into the air. "'Morning, Mr. Henley," he said, offering Thomas his hand.

Thomas shook it. "Good morning, Harry," he said. "I want to introduce you to Gwen Humphreys. She's a local artist, and I'm showing her around the site with the idea that she might come back to draw some pictures of the dam as it goes up."

"Very nice," Harry said. He turned to Gwen and offered her his hand too. "Harry Weston. Pleased to meet you, miss."

"Thank you, Harry," Gwen said.

"Harry's one of our gangers," Thomas explained, "which means he's in charge of one of the cranes and a certain number of masons and laborers." Ignoring the coating of dust on Harry's jacket, Thomas placed his hand on the older man's shoulder. "Harry's a good man and can be trusted. If you ever come to sketch when I'm not available, Harry here will watch out for you."

Harry shuffled his feet awkwardly. "I'd be 'appy to, miss."

"That's very kind of you," Gwen said.

The ganger bobbed his head in her direction before turning back to Thomas. "Will you be needing anything else, sir?"

"No, thank you, Harry. You've been most helpful. I'll let you get back to work."

"Thank you, sir," Harry said before hurrying back to his waiting crane.

Thomas and Gwen made their way over to the railroad ties Gwen had included in her earlier drawing. The pile was significantly bigger than it had seemed from the mountain. Gwen stepped up onto the third tier of wood. From that spot, she could see the entire length of the dam.

"Well," Thomas asked from below, "will you come back and draw this?"

Gwen watched the long arm of Harry's crane swing to the right as the men below gathered around a boxcar full of rock. Her fingers were itching to start sketching all that she'd already seen. "You're sure it's all right that I be here?" she asked.

"If ever it's not, Harry or I will inform you," he said.

"Then I'll come," she said. "I'll do as you suggested and draw what I can see from this spot."

Thomas gave a broad smile. "Excellent," he said, holding out his hand to help her down from the logs. "I look forward to seeing your work."

A little hesitantly, Gwen accepted his hand. She was fairly sure this wasn't the decorous distance her aunt had had in mind, so she relinquished his hand as soon as her feet were safely on the ground, then moved a few steps back.

"May I ask you a question now?" Gwen ventured.

"Of course."

"How do you know my last name? You introduced me to Harry as Gwen Humphreys, but I made a point of not telling you my full name when we met."

"So I noticed," Thomas said, his mouth quirking up as he fought back a smile.

"But you know it."

This time he chuckled. "It was very easy to discover," he said. "I simply walked into the local shop and asked the proprietor if she knew a Gwen with long, chestnut-colored hair who lived in Llanwddyn. We had a little problem translating *chestnut*, but when I changed the word to *pretty*, she said, 'Ah, yes, Gwen Humphreys from the post office.' I walked straight from the shop to the post office, and there you were."

Not quite sure how to respond to his description of her hair, Gwen quickly decided her best recourse was to focus on the translation issue rather than his choice of words. "You've probably noticed the younger people in the village speak better English than the older ones," she said.

Thomas nodded. "Yes, but your English is far better than anyone else's I've met. You seem to understand everything I say, and you speak it well."

"I've had more exposure to English than most people in Llan-wddyn," she said. "The younger ones have picked it up from the navvies, but I spent some time at a school where English was taught and where I had English-speaking friends."

"Well, I'm very glad," Thomas said, "because I like talking to you."

At that moment, Gwen realized she could echo his sentiment; she'd genuinely enjoyed her time with Thomas. "Thank you," she said, giving him a shy smile.

A rumble sounded in the distance, but this time it had nothing to do with the construction and everything to do with the gray skies. They both looked up.

"Come on," Thomas said. "I'd better get you back to the village before the rain starts."

Half a dozen huge drops fell at their feet.

"I think it might already be too late," Gwen said.

He groaned. "And that's why this is such a great place for a reservoir."

Gwen raised her shawl so it covered her head. "There's no point in you getting wet when you don't need to. I can run home in no time. "

"I can't let you go on your own," Thomas said, looking shocked.

"Of course you can." She laughed. "I'm very used to this. I'm out in the rain all the time." She backed up a few paces. "Thank you for showing me everything . . . and for inviting me back."

"But, Gwen . . ." he began.

"I'll return when the weather clears up," she said, and with a wave, she started running down the path that led to the village road.

"Gwen!"

She heard him call her name again, but she ignored it. It really was quite pointless for him to go back and forth in the rain when she was perfectly capable of getting home on her own.

Chapter 22

APRIL'S SHOWERS CONTINUED INTO MAY, but whenever there was a break in the wet weather for more than an hour or two, Gwen made her way to the dam with her sketchbook in hand. Just as she'd earlier claimed the boulder on the mountain as her own, she now claimed the pile of railroad ties that overlooked the construction. From this spot, she drew the ever-growing retaining wall, the movement of men and machines, the latticework of scaffolding and wooden ladders, the coming and going of the locomotives from the quarry, and the changing face of the nearby hillside.

On most of her visits, Thomas left his office for a short time to sit with her. He was always anxious to see her latest project and was happy to explain the newest developments at the site so she could anticipate what the men would be working on next. Sometimes, however, he steered the conversation to more personal topics and asked about her family and her interests beyond drawing.

Gwen told him about her parents' deaths and her subsequent move to Llanwddyn, about living with Aunty Jane and her feeling of loss when her brother left for sea, and about some of her experiences at school in Llanfyllin. But even though their talks were often long and Thomas was a good listener, she never once talked about Lewis. She wasn't sure how to explain her relationship with Lewis—she didn't understand it herself—so it was easier not to bring it up at all.

Sometimes she wondered if her decision to spend more time drawing at the dam site than on the mountain was a form of self-preservation. She associated the boulder in the clearing with Lewis, and returning there without him was not always easy. But if she ever felt any misgivings over abandoning that special place, she reminded herself that the scope and variety of her sketches were so much greater from her new vantage point.

She also enjoyed learning more about Thomas. He told her of his home in Liverpool, where he lived with his widowed mother and younger sister, Cecilia. He shared some of his experiences at an all-boys boarding school and at college before working under the tutelage of Mr. Wainwright, but she liked it best when he described some of the projects he'd worked on over the last few years. That was when his expression became animated and the passion he felt for his vocation was manifest.

It was obvious that even though he was considerably younger than many of the men working at the dam, Thomas was well respected; he was often called upon to check on problems that arose. When that happened and Thomas was unable to join her at the logs, Harry would inevitably wander over to check on her. Harry never stayed long, and his conversation was usually limited to one or two lines.

"All right, Miss Humphreys?" he would ask.

When Gwen responded in the affirmative, he quickly followed his question with, "Good to know. Just needed to be sure."

Harry always made her smile. He didn't want to be found neglecting his unusual assignment, but he obviously didn't know quite what to do with it either. Gwen often reflected that he probably thought he never did anything for her, while, in fact, the opposite was true. Harry's quiet consideration had done a great deal to restore Gwen's faith in the worth of at least some of the English workmen who had flooded her valley. She was still wary of the navvies who roamed the village streets after having been at the pub, but her opinion of them as a whole had improved.

She'd never considered the fact that any of these men could be churchgoers until one Saturday when Thomas broached the subject. He'd been sitting quietly beside her as she'd finished her sketch of the two closest overflow archways, but when she started putting her pencils away, he spoke. "Do you always go to church on Sunday?" he asked.

"Yes," Gwen said. "I go to the Methodist chapel in the village."

He thought about that for a moment. "Even though I'm not a Methodist, do you think I could join you there tomorrow?"

Astonished, Gwen turned to look at him. "I'm sure you could. The minister is always happy to have visitors." She paused. "But you realize the entire meeting is in Welsh—the sermon, the prayers, the singing, everything."

"Yes, I know that," he said. "But it's been almost two months since I was able to attend a Sunday service, and since there are no meetings held in English anywhere near here, I thought that even if I can't understand the words, it would be better to go somewhere than not to go at all. Besides, I've heard great things about how the Welsh sing, so perhaps I can enjoy the music regardless of the language spoken."

Gwen smiled. "The singing is quite marvelous," she said. "Our worship service starts at ten o'clock. You can sit with me and my aunt if you'd like."

"Thank you," Thomas said, looking pleased. "Can I meet you at your home and walk to the chapel with you?"

Gwen could only imagine the tongues that would start wagging the moment she and Aunty Jane arrived with Thomas. But there was nothing she could do about it. She certainly couldn't deny the man his right to attend a Sunday service because of her dislike of village gossip. "That would be fine," she said. "It's the gray rock house with the dark green door, about two hundred yards down from the post office."

"The one with all the rose bushes?" he asked.

"Yes, that's the one," Gwen said. "Be there about quarter to ten. It's not far to the chapel, but my aunt isn't able to walk very fast."

"I'll look forward to it," he said, offering her his hand as she stepped down from the logs.

She gave him a hesitant smile. "I'll see you tomorrow, then."

He released her hand, and with a quick wave, she hurried away, trying to ignore the sinking feeling that something was on the verge of spinning out of control.

◆

Aunty Jane accepted Thomas's presence on their pew at chapel much more readily than Gwen had anticipated. Perhaps her zealous heart truly was more concerned about saving a man who had not been able to attend Sunday services for weeks than it was about appearances. Gwen wished she could claim the same indifference, but she was all too aware that their arrival with Thomas that morning had caused a stir. It was not that she wasn't glad Thomas was there. Quite the opposite, in fact. She enjoyed being with him. She simply dreaded all the questions, the speculation, and the talk.

Thomas had taken Aunty Jane's arm at the front door of their house and had helped her all the way to their bench near the front of the chapel. He had stood back, allowing Gwen to slide in next to her aunt before joining them on the pew, and had then sat quietly through the service, relying on Gwen to give him a prompt before the congregation stood, sat, or kneeled. John Ellis's sermon had been based on the story of the Good Samaritan, which may have worked in Thomas's favor because when everyone filtered out of the chapel at the end of the meeting, several members of the congregation went out of their way to greet him and introduce themselves.

By the time Thomas walked Gwen and her aunt home, everyone in the congregation knew Thomas by name, profession, and association with Gwen. And Thomas, who was most gratified by the warm reception he'd received, announced that even though he hadn't comprehended a single word during the meeting, he was looking forward to returning the next week. Gwen didn't understand how it had happened; she and Thomas had gone to the same meeting and had talked to the same people, but for some reason, the experience had left him feeling delighted while she felt exhausted.

After Thomas left, Gwen slowly made her way upstairs to her bedroom. Closing the door behind her, she walked over to the chest of drawers, opened the top drawer, and lifted out the folded petticoat inside. Underneath, lying on top of her winter nightgown, was her rose. Making sure she didn't catch the metal thorns on anything, Gwen gently lifted the rose out of the drawer and walked over to her bed. She lay down and placed the metal flower on the pillow beside her. She studied it for a few minutes, her eyes following the gentle lines of the curling petals. Then, with a sigh, she turned her back on it, closed her eyes, and tried to empty her mind of everything so sleep could come.

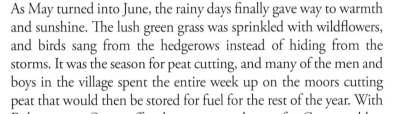

As May turned into June, the rainy days finally gave way to warmth and sunshine. The lush green grass was sprinkled with wildflowers, and birds sang from the hedgerows instead of hiding from the storms. It was the season for peat cutting, and many of the men and boys in the village spent the entire week up on the moors cutting peat that would then be stored for fuel for the rest of the year. With Robert gone, Owen offered to cut enough peat for Gwen and her aunt, along with what he needed for his family and the smithy furnace. In exchange, Gwen insisted on taking lunch to Rowland and him while they cut.

Gwen enjoyed the excuse to be outside, and even though her basket was weighed down with food on the way there, her return trip through the pastures was lovely. There was also something quite stirring about seeing all the men of the village working together for a common goal. She could usually hear them singing or whistling before she reached them. It was a backbreaking job, but they worked hard and well together.

Rowland was always particularly glad to see her. He didn't seem to mind that she didn't provide his mother's bara brith; he was excited for the arrival of any food. All that mattered to him was that there was plenty of it. He'd grown a lot while she was in Llanfyllin, and Gwen guessed that his enormous food intake had something to do with the fact that his height and shoulders were starting to resemble his older brother's.

When she spotted Rowland on the third day of peat cutting, he was lifting the heavy blocks of peat into the back of a cart several yards from the area where his father was still cutting. Gwen took Owen his lunch first, then she continued up the hill to Rowland. He took the basket from her and walked over to an old tree that had fallen to its side not far from the cart.

"Can you stay for a bit?" he asked, sitting down on the wide trunk and making sure there was room for her.

"And risk having your dad tell me off for stopping you from working?" Gwen said.

Rowland laughed. "Dad would never do that to you."

"I wouldn't be too sure." Gwen raised her skirt a couple of inches and walked across the squelching, waterlogged earth until she reached the tree trunk. "I'll stay until you finish your sandwich."

"Right," Rowland said, unwrapping the wax paper. "I'll eat as slow as I can." He took a big bite. "That will be hard, mind, because I'm starving."

Gwen rolled her eyes. "You're always starving, Rowland."

His mouth was full, but he nodded. She waited quietly while he chewed and swallowed.

"So tell me about Thomas Henley," he said.

Sitting had been a bad idea. "He's from Liverpool, and he's an engineer at the dam."

"I know that stuff already," Rowland said.

"There's not much more to tell."

Rowland gave her a searching look. "Is he courting you?"

Gwen felt color flood her cheeks. Thomas had accompanied her to worship service for the last three weeks, and she'd heard the whispers as they'd walked in and out of the chapel and noticed the curious looks directed her way at the post office, but up until now, no one had dared say anything to her face. She'd hoped interest in her and Thomas would die down as people got used to seeing him on Sundays. She should have known it was a forlorn hope. But why, oh why, did her first inquisitor have to be Rowland Morgan?

"He's a good friend, and he enjoys going to chapel with Aunty Jane and me," she said.

"With you," Rowland corrected her. "He enjoys going to chapel with you. He likes you a lot."

Gwen got to her feet. "Talking is making you eat too slowly. Your dad will be after you in a minute."

Rowland groaned and stuffed the last piece of bread into his mouth. Gwen picked up the empty basket. She would leave before he was capable of saying anything more.

"I'll see you again tomorrow, Rowland."

Still chewing, Rowland nodded his agreement, and Gwen made her getaway as quickly as she could.

Chapter 23

IF GWEN HAD ONLY KNOWN that Rowland's questions were simply a portend of what was to come a few days later, she would have undoubtedly found a reason to miss the worship service on Sunday. Instead, she attended the meeting with Aunty Jane and Thomas, and when it was over, she waited patiently for the pews ahead of them to empty before guiding her aunt into the aisle.

Since Aunty Jane's measured pace was considerably slower than anyone else's in the congregation, by the time they arrived at the door to the rear of the chapel, everyone else had already exited the building. With none of his flock still waiting to greet him, the minister exchanged a few words with Aunty Jane before offering her his arm to guide her down the step and out of the chapel. Thomas, in turn, offered his arm to Gwen, and she allowed him to lead her outside.

After the relative gloom of the chapel, the bright midday sun was blinding. Gwen raised her free hand to shade her eyes, and Thomas guided her a few steps to the left. Up ahead, Aunty Jane and the minister had stopped to talk to someone. Gwen looked their way—and froze. She would have recognized that dark hair and those broad shoulders anywhere. With unaccountably rising discomfort, she watched Lewis shake the minister's hand before turning to see her for the first time. For a split second, she saw his blue eyes light up with pleasure, and then he noticed Thomas, and the light was doused.

Gwen removed her hand from Thomas's arm and forced herself to move forward. Giving her a puzzled glance, Thomas followed.

"Hello, Lewis," she said.

"Hello, Gwennie."

Her stomach clenched. She'd only seen this expression on Lewis's face once before, in the clearing the night before she'd left for Llanfyllin. And now, as then, she desperately wanted it to go away.

"Are you going to introduce me to your friend?" he asked.

His politeness sounded forced, but it shocked Gwen into remembering her own manners. "Lewis Morgan, this is Thomas Henley," she said in English. "Thomas is an engineer at the dam." She turned to Thomas. "Thomas, this is Lewis. He's my brother's best friend and is a blacksmith at Pen-y-Bont Fawr."

Thomas immediately offered Lewis his hand. "Very nice to meet you," he said. "Any relation to Rowland Morgan?"

"He's my brother," Lewis said, accepting Thomas's hand a little more slowly than it had been offered.

"I see the resemblance," Thomas said. "Rowland helped mend a chain that broke on one of our cranes a while back."

"That's good."

Gwen frowned at Lewis. What was wrong with him? She knew he spoke English well enough to maintain a conversation. Couldn't he make a little more effort to be friendly?

"Are you back in Llanwddyn for very long?" Thomas asked.

Gwen saw Lewis wince at Thomas's pronunciation, and even though she'd had the same reaction, it made her cross.

"You can answer this question in more than two or three words if you like," she said in Welsh.

Lewis swung to face her, and the pain in his eyes took her breath away. "An Englishman? Really, Gwennie? And working on the dam, no less. I never would have believed it."

Before she had a chance to respond, Lewis turned back to Thomas and spoke in English again. "No, Mr. Henley, I won't be here long. In fact, I leave for Pen-y-Bont Fawr within the hour."

"Well, safe travels," Thomas said, a look of concern crossing his face as his eyes darted between Lewis and Gwen.

"Uh, sorry to interrupt."

Still reeling from Lewis's stinging words, Gwen looked up to see Rowland approaching.

"Mam asked me to come tell Lewis that if he's to eat before he starts back, he should come home right away," he said.

"Thank you, Rowland," Lewis said. "I'll come with you now."

Rowland hovered uncertainly, as though he wasn't sure if he was to wait for his brother or not.

"Good-bye, Mr. Henley. Good-bye, Gwennie," Lewis said.

"Good-bye, Lewis." Gwen's voice was little more than a whisper, and in the end, she wasn't sure if he heard her because he'd already turned and walked away.

Just before the brothers reached the chapel gate, Rowland placed his hand on Lewis's shoulder, and she saw Lewis's head drop. Tears pricked at the back of Gwen's eyes. It felt as though she'd just lost something precious, and as badly as it hurt, she had no idea how to get it back.

"What was that all about?" Thomas asked.

"He had to go home for dinner because he's leaving soon," she said.

Thomas gave her a long look. "I was actually referring to what happened before Rowland arrived. The part of the conversation that turned your face and Lewis's knuckles the same color white," he said.

"It was nothing," Gwen said, hoping that she could be forgiven for such a lie. It was far from nothing, but she was not about to discuss the matter with Thomas.

"We should be getting home, Gwen." Aunty Jane's insistent voice brought Gwen back to her current situation. "It's getting late."

"Of course, Aunty Jane," Gwen said. "We can leave straight-away."

The walk home was agonizingly slow. More than anything, Gwen wanted to be alone to sort out her thoughts and feelings and to work on making the pain in her chest disappear. Instead, trapped by her aunt's inability to speak fluent English, she found herself forced to translate a long, drawn-out conversation between Thomas and Aunty Jane. And just as they reached the front door and she thought the ordeal was coming to an end, her aunt asked her to invite Thomas to stay for a cup of tea and a scone before he returned to his lodging.

At Thomas's acceptance, Aunty Jane led the way to the sitting room and carefully lowered herself into her favorite chair. "If you wouldn't mind bringing the tea things in here, bach," she said to Gwen, "we'll see if Mr. Henley would be so good as to stoke the fire."

Gwen nodded. If she kept her mind on menial matters and her hands busy, perhaps it would help. She pointed Thomas in the direction of the peat and the poker and headed for the kitchen. By the time she returned with the heavily laden tray, the fire had perked up and the chill in the room was gone.

Thomas rose from his seat, took the tray from Gwen, and set it on the small table next to Aunty Jane. Gwen poured everyone a cup of tea before passing Thomas a scone.

"Did you make these?" he asked.

"Yes," she said, "but Aunty Jane made the jam."

"They're both excellent," he said.

Gwen gave him a weak smile. Last night, she'd been quite proud of them. Now she didn't think she'd be able to swallow a bite.

Thomas gave her a worried look. "I don't mean to be forward," he said, "but are you feeling ill?"

"I have rather a bad headache," she said. "I'm sorry. I'm afraid I'm not very good company at the moment."

"It's quite all right," he said, coming to his feet. "I should be on my way and let you get some rest."

Gwen rose too. "Thank you, Thomas. You're very kind."

No matter what Lewis thought, Gwen knew Thomas Henley was a good man. He'd been nothing but considerate in every interaction she'd ever had with him.

"I hope you feel better very soon," he said. He turned to Aunty Jane. "Thank you for the lovely tea, Mrs. Jones."

Aunty Jane looked pleased. "You're welcome."

After walking Thomas to the door, Gwen slowly returned to the sitting room and started gathering the teacups.

"A nice boy, that," Aunty Jane said.

Gwen placed the teapot on the tray. "Yes," she said, "but I'm surprised you like him so much. You barely understand each other."

"He has excellent prospects," Aunty Jane said, "and that's what's most important."

Gwen stared at Aunty Jane. That was her aunt's measure of the worth of a man? His financial future? The teacup sitting on the saucer in her hand rattled, and Gwen lowered it back onto the table before her aunt noticed it was shaking. Why would she say such a thing?

"You mark my words, Gwen." Aunty Jane was now wagging her index finger to emphasize her point. "There'll be several young men from this village and the surrounding ones who'll want to court a pretty, well-educated young lady like you. They'll try sweet-talking you into believing you're in love, but that means nothing if they don't have the income to take care of you."

Gwen stood in stunned silence. Had her aunt's view on marriage always been so jaded? She wracked her brain for anything she'd been told about Aunty Jane's husband, Arthur. He'd been a laborer for one of the local farmers and had died in an accident with a horse and cart only three years after they'd married. Undoubtedly his income had been small. Had she fallen in love with him only to live in poverty while they were together and been left penniless as a widow?

"But to get married without being in love . . ." Gwen said.

"Love can come later," Aunty Jane said firmly. "All you need before getting married is basic common sense." She gave Gwen a pointed look. "And in case you were wondering, common sense would tell you not to bother with any of the young men from Llanwddyn. Within four years, the local farmland will be underwater and so will the businesses. Everyone will have to start fresh somewhere else, and there's no guarantee in that." She leaned back in her chair with a satisfied sigh. "I daresay Mr. Henley already has more money in his bank account than anyone from this village will make in a lifetime. And on top of that, he's well mannered, attentive, and obviously quite fond of you."

Gwen put a shaky hand to her head. Did Aunty Jane really think Thomas was interested in marrying her? That he was her best hope for happiness? Gwen refused to believe that all the young men in the village were doomed to a lackluster future simply because of the construction of the Vyrnwy Dam. Not when there were men like Robert and Lewis who relied on personal integrity and hard work to reach their goals.

A queasy stomach now joined her pounding headache, and just thinking of Lewis and remembering their interaction outside the chapel was making her feel even worse. She steadied herself against the back of the chair. "Aunty Jane, I'm very sorry, but I think I may have to go to my room," she said. "I really don't feel well."

Her aunt pursed her lips. "You do look pale," she said. "With all that walking up to the peat fields, perhaps you've overdone it a bit this week. See if a rest helps."

With a grateful nod, Gwen slipped out of the sitting room and headed straight for her bed.

Chapter 24

GWEN WASN'T SURE HOW LONG someone could go before lack of sleep really took its toll, but two weeks later, she was beginning to think she was close to reaching her breaking point. Every morning, she went to the post office and sorted the letters, greeted customers, and helped her aunt with the bookkeeping. At noon she returned home to do housework or schoolwork or to prepare something for supper. She went through the motions of everyday life as though nothing was wrong, but physical and emotional exhaustion were definitely starting to affect her.

She saw the dark circles under her eyes each morning, and she no longer had the stamina or concentration to draw for more than half an hour at a time. If she went to the dam and Harry asked if she was all right, the question was no longer cursory but an inquiry of genuine concern. And Thomas was especially solicitous. Whenever he was able to join her, he'd sit beside her on the logs, even if she'd put away her pencils and didn't want to talk. He never pushed her to tell him what was wrong, perhaps because he sensed she didn't know the answer herself.

The only thing Gwen did know was that she was haunted by the pain she'd seen in Lewis's eyes when he'd last spoken to her and that the memory of his disappointment that she'd been with Thomas was constantly at odds with her aunt's counsel to consider Thomas as more than a friend. Her nights were filled with stress-filled dreams, and more often than not, she woke up crying, desperately wishing her mother were there to comfort and guide her.

She'd thought a lot about her parents since her conversation with Aunty Jane, and even though she was only able to draw on childhood memories, she was convinced her mother and father had loved each other deeply. She'd seen her father hold her mother tenderly on more than one occasion, and sometimes she'd caught them holding hands when they were sitting near each other. She also remembered their joy at being reunited, even if they'd only been apart for a few hours. Losing them both in one week had been devastating for her, but for her parents, it had been an incredible blessing. Neither would have wanted to be without the other.

That was the kind of relationship Gwen wanted. She could not believe that Aunty Jane's cut-and-dried approach to marriage was right. There had to be an emotional attachment between a husband and wife, and she still believed it could be a love like no other. Thomas had been unfailingly good to her, and she certainly considered him a valued friend, but would she ever feel more than friendship for him? The question tortured her.

Then her traitorous thoughts would turn to Lewis. He'd never asked to court her, and she was convinced he didn't see her as anything more than Robert's little sister. But no matter how hard she tried, she couldn't put aside all they'd shared as though none of it mattered anymore. And at night, when doubts and dreams wove together, she'd think of the rose he'd given her and wonder if there could be something more between them.

There had been times when they'd been together—like the evening he'd walked her home from the St. John's Day dance—when it had been as if he'd known what she was feeling and he'd felt it too. She thought that perhaps he'd been as reluctant to part as she had when he'd held her for a few minutes in the clearing the night before she'd left for Llanfyllin, but then he'd started spending time with Mabel, and after the first letter, he'd never written another. Gwen didn't know what to think anymore. In fact, if she could just stop thinking altogether, perhaps she would be able to sleep again.

She hadn't spoken to Mabel for a few weeks, but her mother, Bronwen, came into the post office regularly to see Aunty Jane. Usually Bronwen came bearing some sort of news, and Gwen always marveled at how many miscellaneous details the woman could remember about everyone in the village. However, on the Wednesday morning two and a half weeks after Gwen had seen Lewis, Bronwen came into the post office in the biggest flap Gwen had ever seen.

"Oh, Jane, I have the worst news!" She puffed her way up to the counter where Aunty Jane was sorting letters. "I had to come tell you as soon as I heard, but quite honestly, I'm going to have to go right back home afterward. My poor Mabel! I've never seen her in such a state."

Aunty Jane lowered the small pile of envelopes in her hand and waited. From past experience, she knew she wouldn't need to prompt Bronwen to continue; she merely needed to give her time to catch her breath.

A few seconds later, Bronwen placed her hands on the counter and leaned forward. "There's measles in Pen-y-Bont Fawr," she said.

All the air left Gwen's lungs. She reached for the shelves behind her and held on until the room righted itself again. Aunty Jane gave her an anxious look, but Bronwen continued talking, seemingly unaware of how her news was affecting anyone else in the room.

"I heard it from Mr. Williams the Shop," she said. "You know he has family in Pen-y-Bont Fawr. Well, he was supposed to go there this morning to make a delivery, but Edward Jones, one of the local farmers, stopped him not more than a mile from the village. Mr. Jones told him the doctor from Llanfyllin had been there yesterday and confirmed six cases of the measles. They're quarantining the village. Mr. Jones was told to turn back anyone approaching from the Llanwddyn road, and presumably they've got someone else monitoring the other roads."

"Did Mr. Jones say how it started?" Aunty Jane asked.

"Gypsies," Bronwen said, her tone expressing exactly how she felt about the nomadic people who wandered the countryside in their colorful caravans. "They arrived in Pen-y-Bont Fawr a week ago. Within four days, one adult and two children had the rash. Now three village children have high temperatures and runny noses."

As Bronwen spoke, a flood of memories washed over Gwen: lying listless on her bed, crying for her mother because her throat hurt so badly, listening to her father coughing, suffering the discomfort of a body covered in red, itchy blotches, and then sitting stoically through her parents' funerals. She would always associate the measles with suffering, sorrow, and death; it terrified her.

"Can anything be done to help?" Gwen already knew the answer, but she had to ask.

"Well that's it, isn't it?" Bronwen said, raising her hands helplessly. "There's nothing to be done. No one can go in or out of the village until the quarantine's lifted, which means the delivery of even letters and basic supplies will be uncertain. Who knows when we'll next get word on what's happening there."

Lewis was in Pen-y-Bont Fawr, and he would not be able to leave. Gwen took a deep breath, trying to push past her fear. *Please, Father*, she prayed silently, *bless the people of Pen-y-Bont Fawr, and please protect Lewis.*

"Have you talked to Mair Morgan?" Aunty Jane was obviously thinking of Lewis too.

"Yes," Bronwen said. "And I must say she's taken the news remarkably well. Much better than my poor Mabel. Poor girl. She's quite beside herself about the possibility of Mair's eldest boy getting the measles."

"Well, maybe you should be getting back to her, then," Aunty Jane said.

Bronwen seemed to suddenly remember her self-imposed injunction to return home quickly. "Yes, indeed," she said. "Thank you, Jane." With a swoosh of her long skirt and the clack of her heels, she left the post office as quickly as she'd entered.

Aunty Jane turned to Gwen, her expression worried. "Are you all right, bach?"

Gwen nodded. "It's a horrible disease, Aunty Jane," she said softly.

"I know, and just hearing about it brings painful memories."

"Yes." Gwen swallowed hard. "I hope they contain it quickly."

"Dr. Edwards will do everything he can to stop it from spreading," her aunt said.

Gwen nodded again. She could only pray it would be enough.

◆

Rather than going straight home at noon, Gwen took the road that led to the smithy. As she crossed Pont Cedig, the distinctive clang of metal hitting metal rang out across the street and brought back memories of the time she'd taken Robert's letter to the smithy for Lewis to read. It seemed like such a long time ago, and if she were to enter the smithy now, she'd find Rowland, not Lewis, working with his father. The thought was a sobering reminder of where Lewis was presently, and she picked up her pace.

She followed the road past the smithy until she reached the third house from the corner, where she stopped. She stood facing the navy-blue door, suddenly filled with indecision. Should she knock? What would she say when Mair opened the door? She didn't really know why she was there. It didn't make any logical sense, but her desire to visit Mair had been so strong when she'd left the post office she couldn't ignore it. She took a small step forward and let the brass door knocker fall before she could talk herself out of it.

The sound of footsteps reached her, and seconds later the front door opened.

"Hello, Mrs. Morgan," Gwen said.

A look of surprise flashed across Mair's face before she hid it behind a welcoming smile. "Well, Gwen, how nice to see you."

"I . . . I . . ." As Gwen floundered to come up with the right words, Mair's eyes met hers. They were red. Mair had been crying. And in that moment, Gwen knew she'd been right to come. "I just heard about Pen-y-Bont Fawr," she said.

"Come inside, bach," Mair said.

Gwen followed as Mair led her down the hall and into the kitchen at the back of the house. Bowls, flour, eggs, sugar, and butter sat on the wooden table, and on the stove, a pan simmered.

"I'm making bara brith," Mair said. "When I first heard the news, I had a good cry, then I decided there were much better ways of working out my worry." She gave a small smile. "It's amazing how much better you feel after you've beaten eggs and batter for a while."

"I pummeled my bread dough for over half an hour when Robert left," Gwen confessed.

A slightly mischievous look appeared on Mair's face. "Can you imagine what the horseshoes will look like today? They'll be banged as flat as pancakes."

"There was an awful lot of noise coming from the smithy when I passed," Gwen said.

The two women looked at each other, then they started to giggle.

"Oh, Gwen," Mair said when she finally had her laughter under control. "I'm so glad you came. I needed that."

Gwen was glad too. She hadn't laughed so much since she'd been with Alice and Rosamond in Llanfyllin, and she'd missed it. Mair's friendliness combined with the inviting warmth of the Morgans's kitchen was a welcome reprieve from the feelings of loneliness and disquiet that had plagued her for so long. Reluctant to leave, she leaned over and peeked into the small bowl closest to her. It was full of raisins. "Would you show me how you make your bara brith?" Gwen asked.

The twinkle was back in Mair's eyes. "I will on one condition," she said.

"What's that?" Gwen asked.

Mair lowered her voice. "You don't tell Bronwen Richards. She's been after this recipe for years."

Gwen smiled. "I promise," she said.

"Right, then." Mair pointed at an apron hanging on a hook behind the kitchen door. "Good bara brith starts with putting on an apron."

With a lighter step than she'd had in weeks, Gwen walked over to the hook and retrieved the apron. When she'd put it on, she moved back to the table and watched as Mair started pouring flour into the largest bowl.

"Here you are," Mair said, handing her the spoon. "Start mixing."

It wasn't long before the batter was ready, poured into the tin, and placed in the oven, and as the two women sat down at the kitchen table to have a cup of tea while they waited for the bara brith to cook, their conversation circled back to the reason for Gwen's visit.

"You know about the measles firsthand, don't you, bach?" Mair said.

Gwen looked down at the brown liquid steaming in the teacup in front of her, fighting back the memories again. "Yes," she said quietly.

Mair reached over the table and placed her hand over Gwen's. "It seems to me that it's human nature to focus on the worst-case scenario," she said. "I certainly did. As soon as Mr. Williams brought us the news, all I could think of was Lewis dying or losing his hearing or some of the other awful things we've heard happen after people get the measles. For you, those things are even more real because you've experienced them personally.

"But I had no excuse, so I took myself to task. We don't even know if Lewis will catch the measles. He's a strong man, and if he does go down with it, I have to believe he will fight it successfully—just as you did."

Gwen nodded. She wanted to believe that too. "Will you let me know if you hear anything?" she asked.

"Of course I will, bach," Mair said. "And in the meantime, we'll all pray for everyone in Pen-y-Bont Fawr."

Chapter 25

THERE HAD BEEN NO LETTER from Robert, and since school had
ended for the summer holidays, there'd been only one letter from
Rosamond and none from Alice. No one in the village had received
anything from anyone in Pen-y-Bont Fawr, and even though it
had been almost a month since the measles outbreak had begun,
there was no sign of the quarantine being lifted. Occasionally Ed
the Post brought secondhand news through his contact with Dr.
Edwards in Llanfyllin, and from what they could tell, at least ten
more cases of the measles had been confirmed.

Even though neither the Williamses nor the Morgans had
heard anything from their family members, everyone was going
on the premise that their loved ones were still free of the highly
contagious disease. Gwen tried really hard to stay positive. The
thought that her final interaction with Lewis might be the angry
words they'd shared outside the chapel was too awful to bear, so she
had to at least pretend all was well.

She tried to refocus her energy on drawing but rarely made
it to the dam site more than once or twice a week. She did see
Thomas more often than that though. He still accompanied Aunty
Jane and her to chapel meetings, and if he hadn't seen her at the
dam for a few days, he would seek her out at home in the evenings,

and they would take a walk. The long summer evenings with their gentle warmth did a great deal to help lift her spirits, but the dark of night was still difficult.

Despite the unsettling feeling that something was not right, nothing could have prepared Gwen for the letter Ed the Post handed her the next Tuesday morning.

"Looks like a foreign stamp to me," he said with a grin.

Aunty Jane immediately stopped what she was doing behind the counter and moved closer. "Is it from Robert?" she asked.

Gwen turned the envelope over. The stamp did look as though it had come from India, but she didn't recognize the handwriting. The sloped letters were even and carefully formed, a far cry from Robert's scrawl.

"I don't think so," Gwen said, her heart starting to pound. Who else would have written to her from India?

"See who it's from, then," Ed the Post said.

Aunty Jane nodded her agreement, and with shaking hands, Gwen slid her finger under the top of the envelope and tore it open. There was one sheet of cream-colored paper inside. Carefully she unfolded it and glanced at the signature at the bottom.

"It's from Captain Tecwyn Owen," she said.

"Isn't that the name of Robert's captain?" Aunty Jane asked.

"Yes," Gwen replied.

Aunty Jane and Ed the Post exchanged a worried look, and like wisps of smoke, fear began to permeate the room. Gwen's attention went back to the letter, and she started to silently read.

Dear Miss Humphreys,
It is with deepest regret that I write to inform you of the passing of your brother, Robert Humphreys . . .

From far away, Gwen heard a plaintive moan, but she didn't realize the sound had come from her own mouth until she became aware of Ed the Post gently lowering her into a chair.

"Deep breaths now, bach," he said. "Deep breaths."

"The letter," she gasped.

"I have it, Gwen." Aunty Jane's face was pale. "You dropped it when you fainted."

"Read it," Gwen said. "Read it out loud to me."

Aunty Jane hesitated.

"Please," Gwen begged. "I have to know what happened."

Slowly her aunt lifted the letter and cleared her throat.

Dear Miss Humphreys,

It is with deepest regret that I write to inform you of the passing of your brother, Robert Humphreys, on 27 March 1886.

Robert suffered an acute appendicitis on board the SS Talookdar *while the ship was becalmed off the coast of South Africa. Notwithstanding the significant efforts of the ship's physician, the infection took his life within thirty-eight hours of its onset, and I hope that despite this tragic loss, you will draw comfort from knowing he did not suffer long.*

Although Robert had been with the SS Talookdar *for only one year, he had earned the respect of the entire crew. He was well liked and known for being honest, hardworking, and cheerful; he will be sorely missed by both his crewmates and his captain.*

According to his wishes, Robert was given an honorable burial at sea, and his personal effects will be shipped to you as soon as the SS Talookdar *makes port in Liverpool.*

On behalf of all those on board the SS Talookdar*, I send our heartfelt condolences.*

Sincerely,

Captain Tecwyn Owen

As Aunty Jane finished the letter, Gwen lowered her face into her hands and started to cry. Robert was gone. He had been for almost five months, and she'd not known. Her brother was never coming home again. Deep, heart-wrenching sobs shook her small frame and would not stop. She was vaguely aware of her aunt's and Ed the Post's voices, of someone leaving, and, a short while later, of someone arriving. Then somebody put a gentle hand on her back and knelt down beside her chair.

"Gwen, I've come to take you home."

Over and over again, the hand softly rubbed back and forth until at last the rhythmic motion began to calm the storm inside. With a shuddering breath, Gwen slowly raised her head. Aunty Jane, appearing more worried than Gwen had ever seen her, sat at the counter behind a forgotten pile of unsorted letters. Ed the Post hovered near the door, looking as though he would rather be anywhere but inside the post office, and beside Gwen's chair, Mair rose to her feet and placed a shawl over Gwen's shoulders.

"Come with me, bach." Mair reached down and took Gwen's hands in hers. "We're going to go home. Ed the Post will stay here long enough to help your aunt sort today's letters, then they'll close the post office early, and your aunt will come home to be with you."

Numbly Gwen came to her feet.

"That's it." Mair released her hands and placed a protective arm around her. "You've had a bad shock, but you'll be all right."

Very slowly Mair started guiding Gwen toward the door. Without a word, Gwen matched her pace.

"Thank you, Mair." Aunty Jane's voice was strained.

"I'm very glad you sent Ed for me," Mair said. "And don't you worry. I'll have her settled in bed in no time." She paused. "Mind you get home as soon as you can, Jane. This has been a shock for you too."

"Yes," Aunty Jane said heavily. "Yes, it has."

"We'll have these letters taken care of in no time," Ed the Post said, sounding as though he'd be glad to be back doing what he knew.

He opened the post office door for the two women, and Gwen blinked as the bright light of morning stung her swollen eyes.

Mair gave her a comforting squeeze. "Let's get you home, bach."

❖

Over the next few days, the stream of callers never stopped. Most of them came and went in a blur. The only ones Gwen remembered with any clarity were Ioan Llanwddyn, whose lined face had crumpled as he'd told Gwen how much he'd appreciated Robert's kindness; Harry Weston, who'd entered the sitting room, nervously wringing his cap in his hands, to offer the condolences of all the men from his team at the dam; John Ellis, the minister, who'd discussed holding a memorial service for Robert; and Owen and Mair, who'd told her what she'd most needed to hear—that they'd written to tell Lewis. She didn't know how long it would be before the letter reached him, but she was grateful it had been sent.

Thomas had been a rock of support the entire time. He'd arrived at the house as soon as he'd heard the news and had returned often. He'd stayed with her when she'd needed someone to talk to and had left her alone when she'd needed quiet. Even though he'd never known Robert, he listened attentively when she recounted stories about him, and he let her cry on his shoulder when the memories became too painful.

Just as she had after Aunty Jane's stroke, Mair had been slipping into the house each day to drop off something small for the two women to eat for supper. Gwen had wanted to tell her not to bother, that eating was the last thing she wanted to do, but she could not bring herself to refuse the woman's kindness. She remembered that Mair had turned to baking to help her overcome her worry for Lewis, and she wondered if perhaps this was the way she was coping with her own grief over the loss of her son's best friend.

Aunty Jane said little. They coexisted in the house, politely helping one another with the few chores that had to be done each day, but they did not share their feelings with one another. Gwen knew her aunt was grieving; she could see it in her drawn expression and emotionless eyes. She wished they were better able to reach out to each other, to buoy each other up, but it had never been in Aunty Jane's nature to open her heart to others, and in Robert's death, she was making no exceptions. Aunty Jane would grieve in private and expected Gwen to do the same.

Her aunt's stoicism continued through the memorial service held on Saturday. Under the direction of John Ellis, the meeting included Robert's favorite hymns, a scripture reading, and a short sermon in which the minister included a few anecdotes from Robert's life. Gwen sat between Aunty Jane and Thomas on the front pew. She wished she could emulate their somber dignity throughout the meeting, but her heart was too fragile. As she listened to the congregation sing the closing hymn, her tears overflowed.

When the service was over, Thomas helped Aunty Jane out of the chapel, and Gwen followed. With no burial to follow, they stood outside, greeting the other mourners as they exited. Most people gave them a solemn handshake and briefly expressed their sympathy. Mabel gave Gwen a quick hug but, for once, seemed at a loss for words, and Rowland stood in front of her as though gathering his courage for a few moments before pulling his hand out of his pocket and showing her a shiny brown conker threaded on a black shoelace.

"Robert gave me his prize conker when he left," he said, his voice breaking slightly. "He told me to use it to beat Lewis." He sniffed and put on a brave smile. "I did too. Smashed Lewis's conker to smithereens."

Gwen managed a returning smile. "I think that would have made him very happy," she said.

Silently Rowland nodded, slipped the conker into his pocket, and moved back. Mair took his place. She wrapped her arms around Gwen and held her tightly. "You know Lewis would have wanted to be here," she whispered.

"Yes." The single word caught in Gwen's throat. Lewis was the one person who would have completely understood and shared her heartbreak. "I've missed him so much."

Mair's grip tightened. "I have too, bach, and I'm sure he'll come as soon as he can."

"I know." Gwen swallowed hard. "Have you heard anything new from Pen-y-Bont Fawr?"

"Ed the Post said that Dr. Edwards has treated twenty-three people. They're hoping the spreading of the disease is slowing, but they won't lift the quarantine until they've had no new cases for two weeks."

Gwen nodded. "I hope that won't be long."

"Me too." Mair stepped back, reached for Gwen's hands, then gave them a squeeze. "And in the meantime, you look after yourself, bach."

Gwen gave her a weak smile. "I'll try."

Chapter 26

AUNTY JANE SET OFF FOR the post office early on Monday morning, telling Gwen that it was time to go back to living their normal lives; it was what Robert would have wanted and expected. On a logical level, Gwen agreed, but getting her emotions to cooperate was another matter. She'd gone from having a constant ache in her heart a few weeks before to feeling nothing but hollow emptiness.

The simplest of tasks at the post office seemed to elude her. She would start by sorting the outgoing letters only to become distracted by needing to put more peat on the fire. She'd add fuel to the fire only to find that twenty minutes later she was still standing at the grate, staring into the flames. Customers asked her the same question two or three times, and she couldn't remember if she'd answered them at all.

She sensed that Aunty Jane was frustrated with her and was biting her tongue rather than doling out the normal reprimand for her absentmindedness, but try as she might, Gwen could not seem to focus on anything. She walked to the dam with her sketchbook in hand but ended up sitting on the logs, watching the work going on around her without even opening it. When Thomas joined her, he gave her a worried frown.

"Gwen, are you eating?" he asked.

"Now?" she said, puzzled by the question.

"No. In general." He studied her face. "You're very pale, and it looks to me like you're losing weight."

She shrugged. "I never feel hungry."

He rested his hand on hers. "Gwen, you need to eat. It's no wonder you can't concentrate on anything. It's a miracle you had the energy to walk here."

With eerie detachment, Gwen looked down at his hand clasped over hers. He was right; she knew he was. She would have to try harder. Perhaps she could manage some oatmeal for supper.

"I'll eat something when I get home," she promised.

Thomas looked at her thoughtfully. "Can I walk back with you? I have an idea, and I'd like to see what you and your aunt think of it."

Gwen felt her curiosity pique. "What is it?" she asked.

Thomas smiled. "Oh no. I'm not telling you that easily. You have to eat something first."

"I have to . . . ? Thomas! That's bribery."

"Call it what you will," he said. "If it makes you put something in your stomach, it's worth it."

Gwen frowned. "Very well. But I choose what it is and how much I eat."

"You can choose what you have, but I have a say on the quantity. My idea is worth much more than one or two bites."

Gwen glanced at the pompous expression he was affecting and started to giggle. "All right, bossy boots," she said. "I'll eat a bowl of oatmeal."

"That's what I wanted to hear," he said with a grin. He rose to his feet and offered her a hand. "Come on, let's see if your aunt is home yet."

Aunty Jane was putting the kettle on the stove when Gwen and Thomas arrived at the house.

"Good afternoon, Mrs. Jones," Thomas said as they entered the kitchen.

"Good afternoon, Thomas," Aunty Jane replied. She gave Gwen a long look. "How are you feeling, Gwen?"

"A bit tired," Gwen said.

"She's going to eat a bowl of oatmeal," Thomas said, earning him a glare from Gwen.

"A very good idea," Aunty Jane said. "There's a pan in the cupboard over there."

She directed Thomas through the process of making oatmeal the best she could with their language barrier, and before Gwen had time to argue, there was a large bowl of steaming porridge sitting in front of her.

Thomas handed her a spoon. "All of it," he said, raising his eyebrows as if daring her to defy him.

Gwen sighed. It might take her all evening, so the sooner she started, the better. She took a spoonful. "Are you going to tell us your idea now?" she asked.

"As soon as half the bowl's finished," he said.

Rolling her eyes, Gwen took another bite.

It actually didn't take as long as Gwen had anticipated to finish most of the oatmeal. It was tastier than she'd thought it would be, and although she wouldn't admit it to Thomas, she did feel better after she'd eaten. She lowered her spoon to the bowl, and Thomas gave her a satisfied smile before turning to her aunt.

"Mrs. Jones, I heard from Mr. Wainwright yesterday."

After Gwen had translated for him, Aunty Jane nodded her head. She probably remembered the letter coming through the post office.

"He wrote to ask that I meet him in Liverpool as soon as possible to go over the developments at the dam. Enough time has gone by since he was able to oversee it in person, I think he feels the need of an update," Thomas said.

After waiting for Gwen's explanation, Aunty Jane nodded again.

Thomas glanced at Gwen. "I wondered whether you would give Gwen permission to accompany me."

Gwen stared at him in shock, and Aunty Jane's eyes flitted from Thomas to Gwen and back before she rapped her knuckles on the table. "What did he say?" she asked impatiently.

"He wants to know if you would give me permission to go to Liverpool with him," she said.

It was Aunty Jane's turn to look at Thomas wide-eyed.

"Everything would be completely circumspect," he said hurriedly. "We would travel by train from Llanfyllin and be met in Liverpool by my own carriage. Gwen would be a guest in my home, but my mother and sister would act as chaperones. When I meet with Mr. Wainwright, she would be at leisure to draw or read or go out with my sister." He cleared his throat nervously. "I have to make the trip anyway, and I thought that a temporary change of scenery might be just the thing for Gwen right now."

As Gwen translated for Aunty Jane, her mind raced. Liverpool. That was where Robert had boarded his ship. "Could you take me to the docks?" she asked.

Thomas looked uncomfortable. "That's not a very safe area of the city," he said. "Especially for a lady."

"But if you were with me? Wouldn't it be all right if you were there?"

"I will find out," he said. "It's been some time since I was there myself. Perhaps things have improved."

For the first time in what seemed like forever, Gwen felt a spark of excitement. She reached for her aunt's hand. "May I go, Aunty Jane?"

Aunty Jane looked down at Gwen's hand and then up at her face. "Is this something you really want?" she asked.

"It would mean a great deal to see where Robert was," Gwen said. "Even if the *Talookdar* is not there, I could stand beside the ocean and imagine him sailing off to India."

Her aunt turned to Thomas again. "How long would you be gone?" she asked.

"Not more than a week or so, I imagine," Thomas said. "It will depend largely on Mr. Wainwright's schedule."

Still Aunty Jane hesitated. Gwen held her breath. She rarely sought out adventure, and she shied from change, but this was different. This was Liverpool. Without any tangible evidence of Robert's passing, she'd struggled to come to terms with his death, but in Liverpool, she could visit the sea and personally touch the water that flowed over the place of his burial. Liverpool was the closest Gwen could hope to come to experiencing some semblance of closure.

"Very well," Aunty Jane finally said. "Gwen may go." She gave Thomas a stern look. "But I shall hold you personally responsible for her welfare and her good name."

Thomas took the admonition seriously. "I will take care of her," he said.

Gratitude welled up in Gwen. "Thank you, Aunty Jane. Thank you, Thomas."

Aunty Jane gave her an accepting nod, but Thomas looked genuinely pleased.

"How soon do we leave?" Gwen asked.

Thomas gave her an amused look. "How soon can you be ready?"

"First thing tomorrow?" she said.

He laughed. "Tomorrow it is. I'll send a telegram from Llanfyllin to have my driver meet us at the train station in Liverpool and to warn my mother and sister that they're going to have company."

At his words, Gwen experienced a pang of misgiving. "Will that be a terrible inconvenience? I don't want to put them out by arriving so unexpectedly."

"They will be happy to have you," Thomas reassured her. "We have plenty of room, and I look forward to introducing you to them."

She wasn't completely convinced that Thomas's mother and sister would be as delighted as he seemed to believe, but she stifled her qualms and smiled at him.

"Well, then, I suppose I should start packing a bag."

Thomas got to his feet. "Yes. And so must I." He walked briskly to the door. "I'll be back to pick you up at six o'clock tomorrow morning."

"I'll be ready," she said.

He waved and disappeared through the door, and Gwen started up the stairs to gather her belongings.

Chapter 27

THE JOURNEY TOOK ALL DAY. Thomas and Gwen traveled by horse and cart to Llanfyllin. Once there, Thomas left the horse and cart at the stable near the railroad station, and they caught the train to Oswestry, changed trains there for Chester, and in Chester changed yet again for a train that would take them into Liverpool. Each train and each railway station got progressively bigger and more crowded, and Gwen was thankful to be with someone who knew how to navigate the throngs of people and the maze of station platforms.

It was the first time Gwen had ridden a train. Experiencing the power and speed of the steam engine firsthand was thrilling, and watching the beautiful scenery go by was mesmerizing, but by the time they neared Liverpool, her enthusiasm for travel was waning. The pastoral views had been replaced by industrial sprawl, and the novelty of the ride had been exchanged for bone-weary tiredness. She felt dirty, disheveled, and more than a little out of her element.

Within minutes of exiting the Liverpool Lime Street Railway Station, Thomas located his carriage waiting just outside the station entrance. It was black and shiny and was pulled by a handsome brown horse. After introducing Gwen to the driver, Thomas helped her inside, and as soon as their bags were loaded, they set off through the streets of Liverpool.

Even though daylight lingered long into the evening in August, it was late enough that the gas lamps had been lit, and their light reflected off the windows of the huge buildings lining the roads. Gwen had never seen such imposing structures. Everywhere she looked there were more buildings; no hedgerows, trees, or grass verges, only buildings.

At last the carriage pulled into a gravel driveway that curved around to the front of a large redbrick house. It stood three stories tall, with dormer windows breaking up the roofline. Half a dozen chimney pots lined the top of the house, with smoke coming from at least four of them. A few shrubs and trees grew on either side of the house, and a narrow path cut between the trees and a redbrick wall, presumably leading to the back garden.

"Here we are," Thomas said as the carriage came to a stop in front of the house. He opened the carriage door and stepped out, then turned to help Gwen descend. "This is where I grew up and the place I still call home."

Gwen stood on the driveway, staring up at the house, trying not to feel intimidated by its size and commanding presence. Other than Powys Castle, where the Earl of Powys lived, it was by far the largest house she'd ever seen.

"It's very impressive," she said.

Thomas smiled and picked up their bags. "Let's go inside."

The front door opened as they approached, and a dark-haired lady in a black dress stepped forward to greet them.

"Welcome home, Mr. Henley," she said.

"Thank you, Margaret," Thomas said. "This is our guest, Miss Gwen Humphreys."

Margaret nodded. "Nice to meet you, Miss Humphreys," she said.

The housekeeper stepped aside so Thomas and Gwen could precede her into the main hall. The polished wooden floor gleamed in the lamplight, and the walls were covered in paintings of horses and hunting scenes. Heavy brocade curtains hung at the windows on either side of the front door, and straight ahead a wide staircase led up to the next floor.

"Have my mother and sister already retired for the night?" Thomas asked.

"Yes, sir. They apologize for not being here to meet you, but your mother does not do well if she stays up too late. She asked that I see Miss Humphreys to her room."

"That would be marvelous. Thank you, Margaret."

The housekeeper nodded again. "Can I get you anything to eat or drink before you retire, miss?" she asked Gwen.

"No, thank you," Gwen said. "I think I'd rather go straight to bed, if that's all right."

She saw the startled look in the housekeeper's eyes before she realized what had caused it.

"Miss Humphreys is Welsh," Thomas said. "She speaks fluent English, but you may detect her accent."

Gwen swung around to face him. *Her* accent? It was the English whose accents were so hard on the ear. Did her speech sound as strange to the English as theirs did to her?

"Indeed, sir," Margaret said, unknowingly answering Gwen's question.

Thomas pointed to a room on the right. "That's the breakfast room," he said. "Whenever you're ready in the morning, come downstairs, and I'll meet you there."

"All right." Gwen was suddenly nervous. Thomas was back in his own sphere, and she was completely out of hers. "Thank you, Thomas."

He smiled. "I hope you sleep well," he said.

Margaret picked up Gwen's bag. "If you'll follow me, miss," she said, heading toward the stairs.

Without a word, Gwen followed the housekeeper up the stairs and onto the landing to the left.

Margaret led her to the second door down the hall and pushed it open. "This will be your room," she said, walking in and placing

Gwen's bag on the floor at the foot of the bed. "You should have everything you need, but if not, just pull the bell. The cord's beside the bed."

"Thank you, Margaret," Gwen said.

"Good night, miss," she said, and she left the room, closing the door behind her.

Slowly Gwen turned in a full circle. She'd never seen a bedroom like this before. The walls were painted the same pale blue as the fluffy quilt that lay across the bed. Ivory lace curtains hung at the windows, and matching fabric hung draped from the top of the four-poster bed. The bed itself was larger than any Gwen had slept in before and was positioned in the center of the room, with an elegant wardrobe, chest of drawers, ornate mirror, and armchair completing the room's furnishings. A cheery fire burned in the fireplace, and two oversized rugs covered the wooden floor, adding to the bedroom's coziness.

Not wanting to dirty either the elegant bed or the armchair, Gwen opened her bag, pulled out her nightgown, and hurriedly changed out of her dusty travel clothes. Using the washbowl on top of the chest of drawers, she washed her hands and face. The soap smelled of lavender and helped her feel clean again. After a short bedtime prayer, Gwen blew out the candle and crawled under the covers. For a moment, she stared up at the shadowy outline of the canopy above her head, then she rolled over and closed her eyes. Llanwddyn felt very far away.

◆

The next morning, Gwen approached the breakfast room with considerable trepidation. She could hear female voices coming from the room as she descended the stairs and guessed that she was about to meet Thomas's mother and sister. When she reached the doorway, she paused and quietly surveyed the scene inside. The two women sitting at the table were obviously related. Gwen guessed there was about thirty years difference in age between them, and even though one of them had graying hair and aging skin, their facial features were virtually identical. Neither of them looked very much like Thomas, but when she saw the younger one frown, she recognized the expression as one she'd seen on Thomas's face only a few days before.

"There you are!"

Thomas's voice made her jump. He'd been standing beside a small buffet table at the side of the room, and she hadn't noticed him there. He walked over to her, took her elbow, and guided her into the room.

"Mother, Cecilia, this is Gwen Humphreys," he said. "Gwen, this is my mother and my younger sister, Cecilia."

Resisting the urge to smooth down her brown woolen skirt and white blouse or check to see if her unruly hair was already escaping the bun she'd attempted that morning, Gwen stood before them and gave a hesitant smile. "Pleased to meet you," she said as both women turned to stare at her. "Thank you for allowing me to come and stay with you. Your home is beautiful."

"I beg your pardon," Mrs. Henley said.

"Your . . . your home is beautiful," Gwen repeated, glancing at Thomas to make sure she hadn't said anything wrong.

"Goodness gracious, Thomas. However do you understand her? I've never heard such an accent."

"Very easily, Mother," Thomas said, his grip on Gwen's elbow tightening. "Gwen speaks excellent English; her Welsh accent simply adds melody to the words."

"Well, it will certainly take getting used to," the older woman said. She waved her hand toward the buffet table. "Make sure she has something to eat, Thomas."

"She can understand you perfectly well if you address her directly, Mother." Gwen had never heard irritation in Thomas's voice before. He seemed to be almost as uncomfortable with this conversation as she was, and she was relieved when he turned away from his mother and led her across the room.

The buffet table was loaded with platters of eggs, bacon, fried tomatoes, mushrooms, and toast. With the way Gwen's stomach was churning, she wasn't sure she could have eaten half a bowl of oatmeal, and she was quite sure she couldn't manage a full cooked breakfast. She put a piece of toast on her plate.

"Gwen," Thomas muttered. "You have to eat more than that."

"Not now, Thomas. Please," she whispered back.

He gave her a searching look. "Do you remember me telling you that your aunt reminded me of my mother?" he asked quietly. She nodded.

"Keep that in mind," he said. "Don't let her intimidate you."

Gwen swallowed past the lump in her throat. Thomas's advice was a lot easier said than done, especially if the criticism was to come every time she opened her mouth to speak. But she knew he was right. Raising her chin slightly, she walked over to the table, took a seat across from Cecilia, and waited for Thomas to join her before taking a bite of her toast.

"I sent word to Mr. Wainwright last night to tell him I was back in Liverpool," Thomas said. "He responded this morning, asking that I meet him at two o'clock this afternoon."

"Excellent," Mrs. Henley said. "I'm glad you don't have to rush over to his office first thing this morning."

"Yes," Thomas said. "It will give me time to show Gwen around first."

Mrs. Henley frowned, but Cecilia perked up. "And you'll be back in time to attend the theatre tonight."

"The theatre?" Thomas asked.

Cecilia's placid expression evaporated. "The Chapmans and the Cluffs will be there. We've had it planned for weeks." She reached over the table and grasped her brother's hand. "Please say you'll come, Thomas. Everyone has missed you at our monthly gatherings."

Thomas looked over at Gwen. "Would you like to go to the theatre tonight?" he asked.

"I've never been before," Gwen said, not sure how she should feel about it.

"Oh, you'll love it!" Cecilia's hands were now clasped together, a rapturous expression on her face. "They're performing a comic opera called *The Mikado*. Everyone's talking about it."

As far as Gwen knew, no one in Llanwddyn had ever heard of *The Mikado*, let alone spoken of it, but it was hard to disregard Cecilia's enthusiasm for the outing. "Then perhaps we should go," Gwen said.

Thomas smiled broadly as Cecilia clapped her hands. "Mother?" he asked. "Would you like to go?"

Mrs. Henley pondered the question for a few seconds. "No, thank you, Thomas," she finally said. "I believe I will stay home this time."

Gwen hid a small smile. Based on the little that Thomas had told her about his mother, she guessed this was a fairly regular exchange between them. She couldn't deny feeling some relief that Mrs. Henley would not be at the theatre with them. The outing was going to be frightening enough without any added criticism directed her way. Trying to block out her insecurities, Gwen turned her attention to something more important. "Do you think we could go to the docks this morning?" she asked Thomas.

"The docks?" Mrs. Henley looked aghast. "Is that what you said? Why ever would you want to go there?"

Cecelia was also regarding her with a mystified expression.

"Gwen's brother passed away a few months ago on a ship that sailed from Liverpool to India. She would like to see if his ship is in dock," Thomas explained.

Mrs. Henley's brow puckered. "But, Thomas," she said, "the docks are—"

"The morning would be the best time to go," Thomas interrupted her. "Don't worry, Mother. I won't take any unnecessary risks, and we will not stay long."

As though wanting to ward off any further argument, Thomas turned to Gwen. "Can you be ready within the hour?"

"I'm ready now," she said.

He chuckled. "Of course. Then I'll have my driver meet us outside in twenty minutes."

"Thank you, Thomas," Gwen said.

Chapter 28

IT WAS FAR EASIER TO see the gradual change in the tenor of the neighborhoods in daylight than it had been the night before. As they drove toward the docks, Gwen watched the upscale homes become more modest town houses and the large shops with alluring window displays become small, rundown establishments with torn awnings and dirty glass fronts. The gray smoke Liverpool's many chimneys produced obscured the blue sky Gwen was used to seeing, and all the buildings seemed to be coated with a layer of soot and grime.

The closer they got to the docks, the more ragged the appearance of the men, women, and children along the roadside, and Gwen started to notice more and more children sitting on the corners of the streets or weaving unsteadily between buildings. At one point, a boy who could not have been more than six or seven years old staggered across the road right in front of their carriage. With a shout, their driver reined in the horse just in time to avoid disaster, but the boy did not even look up and the carriage moved on.

"I don't understand," Gwen said, shaken by the incident. "Why didn't that boy run out of the way? He didn't seem to even notice how close he came to being trampled by the horse."

"He was drunk," Thomas said.

Gwen stared at him in horror. "Drunk? But he's a young boy!"

Thomas pointed at the three children slumped together on the ground at the next corner. "They're all drunk."

She clutched the side of the carriage. What kind of place had she come to? Where were these children's parents? How could they allow this to happen?

Her distress must have shown on her face because Thomas took her hand. "As difficult as this is to witness," he said, "perhaps it will help you realize why it is so important that we build the Vyrnwy Dam."

"The Vyrnwy Dam?" Gwen could not see the connection.

Thomas nodded. "The reason those children are drunk is because they don't have access to drinking water. The water shortage in the city is so bad water only runs through the pipes two or three times a week for two or three hours at a time. And even then it's not clean. These children have learned from painful experience that if they drink the water, they're likely to end up with dysentery, cholera, or typhoid. They've seen the devastating effects of those diseases, so they turn to the only other liquid available to them—alcohol."

Gwen covered her mouth with her hand, hoping the gesture would hold back her tears along with her cry. She was starting to understand why Robert had expressed gratitude for his Welsh-village upbringing in the first letter he'd sent from Liverpool.

"Can nothing be done to help them now?" she whispered.

Thomas shook his head. "The problem is too widespread. But the sooner we can start pumping from the Vyrnwy reservoir, the sooner they'll have access to clean water."

Gwen turned her head away as though she was gazing through the carriage window, but instead of seeing the rundown buildings and dark alleyways, she was picturing the green hills, running streams, and gray-stone houses of Llanwddyn.

A little girl with tangled hair and a torn dress stood at the curb, watching the carriage go by, and a tear rolled down Gwen's cheek. Her own childhood had been spent chasing Robert and Lewis through the heather and making daisy chains while they fished. She would never take those things for granted again.

The carriage wheels groaned in protest as they rolled from the hardpacked road onto the cobblestones of the dock. Thomas pushed open the window, and immediately the sound of seagulls, creaking timber, splashing waves, and shouting men filled the carriage.

Gwen sat on the edge of her seat, her eyes scanning the forest of masts that stretched as far as the eye could see. "Can we get out here?" she asked.

She could see Thomas's concern, but he gave a reluctant nod. "We'll ask about your brother's ship, but we mustn't stay long."

He opened the door and helped Gwen out, then he placed her arm in his and walked toward a large warehouse. The sign above the door read "Sail repairs," and an old man was sitting on a stool, sewing an enormous piece of white canvas. As they approached, the man looked up.

"Mornin'," he said.

"Good morning," Thomas replied. "Can you tell us if the SS *Talookdar* is in port?"

The older man rubbed his white stubbly beard and considered the question for a moment. "*Talookdar*," he repeated thoughtfully. "She's the newest ship in the Brocklebank line, I'm thinkin'. A Welsh captain, no less."

"Yes, that's right," Gwen said.

The man's tongue made a sucking sound against the gaps in his teeth. "Left port three days ago," he said. "Weren't here long this time 'round."

Disappointment hit Gwen like a lead weight.

"Can you tell us where she was berthed?" Thomas asked.

The man waved his hand toward the other end of the dock. "Not far," he said. "Right next to the *Mahanada*, I reckon she was."

"Thank you," Thomas said. "You've been most helpful."

Tightening his grip on Gwen's arm, Thomas turned and began walking in the direction of the anchored ships.

"I'm sorry, Gwen," he said. "I wish we'd arrived in time."

"I'm glad we came, even if we didn't see his ship," she said, trying to remain positive. "At least now I can say I've seen the sea and stood at the dock Robert left from."

They walked until they reached the SS *Mahanada* and stood in front of the empty berth beside the gently swaying ship. Waves slapped against the dock, the greenish-gray water stretching out far beyond the row of vessels at anchor. Gwen knelt on the cobblestones and reached her hand into the water. It was cold.

"Do you think the ocean is warmer near South Africa?" she asked.

"Perhaps," Thomas said.

Gwen nodded and rose to her feet again. She wanted to believe Robert was buried somewhere a little less forbidding, but as she gazed out at the ocean that had beckoned to her brother for so long, she realized he was where he would have wanted to be. She put her hand into her skirt pocket and drew out a folded piece of paper. She carefully pulled back the corners to reveal a small pile of pink and yellow rose petals.

"They're from Aunty Jane's bushes," she said. "I picked them yesterday morning before we left."

Thomas gave an understanding smile. "Would you like help?" he asked.

Gwen poured half the petals into his open hand and kept the rest for herself. They stepped up to the edge of the dock and scattered the petals onto the water below. Gwen stood silently for a moment, watching the petals bob up and down before swirling out to sea.

"I love you, Robert," she whispered. "Rest in peace."

Thomas touched her elbow. "I'm sorry, Gwen, but we should probably be on our way," he said.

Over the sound of the waves and the creaking of the ships, the sound of coarse laughter reached her. Gwen looked to her right to see half a dozen men sauntering toward them. Memories of her encounters with the navvies in Llanwddyn filled her mind, and she felt a flicker of fear. "Yes," she said. "We should go."

Thomas took her arm, and they walked briskly toward the waiting carriage. Gwen heard one of the men call out to her, but she ignored him. Quickening her step, she reached the carriage within seconds, and as Thomas closed the door behind them and the wheels began rolling over the cobblestones toward the city, she breathed a grateful sigh of relief.

.... ◆ ....

The next two hours passed in a blur. Thomas had his driver take them through the streets of Liverpool so Gwen could see some of the city's landmarks. They passed one magnificent building after another: the Walker Art Museum, the World Museum, the St. George Hall, and the Philharmonic Hall. With towering stone pillars and grand staircases, water fountains and domed roofs, each new edifice seemed more imposing than the last, and Gwen found herself struggling not to feel overwhelmed by the size of the city and the throngs of people filling the streets.

From her position in the slow-moving carriage, it was hard to reconcile her view of the well-groomed gentlemen and perfectly dressed ladies going about their business in town with the hollow-eyed men, women, and children wearing ragged clothing at the docks. And no matter how hard she tried to focus on all that Thomas was showing her, no architectural wonder could replace in her mind the face of the drunken young boy they'd passed earlier.

Perhaps Thomas, with his usual sensitivity for her feelings, suspected she needed time away from the busy thoroughfares and buildings because he ended their tour with a drive through the carefully tended lawns, rocky terraces, and formal flower gardens of Stanley Park. The manicured landscape was different from the wild Welsh hills Gwen was used to, but the greenery was a welcome balm, and as the carriage rolled along the banks of one of the park's small lakes, Gwen found herself beginning to relax.

"This is lovely," she said as the road rounded a small copse of trees and entered yet another garden.

Thomas looked pleased. "I'm glad you like it." He pulled his watch out of his front pocket and glanced at it, his forehead creasing into a slight frown. "I'm sorry, Gwen. I wish we could stay longer, but . . ."

"Please don't apologize. You've already spent far longer on this outing than you should have, and I don't want you to be late for your appointment."

He gave her a grateful smile. "I will look forward to spending time with you this evening."

·······································◆·······································

A few hours later, Gwen stood in front of the mirror in her bedroom and studied the young woman reflected there. She was wearing her Sunday-best navy skirt and white blouse, and she'd rolled her hair into a twisted knot. A few curls were already escaping the hairpins, but she'd noticed that Cecilia had curls framing her face, so she let them be. She was thankful that her eyes didn't show obvious signs of her tears. It had been a long, emotionally draining day, and unfortunately, it wasn't over yet.

When she and Thomas had returned from their outing, she'd been glad to escape to her room for a while. She'd needed time alone to process all that she'd experienced that morning. The vastness of the city made her feel small and insignificant, and the disparity between the affluent and the destitute among its population filled her with helplessness. But it was her final farewell to Robert and her sorrow over the plight of Liverpool's children that had brought her to tears.

At last, when she could cry no more, she'd lain on the bed, thinking about home, wondering how Aunty Jane was faring without her, wondering if the quarantine had been lifted in Pen-y-Bont Fawr and whether Lewis had remained healthy.

Her longing for home and all that was familiar had intensified when she'd joined Mrs. Henley and Cecilia for dinner. Thomas had still not returned from his meeting with Mr. Wainwright, which meant she didn't have his support when his mother insisted that she repeat everything multiple times. She also had to face the daunting task of eating a formal meal without coaching. There were more dishes on the table than she'd ever seen in her life, and the rows of knives, forks, and spoons at her place setting were baffling. It didn't take long for her to realize that her only recourse if she were to make it through the meal without too many social gaffs was to surreptitiously watch to see which utensil Cecilia used for each course before choosing a matching one of her own.

By the end of the meal, keeping up appearances with the Henley women had further exhausted her, and she was more than happy when Cecilia declared that they needed to return to their respective rooms to get ready for the theatre. Gwen wasn't sure what more she could do to prepare. She was already wearing her nicest clothes and didn't think she could do much to improve her hair, but she was glad of the excuse to leave the dining room and to remove herself from Mrs. Henley's critical eye.

She didn't know exactly what time she was supposed to go downstairs again, but concerned that she not be the one to keep everyone waiting, she gathered her shawl and slipped out of the bedroom as soon as she heard the front door close and footsteps crossing the main hall. She hurried down the stairs, following the sound of voices until she reached the door of the sitting room. The low rumble of Thomas's voice was followed immediately by his mother's shrill exclamation.

"You cannot be serious, Thomas! She's just a chit of a thing, has no breeding, no sense of social decorum, and can barely speak the Queen's English."

Gwen froze.

"I will not have you speak of Gwen that way, Mother," Thomas said. "You are the only person I know who has struggled to understand her speech, and if you were being reasonable, you'd acknowledge that her fluent English is a credit to her."

"And if you were being reasonable, you'd consider that the woman you marry will need to take on the role of hostess for all the social functions your position demands," Mrs. Henley retorted. "That Welsh girl barely knows what knife and fork to use, let alone how to oversee a dinner party."

Taking two steps back, Gwen leaned against the wall, praying that her shaking legs would not fail her.

"Listen, Mother." It sounded as though Thomas was barely controlling his anger. "I did not come here to ask your permission on this matter. I came merely to show you the courtesy I thought you deserved. When Mr. Wainwright told me he has recovered well enough to resume his position at the Vyrnwy Dam and that I will be returning to the Liverpool office, I determined then and there to ask Gwen to marry me. I love her; she is quite simply the most remarkable young woman of my acquaintance. And despite your objections, I have no doubt she is capable of rising to any challenge our marriage might afford."

Gwen closed her eyes and focused on keeping her breathing even. Whatever happened, she could not be found here eavesdropping on this conversation, but she was terrified that if she as much as moved a muscle, the sound would give her away. She took a deep breath and slowly let it out, willing her racing heart to calm. Thomas was moving back to Liverpool. He wanted to marry her and bring her back here permanently. She took another breath. Why was she so shocked? Wasn't this what Aunty Jane had hoped for all along? But was this what *she* had hoped for? As though sent to torture her, the question circled around again. Was marriage to Thomas what she'd hoped for?

She opened her eyes and turned her head. At the foot of the stairs, an upholstered chair had been positioned beside a large vase of flowers on a pedestal table. Splaying her fingers out against the wall to keep her steady, she took a tentative step in that direction. Another step followed and then another. Within seconds Gwen had reached the chair and carefully lowered herself onto it. Less than a minute later, Thomas exited the sitting room. Oblivious to the fact that Gwen was sitting behind the flower display, he marched across the hall and took the stairs two at a time, disappearing from view as soon as he reached the top.

Chapter 29

Gwen was so consumed in her own thoughts that she didn't hear Cecilia until the young woman spoke to her.

"Are you not coming to the theatre after all?" Cecilia asked.

Gwen stood, thankful that her initial shock over Thomas's conversation with his mother had passed and she could stand without fear of falling.

"Yes," she said. "I'm ready."

Only then did she notice how Cecilia was dressed. Her dress was of pale-pink silk and was cinched tightly at the waist, with layers of fabric gathered over a prominent bustle at the back. The dress's neckline was cut low, and the flimsy cap sleeves covered almost none of her arms. Gwen did her best not to gasp. She knew Aunty Jane would be appalled at such a flagrant show of skin.

"Did you not pack an evening gown?" Cecilia said.

Gwen glanced down at her practical but modest attire. "No," she said, not sure that this was the right time to admit that she didn't own one or that her Methodist minister father would turn over in his grave if she were to ever put something like that on.

"Oh dear." Cecilia seemed quite distressed. "If you'd only told me earlier, we might have made one of my old dresses do for you."

Seeing as Cecilia was at least four inches shorter than Gwen and probably that much wider, Gwen thought the likelihood of one of her dresses fitting was unlikely at best.

"That's very kind of you," Gwen said, "but I'm quite all right making do with these clothes."

Cecilia looked uncertain. "Well, if you're sure."

A clatter of footsteps on the stairs had both women turning their heads to see Thomas hurrying toward them.

"I'm sorry to keep you waiting," he said.

He smiled at Gwen, and she felt herself relax. He was not aware that she'd heard anything, and it appeared that for now, at least, he would treat her as he always had. Cecilia placed a shimmery wrap across her shoulders and reached for her brother's arm, then Thomas turned and offered his other arm to Gwen.

Gwen sat opposite Thomas in the carriage, and as his sister told him all about what their friends had been doing while he'd been in Wales, Gwen studied him. He was a handsome man with a pleasant smile and an easy demeanor. His clothes were well cut and of high quality, and she could now quite assuredly report to Aunty Jane that Thomas had more money in the bank than all the young men in Llanwddyn combined. He was kind, attentive, and thoughtful and had proven himself a true friend.

Her personal experience with romantic relationships was sadly lacking, but Gwen was beginning to realize that if Thomas wished to marry her despite his mother's objections, his feelings for her were far deeper than the feelings of comfortable companionship she felt for him. When Thomas had walked down the stairs to greet her and Cecilia, she'd been happy to see him, but his appearance hadn't done anything to her heart rate. When she'd taken his arm, her fingers hadn't tingled the way they had when she reached for Lewis's—

Gwen didn't realize she'd audibly gasped until Thomas and Cecilia stopped their conversation midsentence.

"Are you all right, Gwen?" Thomas asked, concern in his eyes.

"Yes." Gwen tried to pull herself together. "Yes, thank you. I'm sorry. I didn't mean to interrupt."

"You're not interrupting," he said. "We're almost to the theatre."

Gwen turned to look out the carriage window. An imposing redbrick building was coming into view, with "The Royal Alexandra

Theatre and Opera House" written in bold letters across the dark-red, semicircular awning. Up ahead, well-dressed men and women were getting out of carriages to join the milling people who were already climbing the stairs to the main entrance. Gwen tried to take in the spectacle, to savor this unique opportunity, but all the while, her mind was whirling.

Lewis! It was Lewis whose smile she wanted to see above everyone else's outside the chapel, whose touch on the way home from the St. John's Day dance had filled her stomach with butterflies, and in whose arms she'd wanted to stay in the clearing on the mountain. She squeezed her eyes closed. Surely she was the most dim-witted girl to ever walk the Welsh hills. Why, oh, why had she not recognized her feelings for him sooner? Before she'd left for school or before he'd left for Pen-y-Bont Fawr?

The carriage rolled to a stop, and Thomas opened the door. After stepping out, he helped Cecilia down and then offered Gwen his hand. "You're sure you're feeling well?" he asked softly.

After the revelations of the last couple of hours, Gwen could only imagine how pale she must appear. She didn't think her fragile composure could handle much more, but for Thomas's sake, she was determined to be a cheerful companion for the remainder of the evening. "Yes," she said. "I'm sorry if I've been quiet." She pointed to the theatre. "This is all very new to me."

"It's been a day full of new things, hasn't it?" he said.

"Yes," she said again. "It's been rather dizzying."

Thomas laughed. "Well, let's see if you can manage one more."

◆

Gwen had been exposed to music and singing from birth, but she'd never seen anything quite like Gilbert and Sullivan's *The Mikado*. The Oriental theme manifest in the costumes, makeup, and wigs, along with the humor-laced lyrics, combined to be disconcerting and mesmerizing at the same time. When the intermission arrived, she, Thomas, and Cecilia rose from their seats and gathered in the lobby, where Gwen was introduced to Thomas and Cecilia's friends. The group included three young men and two young women, but the only one who paid her any attention after the initial introductions was a blonde woman named Edith.

Edith's dress was similar in style to Cecilia's, but it was a deep purple. Her hair was piled prettily on her head, and her pale blue eyes sparkled as she talked. Compared to Edith, Gwen felt plain in both appearance and personality, but to her surprise, the juxtaposition didn't leave her feeling inadequate. Edith seemed to have a gift for making all those around her feel important, and Gwen noticed she was particularly adept at including Thomas. At that moment, Thomas was laughing at something Edith had said.

Cecilia leaned over to whisper in Gwen's ear. "She's been sweet on Thomas since they were children."

Gwen looked at her wide-eyed. "Does he know?"

Cecilia shook her head. "I think he might be the only person who doesn't."

As Gwen turned back around, Thomas was talking to Edith, who was listening with rapt attention. There was something in Edith's eyes that Gwen had rarely seen before. She didn't know how to define it—it fell somewhere between sincere longing and deep caring, but she knew that as close as she and Thomas had become, she'd never felt an emotion that intense for him and that he deserved to be with someone who did.

It was even more difficult to concentrate during the second half of the production than it had been during the first. Gwen's recent epiphany had helped her make a difficult decision, but it had not lessened the risk of hurting Thomas. More than anything, she wished to spare him that. She knew she needed to talk to him soon, before he moved forward with his plans. She could only hope the opportunity would arise in a timely manner and that she could do what she needed to do without damaging the heart of a very good man.

When the production was over, they returned to Thomas's home, and as the three of them entered the main hall, Thomas pulled her aside. "Could I have a word with you before you go to your room, Gwen?" he asked.

Cecilia glanced at her brother with raised eyebrows but started up the stairs without comment.

Gwen nodded. "Yes. I've been hoping to speak to you," she said.

He pointed to the sitting room, and Gwen followed him there. The fire had died down, but the coals still glowed, and the room was warm. Thomas lit a lamp and placed it on a small table between a couple of armchairs, then indicated that she take a seat.

"What did you wish to speak to me about?" he asked curiously.

Gwen clasped her hands tightly and offered a silent, fervent prayer that the right words would come. "I can't thank you enough for bringing me to Liverpool, for inviting me to your home, showing me the city, and taking me to the docks and the theatre. It's been an incredible, eye-opening experience that I couldn't have had any other way." She gave him a tremulous smile. "But I think that I've stayed as long as I should, and it would be best if I returned home as soon as possible."

Thomas's surprise showed on his face. "Have you been unhappy here?" he asked.

"No," Gwen said. "A little homesick, perhaps, but not unhappy. You've been too good to me to allow that to happen. But I do feel my presence here is stressful for your mother, and I don't want that."

"I told you to pay no heed to my mother," Thomas said.

"Yes, you did, but it's not just that, Thomas," she said, hoping she could make him understand. "Being here has helped me realize what different worlds we come from. While you were in Llanwddyn, you did a remarkable job of fitting in with the locals, but all the while, you knew the situation was temporary, that you'd eventually return to your work and your life here."

She spread her arms to encompass the beautiful furnishings in the elegant room. "This is where you belong, Thomas, and you thrive here. Through your work and social standing, you'll make a difference in the lives of others in a way that I could never dream of doing.

"My path is different. I know that now. I'm not completely sure where it will take me, but I hope it will be as fulfilling to me as your path will be to you."

Thomas leaned forward, and she could see the anguish in his eyes. "You're right about me leaving Llanwddyn," he said. "Mr. Wainwright has asked me to return to the office in Liverpool, but I was hoping I could persuade you to join me here."

Gwen reached out and took his hand. "You and I are good friends, and if I were to agree, we would probably muddle along for a while, but at some point you would start to resent my inexperience. I would be a hopeless hostess, I would dress too simply, my conversation would be sadly lacking, and . . ." She gave a small smile. "My Welsh accent would only make things worse."

"Those things would change with time," Thomas said. "I could help you."

"I know you could—and you would," she said. "But at what price? At every high-society function, you would be anxiously hoping that I not make a terrible mistake, and I would be desperately wishing I were somewhere else. Somewhere outside in the fresh air, climbing the hills or picking the wildflowers."

Thomas searched her face, looking for any hint of hesitation. When he found none, he jumped to his feet and paced over to the fireplace before turning to face her again. "Is there anything I can say or do to make you change your mind?" he asked.

She shook her head. "No. I believe this is the right course for both of us. I'd like to think that you've benefited in some small measure from your time in Llanwddyn, and I will never forget what I've learned from you and from my experiences in Liverpool, but the time has come for each of us to return to our rightful places."

Thomas rubbed his hand across his face as if doing so would erase the regret etched there. "I care about you too much to force my wishes upon you, Gwen. If that's really what you want, I'll take you home."

Gwen rose from the chair and clasped her trembling hands together. She had a fairly good idea of how much this was costing him. "Thomas Henley, you are by far the finest Englishman I have ever met," she said.

Thomas gave her a ghost of a smile. "If only that were enough," he said softly.

Chapter 30

THEY WERE ON THEIR WAY to the railway station by seven o'clock the next morning. Mrs. Henley and Cecilia had still not arisen, so Gwen asked Thomas for some paper and left notes of explanation and thanks for both of them. She guessed Mrs. Henley would breathe a big sigh of relief at Gwen's departure, but she hoped Cecilia might be sorry. Gwen thought that given more time together, they would have become friends.

Thomas was extremely quiet. She could sense his disappointment but was very grateful that he'd accepted her wishes, even though he was still trying to come to terms with how they impacted his future.

The journey was long, but apart from changing trains in Chester and Oswestry, it was uneventful. Gwen felt her heart lighten as the passing scenery changed from rows and rows of buildings to rolling green hills, and when the train finally pulled into Llanfyllin, she embraced the feeling of homecoming, even though she still had twelve miles to go.

The horse and cart they'd used two days before was still at the stable, so it didn't take long to hitch up. Dusk was falling, and though the summer evening was warm, Thomas hurried the horse along, hoping to minimize the time they would have to travel in darkness. Most of the time, the silence between them was the comfortable kind usually had among good friends, but occasionally Thomas's expression would become troubled, and Gwen would ask about his work or his friends or his plans when he returned to Liverpool, anything to take his mind off the fact that he was taking her home to stay.

Despite her best efforts, Gwen couldn't completely prevent the discomfort that grew between them as the cart rolled through Llanwddyn and came to a halt outside Aunty Jane's house.

"Well, this is it," Thomas said as the reins fell slack in his hands.

"Yes," Gwen said. She paused, struggling to know what else to say. "Thank you for bringing me home, Thomas."

Without a word, Thomas climbed down and walked around the cart. He reached up, put his hands around her waist, and lowered her to the ground.

"I'll miss you, Gwen," he said, his hands still on her waist.

Even in the dark, she could see the sorrow in his eyes. "I'll miss you too," she said. "I hope you'll write and tell me how you are every once in a while."

He leaned over and kissed her cheek. "Take care of yourself," he whispered before taking a step back.

She watched as he reached into the back of the cart to retrieve her bag.

"Thomas," she said.

He turned to look at her. "Yes?"

She gave him a sad smile. "Edith would be a wonderful hostess."

"Edith?" he said with a puckered brow.

"Yes. She's lovely."

It was as if she could see the cogs turning in Thomas's mind, and she knew the moment he understood. He tilted his head, his mouth quirking into half a smile. "She is nice, isn't she?"

This time Gwen's smile was genuine. "Good-bye, Thomas."

He climbed back up onto the cart. "Good-bye, Gwen."

With a snap of the reins, the horse moved forward. Gwen stood and watched until Thomas crossed Pont Cedig, then she picked up the bag at her feet. She was opening the gate that led to the back door when she heard the sound of hurried footsteps behind her. Startled, she swung around. On the other side of the road, someone was getting closer. Her hand on the gate tensed, and she strained to see through the dark.

"Evening, Gwen," Rowland greeted her, the fishing rod in his hand casting a long, thin shadow across the road.

Her shoulders slumped with relief. "Good evening, Rowland," she said. "Have you been out fishing this late?"

"It was still light when I was fishing, but the walk home took a long time." He lifted a dark bundle in his other hand. "I caught eight big ones though," he added proudly.

"Your mam will be pleased," she said, smiling into the darkness.

"As long as she's not too cross about me getting back so late," he said.

Gwen laughed quietly. "You'd best be on your way, then."

"Yes," he said, already picking up his pace. "Bye, Gwen."

"Good-bye," she replied.

$$\cdots\cdots\cdots\cdots\cdots\cdots\cdots\cdots\cdots\cdots\;\blacklozenge\;\cdots\cdots\cdots\cdots\cdots\cdots\cdots\cdots\cdots\cdots$$

The next morning, Gwen had just started to explain her unexpected presence in the kitchen to her perplexed aunt when she was interrupted by a loud rap on the front door.

"Good gracious," Aunty Jane said. "Whoever could that be so early in the day?"

Sensing urgency behind the knock, Gwen hurried down the hall to answer it. When she pulled open the door, Mair was standing on the front step, and one quick glance told Gwen something was terribly wrong. Mair was panting hard, as though she'd run all the way from her house to theirs. Her hair was pulling out of the braid she must have slept in, and the moment she caught sight of Gwen in the doorway, her eyes filled with tears. "Oh, Gwen, I'm so glad you're back! This morning when Rowland said he'd seen you, I wasn't sure I could believe it, but I prayed I'd find you home."

"Mrs. Morgan!" Gwen stepped toward her. "Whatever's the matter?"

"It's Lewis," she said.

Gwen reached for the doorframe. *No! Please, God, not Lewis.* Not when she'd only just discovered the depth of her feelings for him. "Is it the measles?" Gwen had to know.

"Yes," Mair said, her voice breaking on the word.

"Come in, Mair." Aunty Jane had joined Gwen at the door and took over for her. "You look like you need to sit down."

"Is he . . . is he . . . ?" Gwen couldn't make the words come.

Aunty Jane gave her a stern look. "Let's go into the kitchen," she said, taking Mair by the arm and leading the way.

No one said another word until they were seated at the table. Gwen was feeling as shaken as Mair looked and was thankful when her aunt finally spoke again.

"Now what's this about Lewis?" Aunty Jane said.

Mair took a shuddering breath. "Dr. Edwards lifted Pen-y-Bont Fawr's quarantine yesterday evening," she said. "No one in the village had come down with the measles for two weeks, and he thought it was safe. Lewis had received our letter about Robert's passing, and he was beside himself to get back to Llanwddyn, so the moment the doctor gave the all clear, he started for home.

"He'd been walking for almost two hours when the sore throat started, and half an hour after that, his temperature was so high he was having difficulty putting one foot in front of the other. He didn't have the endurance to turn back, so he kept walking. It took him an hour longer than usual, but he arrived in Llanwddyn in the early hours of the morning.

"As feverish as he was, he knew he couldn't risk coming in contact with anyone else, so he went straight to our front room because he knows we hardly ever use it."

She paused, trying to compose herself. "When Owen got up this morning, he saw that the front room door was ajar and went to close it, and that's when he spotted Lewis lying on the sofa, shivering like a wet dog.

"Owen went to go in to him, but Lewis shouted at him to go back. He's still coherent enough to tell his dad what happened and to make sure none of us go past the doorway." Tears were now streaming down Mair's face. "He keeps saying that no one else must become ill because of him, but he's in that cold room by himself, with no blankets or food or water."

Lewis wasn't dead. Gwen's relief was so overwhelming she wanted to weep along with Mair. If he was still alive, there was still hope.

"But how did he come down with the measles if it's been two weeks since anyone in Pen-y-Bont Fawr's been ill?" Aunty Jane asked.

"Owen asked him that," Mair said. "Lewis said he repaired a wheel on one of the gypsies' caravans a week ago. The gypsy children followed him around as he worked, and he's guessing their parents wanted to move out of Pen-y-Bont Fawr so badly they didn't let on that they still had illness among them. Because of the quarantine, they'd already stayed much longer than usual."

Aunty Jane muttered something unintelligible under her breath, put her hands on the table, and pushed herself upright.

"We'll decide what's to be done over a cup of tea," she said, reaching for the kettle. "I think we could all use one."

"There's nothing to decide," Gwen said, coming to her feet too. "I'm going to take care of Lewis." Her aunt's hand froze over the teapot, but Gwen didn't even look at her. "That's why you came, isn't it, Mrs. Morgan?"

"Am I asking too much of you, Gwen?" she said brokenly. "You were the only person I could think of that Lewis might let into the room because he knows you've already had the measles. I saw how well you cared for your aunt when she was so poorly and . . . and I know you could nurse him back to health."

"I'll come right away," Gwen said, more grateful than she could express that she could do something tangible to help. She hurried over to the coatrack to retrieve her shawl.

Mair stood and wiped the moisture from her eyes. "Thank you, bach," she said softly.

"Gwen, this is too much for you to do alone." Aunty Jane's voice was firm. "Ill or not, you cannot spend the nights with Lewis unaccompanied. We must think hard. Who else in Llanwddyn has already had the measles?"

Gwen shook her head helplessly. "I don't know. Did anyone say anything about having had the measles when Robert and I arrived here after Mam and Dad died?"

Her aunt frowned, trying to remember. "Let me talk to Bronwen," she said. "If anyone around here knows, it will be her." She turned to Mair. "Your responsibility will be to make sure that only people who've already had the measles go anywhere near your front room. For now, Gwen will make sure Lewis is cared for, and even if we have to send for help from Pen-y-Bont Fawr, I'll find someone to stay with him at night."

"I don't know how I'll ever repay you both," Mair said.

Aunty Jane gave her an incredulous look. "Mair Morgan, we've been in your debt for months. If it weren't for you and your husband, I probably wouldn't be standing here today."

Gwen reached for Mair's hand and squeezed it tightly. "Aunty Jane's right," she said. "Take me to Lewis."

Chapter 31

OWEN WAS WATCHING FOR THEM, and as Mair and Gwen approached the house, he opened the door. "Thank you for coming, Gwen," he said.

"How is he?" Mair asked, hurrying to stand at the doorway to the front room.

"He's been sleeping fitfully since you left," Owen said, rubbing his hand across the worry lines on his face. "I've brought in some peat, Gwen. You'll need to light a fire to take the chill off the room. There's blankets, sheets, a jug of water, and cups. You let me know what else he needs, and I'll get it for you."

"Thank you, Mr. Morgan," she said.

"Let her go in to him now, Owen," Mair said anxiously.

Owen immediately stood aside, and Gwen stepped into the room. It had the cool, damp feel of a room that had been shut up for some time. She pulled her shawl more tightly around her shoulders and quietly approached the sofa. Lewis was sprawled across it, his long limbs hanging off the side. His face was pale, and sweat glistened across his forehead. His dark hair lay limp as though he'd run his fingers through it over and over again, and he was muttering incoherently, tossing his head back and forth as if arguing with someone.

Gwen dropped to her knees beside the sofa and placed her hand gently on his forehead. He was far too hot.

"No, Mam." Lewis's eyes were still closed, his voice hoarse. "No, you mustn't be here."

"It's all right, Lewis," she said. "It's Gwen. You don't have to worry; you can't give me the measles."

His eyelids fluttered open, and he looked at her with glassy eyes. "Gwennie?"

"Yes," she said, softly stroking his hair back from his forehead.

His eyelids closed again, but this time his breathing was more even.

Gwen scrambled to her feet and ran back to the doorway. "His temperature's very high," she told his waiting parents. "I have to cool him down somehow. Can you bring me a bucket of water and some rags?"

Instantly, Owen took off toward the kitchen.

"You must strip him down to his trousers," Mair said.

Gwen swallowed hard. Mair was right; she knew it. But the thought of taking off Lewis's shirt . . . She wasn't sure if she could.

"Do it, Gwen."

Mair's urgency cut through Gwen's discomfort. She raced back to the sofa. Lewis had already taken off his boots; they were lying in a heap on the floor beneath a small table. Quickly she peeled off his socks and added them to the pile. Then she moved up to the other end of the sofa. The top two buttons on Lewis's shirt were already undone. Gwen knelt and, taking a quick, fortifying breath, started to undo the next button. Her fingers trembled as they came in contact with his chest, but the heat emanating from his skin and his sweat-drenched shirt helped keep her focus on the desperate need to bring down his fever.

She was working on the last button when Lewis's hand suddenly reached out and grabbed her wrist.

"No, Gwennie. What are you doing?" he mumbled.

"You have a fever," Gwen said, biting her lip to stop the tears from coming. Her chest hurt to see him like this. "Please, Lewis. I have to take your shirt off."

"Shirt off," he repeated, letting her go and struggling to raise himself.

The moment Gwen had the button undone, she placed her arm around him and tried to help him sit upright. By the time he was sitting, he was shivering violently, and sweat was dripping off his face. Gwen grabbed one sleeve and tugged. It slid off his arm. Quickly she pulled the fabric around his back and pulled on the second sleeve. It was harder to work around the sofa cushions, but at last she pulled it free. She wadded up the shirt and used it to wipe his forehead.

"I have them, Gwen," Owen called from the doorway.

"Can you stay upright a few more minutes, Lewis?" Gwen asked.

He gave a faint nod, lowering his head to his chest as though the effort of holding it up was too much.

Gwen ran to Owen, seized the bucket and small pile of towels from his extended hands, and rushed back. Placing the bucket beside the sofa, she dunked one of the towels into the water.

"This might not feel good at first," she warned Lewis.

Again he gave a small nod. She rung out the towel just enough that it wouldn't drip all over the sofa, then she laid it across his shoulders.

Lewis's head jerked upright as the wet towel touched his burning skin. "Cold," he said through gritted teeth.

"I know it is. I'm so sorry," Gwen said, already dropping the next towel into the water.

She wiped his neck and draped the towel over his chest. She wasn't sure what had happened to the scrawny little-boy body he'd had when she'd watched him and Robert swimming in the Vyrnwy River years ago. The muscular torso currently under the wet towel was much harder to ignore. She turned away to soak another towel in the bucket.

This time, after she'd rung it out, she began to gently wipe his face. He kept his eyes closed as she moved the damp cloth along his hairline and across the stubble developing on his chin. Red dots were starting to emerge around his ears.

"I'm going to get you a drink of water before you lie down again," she said.

He nodded his understanding and sat silently until she returned with a cup. She tried offering it to him, but his hand shook too much to grasp it properly, so she raised the cup to his lips herself. He took a tiny sip and moaned.

"I know it hurts to swallow," Gwen said, "but you need to get as much down as you can."

Lewis opened his mouth again, and she tipped the cup. He managed to drink half of it before pushing it away. Gwen put the cup on the floor and took the wet towels off his body.

"Go ahead and lie down," she said, holding on to one arm to help support him as he lowered himself onto the sofa.

As soon as he was prone, she covered him with a clean sheet and placed another folded wet towel across his forehead.

"Try to sleep now," she said quietly, but his eyes were already closed, and when she tucked his hand under the sheet, he didn't move.

Slowly Gwen got to her feet and walked over to the doorway.

"Bless you, bach," Mair said as Gwen stopped a few feet from her. "Watching from a distance may be the hardest thing I've ever done; I can't tell you how grateful I am that you're with him."

"I hate to see him so poorly," Gwen said, suddenly overwhelmed by the magnitude of her task. "I just hope I can . . ."

"Of course you can," Mair said, interrupting her. "In two weeks' time, this will all be behind us, and Lewis will be back to his normal self."

Trying to draw strength from the older woman, Gwen reminded herself that just because her parents had both died from measles complications did not mean Lewis would suffer the same fate. He was capable of a full recovery, and she would do everything in her power to help him attain it.

"Now," Mair said. "I have to feel as though I'm doing something to help, so I'm going to go to the kitchen to make up some broth. When Lewis wakes, perhaps you can see if he'll take any of it. The more fluids we can get down him, the better. Owen has gone to open the smithy, but he can be back right away if we need him."

"I'll start a fire," Gwen said. "I know the room mustn't be too hot, but it will be good to get rid of the chill in the air."

"That's it," Mair said. She gave Gwen an encouraging smile. "Come to the kitchen and get me if you need anything or if there's any change in Lewis."

Mair headed down the hall to the back of the house, and Gwen picked up the basket of peat and carried it to the fireplace. The grate had been swept clean, so it was not difficult to lay the peat in place and start it burning. Gwen sat back on her heels for a few minutes, watching as the tiny flames begin to lick the dry fuel. When she was sure the fire had taken, she put the basket on the hearth so she could replenish the peat as it was consumed, then went back to the sofa.

She carefully removed the towel from Lewis's forehead, rinsed it in the bucket, squeezed some of the water out, and replaced it. He didn't move. Thankful that he was sleeping more peacefully, she picked up his boots, socks, and shirt and put them in a small pile far from the door so Mair would not be tempted to wash the contaminated clothing herself. Then she sat on the floor and leaned against the sofa, listening to the comforting sound of Lewis's breathing.

Gwen replaced the damp cloth on Lewis's forehead three times before he stirred. She'd just returned to her spot on the floor when she became aware that his eyes were open and he was watching her.

"Hello," she said, unexpectedly shy. "How are you feeling?"

"I'm sorry, Gwennie," he said. His voice sounded a little stronger, but perhaps he still wasn't thinking clearly.

"It's not your fault you're ill, Lewis," she said.

"I never should have said those things to you outside the chapel."

Gwen frowned, trying to follow his train of thought. "Outside the chapel?" As soon as she said the words, the shock and distress she'd experienced after their last interaction came flooding back.

Lewis's meeting with Thomas after their Sunday service had sparked something in Lewis she'd never seen before.

"Thomas is a good man," she said quietly. "He's nothing like the navvies we dealt with before."

"Rowland told me as much," he said, his voice weakening. "But I didn't want to hear it. I was completely out of line, and it's haunted me ever since. Please forgive me." He closed his eyes, and for a moment, Gwen thought that perhaps he'd gone back to sleep, but in the fleeting seconds before exhaustion overtook him, he spoke again, this time so softly she had to strain to catch the words. "It was just that I'd waited *so* long." He paused. "And then before I knew what had happened, I'd waited *too* long."

"He's been in love with you for ages, you know," came a subdued voice.

Gwen swung around. "Rowland," she said, "don't—"

"Come in," he said. "Yeah, I know." He stood at the doorway. "How is he?"

"I think his temperature's gone down a bit," she said, rising to her feet.

"That's good," he said. He tucked his hands into his pockets, suddenly looking uncomfortable. "He'll probably kill me for telling you that, but I think he's daft for keeping it to himself for so long."

"That he . . . he . . ."

"Loves you." Rowland finished her sentence again.

Gwen's heart felt as though it was going to pound out of her chest. "Why would you say such a thing?" she asked. "He's only seen me two or three times in the last year, he never wrote to me, and he was with Mabel the whole time I was away."

Rowland rolled his eyes. "The only good thing about Lewis moving to Pen-y-Bont Fawr was that Mabel stopped coming by the smithy every single day. Dad was surely going to go mad with her always interrupting us in the middle of our work. Like a puppy, she was, following Lewis around and yapping nonstop, and it didn't seem to matter what Lewis said to discourage her; she was back again the next day."

Gwen put a shaky hand to her cheek. Could it be true that Lewis hadn't returned Mabel's affection?

"But why didn't he write to me?" she asked.

Rowland shrugged. "You'll have to ask him that one," he said. "I told you I think he's daft. When it comes to you, he can't think straight."

"Rowland!" Mair's voice came from the kitchen. "You're not getting too close to the front room, are you?"

"No, Mam," Rowland called.

"Come and eat your dinner, then, so you can get back to the smithy and let your dad come for his."

"I'd better go," Rowland said. He looked past her into the room, where Lewis lay asleep on the sofa. "Take good care of him."

Gwen nodded, not trusting herself to speak. With her thoughts and emotions in turmoil, she walked over to the fireplace, poked at the fire, and added another block of peat. Regardless of her confusion over Lewis's words or Rowland's claims, she could not deny that they had both lit a tiny spark of hope within her. After all this time, was it possible that Lewis's feelings for her ran deeper than simple fondness for his best friend's sister?

She glanced at Lewis and took a steadying breath. Even though he was rarely conscious and barely coherent, she wouldn't want to be anywhere else but here with him. She loved him; she knew that now. And even if his responses to her questions ended up breaking her heart, as soon as he was stronger, she would find out what she needed to know.

Chapter 32

EVERY TIME LEWIS WOKE, GWEN offered him a drink, and by early evening, she'd managed to persuade him to consume four cups of water and one bowl of broth. His temperature, although still higher than it should be, had not returned to the dangerously high level it had been at when she'd first arrived that morning, and with a small fire in the grate, the front room was a much more comfortable place to be. The sofa seemed more like a bed now that it had a pillow, sheet, and blanket, and even though Lewis's legs still hung off the end, he was resting more peacefully.

When Owen and Rowland finished work at the smithy, they brought home the cot that Ioan Llanwddyn occasionally slept on and set it in the hall. An hour later, Rhys Jones arrived and carried the cot into the front room, positioning it not far from the sofa. Aunty Jane and Bronwen had done their job. Bronwen had been fairly sure that Rhys had had the measles as a boy, when he'd lived in Porthmadoc. Aunty Jane had visited the tailor to confirm that it was true, and upon hearing of the Morgans' plight, Rhys had agreed to spend the nights with Lewis until he was well enough to sleep alone.

With Mair overseeing things from the hall, Gwen gave Rhys basic instructions on keeping Lewis cool with wet towels on his forehead and regular drinks of water, then left with a promise to return early enough that Rhys could go home for breakfast before opening his tailor shop for the day.

··◆··

When Gwen returned to the Morgans' house the next morning, she discovered good and bad news. The good news was that with Rhys's help, Lewis had been able to bathe and wash his hair, and his temperature was remaining steady. The bad news was that he was now covered in little red dots from his head all the way down to his feet.

"Hello, Spotty," Gwen said when she entered the front room to find Lewis sitting up on the sofa, wrapped in a blanket.

She was rewarded by a small chuckle. "I do look awful, don't I?" he said.

"Not awful," she said, moving closer to touch his forehead. "Awful was yesterday. I'd rather have you covered in spots and sitting up than pale with a fever so high you're barely functioning."

Lewis grimaced. "I don't remember much about yesterday," he said.

Gwen looked away. "That's probably good."

For a moment, neither of them spoke, and then Lewis broke the silence. "I wish I could have been here for Robert's memorial service."

She sat beside him. "I do too," she said sadly. "I missed you."

"Finding out that he'd died and that I'd not been here for you made for one of the worst days of my life."

Gwen looked down. "The service was very nice," she said. "Mr. Ellis spoke, and we sang some of Robert's favorite hymns, but it was a little strange to have it all over at the end of the chapel meeting rather than going on to the cemetery. It felt like something was missing."

"I can understand that," he said.

"Going to Liverpool helped. I think that touching and seeing the same ocean that flows over Robert's burial spot gave me some closure."

"You went to Liverpool?" Lewis said, his shock evident.

"Yes. Thomas took me to the dock. Robert's ship had already left, but I dropped some rose petals from Aunty Jane's garden into the sea. I'd like to think they might float all the way to India."

Lewis cleared his throat uncomfortably. "It was good of Thomas to do that for you," he said. "I must thank him the next time I see him."

"I'm not sure if or when he'll be back," she said.

"Why?" he asked with surprise. "Where is he?"

"Liverpool," she said. "The chief engineer wanted him back at the office there."

"I see." He paused. "How do you feel about that?"

Gwen wasn't sure if the strain in his voice came from weakness brought on by his illness or the question itself.

"I'll miss him," she said. "But he belongs there, just as I belong here."

Lewis stared at her as though he was still trying to process what she'd said. "You really believe that?" he said.

"Yes," she said. "It was hard to say good-bye to a friend, but it was best for both of us."

It looked as though Lewis was about to say something more, but instead he started coughing. Gwen grabbed the cup of water on the small table beside the sofa and held it out to him. He took a drink, and Gwen took back the cup until the coughing slowed.

"Perhaps you should rest a bit," she said.

Lewis nodded. "This coughing began a few hours ago," he said croakily. "Once I get started, I can't seem to stop."

Gwen tried to hide the panic welling up inside her. She'd heard a similar cough coming from her parents' bedroom for days before they'd died. And she recognized the drawn look that the recent coughing attack had put on Lewis's face.

"Has anyone sent for Dr. Edwards?" she asked.

"Dad sent word with Ed the Post," he said.

"Hopefully he'll be here before too long, then," she said, more to herself than to Lewis.

"I daresay," Lewis mumbled, his eyes already closed.

Gwen pulled the blanket up over his shoulders and stepped away. Saying a silent prayer for strength to overcome her fears, she knelt at the fireplace and started clearing out the ashes. Soon she had a fresh fire going and had moved Rhys's temporary cot to the corner of the room. Mair came to check on her a couple of times, talking to her from the hall and handing her two bowls of warm custard, one for her and one for Lewis.

Lewis slept through the morning, and although Gwen knew it was the best thing for him, the time seemed to pass slowly for her. Every once in a while, he would cough in his sleep, and Gwen would hold her breath, hoping that one cough would not develop into a full-fledged coughing attack.

Occasionally she would stand beside the front room window. It gave her a good view of the road, and she could watch the villagers going about their daily activities. She kept an eye out for Dr. Edwards, but when the knock came on the front door, she was changing the damp towel on Lewis's forehead, and he caught her by surprise.

Mair let the doctor into the house and then hovered in the hall while he entered the front room.

"Well, Lewis," he said. "This is not the way I wanted to see you next."

"No, doctor," Lewis said, struggling to pull himself upright on the sofa.

"It's all right, lad," Dr. Edwards said, placing a hand on Lewis's shoulder to prevent him from rising. "Let's take a look at you while you're lying down."

The doctor pulled a stethoscope out of his black bag, and Gwen silently stepped out of the room to join Mair in the hall.

"He's been coughing," she whispered.

Mair nodded, looking worried. "I could hear it from the kitchen. I'm glad the doctor's come. Perhaps he can do something to help."

The two women waited anxiously while Dr. Edwards checked Lewis. When he joined them in the hall, he sighed.

"It's a bad case, Mrs. Morgan. I'm not going to lie," he said. "But he's a strong lad, and given the good care he's getting, I think he'll pull through. Keep using the wet towels to control his temperature, and give him lots of fluids. As soon as he's willing, give him some soup or oatmeal to build up his strength."

"What about his cough?" Gwen asked.

Dr. Edwards frowned. "Walking all the way home with a raging temperature certainly didn't help his symptoms. His lungs are still clear, and that's the main thing. We just have to keep them that way. Give him some hot water with honey to drink; that should soothe the irritation. " He shook his head. "I hate to see another village go through this. I'm not going to do anything now since you seem to have Lewis isolated, but if anyone else goes down with the measles in Llanwddyn, I'll have to order a quarantine."

"We'll do everything we can to keep it contained," Mair said.

The doctor gave a reluctant nod. "Very well. I'll stop by again in a few days, but if things get any worse, send word with Ed the Post immediately."

Mair walked Dr. Edwards to the door, and Gwen went back to Lewis. He was sitting up on the sofa, looking miserable.

"How are you feeling?" she asked.

"I'm not a patient patient," he said glumly.

Gwen smiled. "Not many of us are."

A knock sounded at the front door again.

"D'you think Dr. Edwards forgot something?" Gwen asked, walking back across the room. She glanced into the hall. It was empty. Guessing that Mair had gone to the kitchen to make a hot-water-and-honey mixture for Lewis, Gwen entered the hall and opened the door. To her surprise, she was greeted by Ed the Post.

"Hello, Gwen," he said cheerfully. "I heard I might find you here. I have a box for you, and I thought I'd drop it off on my way rather than having it sit on the doorstep at your aunt's house."

"A box for me?" Gwen looked at the small wooden crate with confusion.

"That's right," he said, lifting it and placing it just inside the door. "How's Owen's boy doing?"

Gwen tore her eyes off the mysterious box to answer him. "Dr. Edwards said it's a bad case," she said, "but we're all hoping for improvement soon."

"Absolutely," Ed the Post said. "You give him my best wishes, you hear?"

Gwen nodded. "I will. Thank you, Mr. Hughes."

She closed the door behind the postman and stood staring at the box. The writing on the address label looked vaguely familiar. Crouching down, she studied it more carefully. *Miss Gwen Humphreys.* Suddenly she remembered where she'd seen that handwriting. It belonged to Captain Tecwyn Owen, and this must be the box he'd promised to send. Slowly she rose and took a big step back, unexpectedly afraid of what it might contain.

"Who was it, Gwennie?" Lewis called from the front room.

Gwen moved closer to the doorway. "Ed the Post dropped off a box for me." She tried to keep her voice even. "I . . . I think it's from Captain Owen. He promised to send me Robert's things."

There was a moment of silence before Lewis spoke again, and when he did, she could hear the compassion in his voice. "Would you like company while you open it?"

Gwen looked over her shoulder at the box and then back at Lewis. "Yes," she said quietly. "I think I would."

Chapter 33

GWEN HAULED THE WOODEN BOX into the front room and placed it on the floor in front of the sofa.

"How do I open it?" she asked.

"Pass me the poker," Lewis said. "It's probably the best we can do in here."

Gwen handed him the poker, and after a few failed attempts, he manage to pop off the lid.

"I hate this," he said with a groan. "I'm as weak as a two-year-old. I hope nobody but you ever knows how long it took me to open this box."

Gwen handed him a damp towel. "Thank you for doing it," she said. "I'm sure it would have taken me longer."

Lewis shook his head and used the towel to wipe the sweat beading up on his forehead while Gwen, with mounting apprehension, stared down at the layer of straw at the top of the box.

"I'm scared," she finally said. "I don't know how I'm going to react when I see what's inside."

Lewis leaned forward and put his hand on her cheek, gently turning her head so she was facing him. "It doesn't matter how you react," he said softly. "It's only you and me. I may be a twelve-and-a-half stone weakling at the moment, but I still have a shoulder you can cry on. If you need quiet, I can do that. If you need someone to talk you through it, I probably have more Robert tales than you do. And if you end up angry, you can throw anything you want, so long as it's not at me."

Gwen placed her hand over his and closed her eyes for a few moments.

"Thank you," she finally whispered.

He lowered his hand, stifling a cough as he moved. Gwen handed him a cup of water and waited until he'd drunk a little before turning her attention back to the box. Then, before she could talk herself out of it, she grasped a handful of straw and pulled.

The first thing she saw was a book. She picked it up and turned it over. "*Treasure Island* by Robert Louis Stevenson," she said in English, lifting it so Lewis could see. "Have you ever heard of it before?"

He shook his head. "It looks new. Perhaps Robert bought it in Liverpool to read on the ship. He probably couldn't find any Welsh books there."

Gwen flipped through the pages. "It's dog-eared," she said. "He must have liked it."

She put the book on the floor and reached for a large object wrapped in a multicolored cotton cloth. Setting it on her knee, she gently unwrapped the fabric. "Oh." She gasped. "It's an elephant!"

The beautifully carved elephant stood about a foot tall and was polished to a shine. She handed it to Lewis.

"I think it's made of ebony," he said, turning it slowly so he could view it from all sides. "With ivory tusks."

He set it carefully on the table, and Gwen reached into the box again. This time she pulled out Robert's bible. She set it beside the other book before returning to the box and withdrawing two bundles of letters, each tied together with string. A quick glance at the fatter bundle revealed that Robert had kept all the letters she'd ever written to him. The second, smaller bundle contained a few letters from Aunty Jane and several from Lewis. Gwen stared at them in stunned disbelief.

"You wrote to Robert?"

"Not as often as I should have," he said.

Gwen's eyes held his. "You wrote to Robert, but you never wrote to me?" Her indignation was rising at an alarming rate. "All that time that I was in Llanfyllin, and then when you were in Pen-y-Bont Fawr, I didn't get any letters. The few times I managed to persuade myself that you hadn't completely forgotten me I told myself it was because you never wrote letters to anyone."

"I did write to you once," Lewis said.

"Once!" Gwen leaped to her feet and marched over to the fireplace. "Do you have any idea how much I longed for a letter from you? How hurt I was when you never replied to mine? How hard it was to be so quickly forgotten?"

Beneath all the red dots, Lewis's face was ashen. "Gwennie, you don't understand," he said.

"Don't understand?" Gwen clenched her fist. "What? That you were too busy with Mabel, or that you were glad of some time off from watching out for me?"

"No!" Lewis threw the blanket aside and pushed himself off the sofa and onto his feet. He staggered, his weakened legs barely holding him up.

Gwen took an instinctive step toward him, then stopped herself. "Sit down, Lewis," she said.

He ignored her. In four shaky steps, he reached the end of the mantelpiece, and using that as a handhold, he kept moving until he was within arms' length of her. She wanted to back up, to keep a safe distance between them, but she couldn't bring herself to do something that would entice him to keep moving, not when his legs were so close to giving way already.

"Lewis, if you collapse, I may not be able to lift you," she warned.

"Then I'll lie there until Rhys comes," he said, turning his head to cough. "I don't care. All that matters is that I'll have explained myself to you." He coughed again, this time for longer, and when he finished, he rested his head against the mantel to catch his breath.

Gwen couldn't stand it anymore. She took his right arm and put it over her shoulder and wrapped her left arm around his waist. "Come on," she said.

Without a word, he let her guide him back to the sofa. Once there, his knees folded, and he dropped onto the cushions.

"Please, Gwennie." He gasped as he lay down. "You have to let me explain."

Gwen pulled the sheet over him and felt his forehead. His temperature was climbing. Her fears rose with it. "I never should have let you get up," she said brokenly. "I'm sorry, Lewis."

"You're sorry?" he cried. "I'm the one who needs to make things right between us."

His coughing returned, and then because he couldn't fight his total fatigue anymore, he rolled onto his side and closed his eyes.

Gwen placed a damp towel across his forehead. "Try to rest," she said, but she needn't have bothered; he was already asleep.

Gwen lowered herself to the floor beside the open box and slid the piles of letters out of the way. Reaching inside, she pulled out the last items: Robert's Sunday-best boots, trousers, his jacket, and the hat he'd worn when he'd come to see her at school in Llanfyllin. She picked up the soft hat and pressed it to her face. Suddenly it was all too much—Robert's death, Lewis's illness, the letters. Pulling her knees up, Gwen wrapped her arms around them, lowered her head, and began to sob.

"Gwen, bach, whatever is the matter?"

Gwen wasn't sure how long she'd been crying when Mair called out to her from the hall, but she recognized the alarm in her voice.

"I'm sorry, Mrs. Morgan," she said, wiping her eyes with her hands as she came to her feet. "I didn't mean to frighten you."

"Is it Lewis?" Mair asked.

Gwen wished she could say, "Yes, my heart is breaking over your son," but instead she shook her head. "His fever's gone up, but he's asleep at the moment." Then, to try to explain her tears, she pointed to the small crate and the various items scattered around it. "Ed the Post dropped off a box from Robert's captain today. It was full of Robert's things. Seeing his bible and his clothes . . . I think it finally hit me that he's really gone."

"Oh, cariad," Mair said, extending her arms from the doorway.

Gwen started across the room but stopped just before she reached Mair. More than anything, she wanted to fall into the woman's arms for a much-needed hug, but with the quarantine hanging over them, she knew she had to hold back.

Mair must have realized it too. With tenderness in her eyes, she slowly dropped her arms. "Now, you listen to me," Mair said. "Lewis is all right for a few minutes, so you take a little time for yourself. I'm going to bring you something to eat. After that, if you put everything back in the box and put the lid on, I'll have Owen or Rowland drop it off at your house later. That way you won't have to look at those reminders again until you're ready. And the moment Rhys gets here, I want you going home to bed. You're absolutely worn out." She handed Gwen her handkerchief. "Now then, mop up, and I'll go make a cup of tea."

"Thank you," Gwen said, her voice breaking on the words.

"Thank *you*, bach. I don't know how we'd manage without you."

◆

Gwen boxed up all of Robert's things except *Treasure Island*, which she left out, thinking Lewis might like to look at it, then she dragged the crate into the hall. It was heavy enough that she was glad she wouldn't have to carry it any farther. Despite the noise she made moving everything, Lewis didn't wake up. He still felt uncomfortably warm to her touch, and when Rhys arrived a little while later, he promised to keep up the wet-towel treatment throughout the night.

As she walked home, she took a moment to soak in the beauty of the warm summer evening, to listen to the birdsong and children's voices, to smell the flowers in the gardens and the faint aroma of supper coming through the open windows of the homes she passed. Roses spilled riotously over the stone wall outside Miss Ellis's old home. The bright colors and sweet perfume were a gentle reminder that many of her neighbors were also experiencing loss and its accompanying sorrow. The dead heads and encroaching dandelions in Miss Ellis's garden told the tale. She was gone, forced by the coming of the dam to take a teaching position elsewhere and to leave her home and beloved prize-winning roses behind.

Gwen had almost crossed Pont Cedig when she heard someone call her name. Too weary to maintain a conversation, Gwen's heart sank when she turned to see Mabel hurrying toward her. A young man was at her side, half running to keep up with her.

"Gwen, I'm so glad I caught you," Mabel said, her breath coming out in little gasps. "How is Lewis?"

"I'm afraid he's quite poorly," Gwen said.

"As soon as I heard about the measles in Pen-y-Bont Fawr, I just knew he'd catch them," she said. "And I suppose he's covered in red spots."

Gwen looked at her quizzically. "Of course."

"Oh dear," Mabel said. "How can you stand to see him like that?"

Gwen knew that in her current state she didn't have the patience for inane questions. She pasted a smile on her face and turned to the young man at Mabel's side. "I don't think we've met," she said.

"Oh, how silly of me," Mabel said. "Hefin, this is Gwen Humphreys. Gwen, this is Hefin Roberts from Llanfyllin. His mother and mine were good friends at school." She gave him an overly sweet smile, and Hefin beamed, giving the appearance of being quite besotted. "Hefin brought his mother to Llanwddyn for a visit a couple of months ago and has been visiting quite regularly ever since."

"It's nice to meet you, Hefin," Gwen said, forcing herself to be polite. "I'm sorry I can't stay to talk. My aunt is expecting me right away."

Mabel gave a little pout and tucked her arm under Hefin's. "Well, that's too bad," she said. "Next time, then."

"Yes," Gwen said. "Next time."

She gave them a quick wave and escaped as fast as her tired limbs would allow. If Lewis hadn't pulled all his hair out or had his brain turn to mush after spending so much time with Mabel, maybe they were meant to be together. Then again, perhaps he'd have to fight Hefin for her now. Either way, she didn't need to be involved.

Chapter 34

WHEN MAIR ANSWERED THE DOOR the next morning, the dark smudges under her eyes and the strain in her smile spoke louder than words. Gwen had had to force all thoughts of Lewis out of her mind in order to sleep the night before, but one look at Mair brought her anxiety for him surging back.

"How is he?" Gwen asked.

Mair shook her head. "I don't know what's wrong," she said. "He didn't even cough that much last night, but when he woke up in the early evening to find you gone, nothing Rhys could do would make him settle back down again. He tossed and turned all night long. I could hear him moaning from my bedroom upstairs."

"Was he feverish?"

"Rhys kept the wet towels on him, but he didn't think there was much change in Lewis's temperature," she said. "Rhys left a little earlier, poor man. I don't think he got any sleep at all."

Gwen didn't wait to hear more. She ran into the front room, slowing down only when she approached the sofa. Overnight, the small dots covering Lewis's skin had multiplied and spread into one great red whole. His face looked raw. Gwen dropped to her knees and reached out to gently brush the dark hair back from his forehead. At her touch, his eyelids fluttered, and suddenly she was staring into his blue eyes.

"You came back," he said croakily.

"Of course I did," she replied.

He swallowed and winced as if it hurt.

"Do you need a drink?" Gwen asked.

He nodded and slowly pulled himself up on one elbow while she reached for the cup of water on the table. Gwen handed him the cup, glad to see that his hand was not as shaky as it had been. After taking a long drink, he handed the cup back to her.

"Thank you," he said, lowering himself to the pillow.

"Do you think you could manage some oatmeal?" Gwen asked. "You might feel a little stronger if you had some food."

"Perhaps," he said.

Mair, who'd been hovering at the doorway, needed no second bidding. "I'll get it right away," she said and immediately disappeared down the hall.

"I heard you had a bad night," Gwen said.

He reached out and ran his fingers down the side of her face before taking her hand. "That's what happens when you believe the most important person in your world has just walked out of your life," he said. "I'm horribly familiar with it because it's occurred before: first when you left for school in Llanfyllin and then when you were with Thomas. But yesterday . . . yesterday was the worst of all because I had nothing to blame but my own failings." He took a steadying breath. "I got no rest last night because I wasn't sure you could ever truly forgive me for hurting you so badly, and that meant that I'd lost you without ever telling you how much I love you."

"You . . . you love me?"

"More than I can express," he said softly. "And as impossible as it sounds, I'm going to try to explain why I can say that even though I didn't write to you while we were apart."

Gwen stared at him, her mind racing almost as fast as her heart. Had Lewis really just told her he loved her? Despite all Gwen's doubts, had Rowland been right about his brother's feelings? She desperately wanted to believe it, but there was so much she didn't understand. "Tell me," she said.

Lewis gripped her hand more tightly. "When I received your first letter from Llanfyllin, I wrote back right away and took the letter to the post office. Your aunt was there, and when she noticed that my letter was addressed to you, she gave me a talking to. She told me I would do well to remember that you were a sixteen-year-old school girl who needed to focus on your studies, that leaving Llanwddyn was going be hard enough for you without receiving letters that would bring on unnecessary homesickness, and that she expected better of me."

Gwen could not hide her shock. "Aunty Jane told you that?"

He gave a faint smile. "Yes, but the worst of it was that deep down, I knew she was right. I realized that if I put my desire to have regular contact with you above your need to make new friends, have new experiences, and discover new strengths, I was the most selfish brute alive. And so I stopped writing."

He looked down at her hand in his. "But I never, ever stopped thinking of you," he said. "Sometimes I'd go up to the clearing, sit on the boulder, and look out at the view we used to share, but it wasn't the same without you there. Then I started making the rose." He gave a wry smile. "It's amazing how much better you feel after you've hit or twisted hot metal for a while."

"I think it may be the most beautiful gift I've ever received," she said.

"I'd planned to give it to you when you came home for Christmas, but then the snow came." He gave an exasperated sigh. "I was lucky to catch Ed the Post when I did. I don't think I could have sent it to you through the post office."

Gwen hung her head. "Aunty Jane never should have spoken to you like that. She may have thought she was being protective, but she was unkind. I missed you so much, and I couldn't understand why . . ."

"I had to wait for you, Gwennie." Lewis's blue eyes pled with her to understand. "You were so young."

"You saw me as Robert's little sister," she said sadly.

He shook his head. "No. You were much more than that." His thumb started to move in gentle circles on the back of her hand. "I think I started falling in love with you that day in the smithy when you gave me an earful for treating you so badly. I knew then that I never wanted to be the cause of that much hurt in your beautiful green eyes again." He sighed heavily. "I haven't done so well, have I?"

"You . . . you fell in love with me that long ago?" Gwen's heartbeat was making it hard to think.

"Yes." Lewis's smile was a little crooked. "You had me completely by age sixteen."

"And now that I'm almost eighteen?" Gwen was suddenly breathless.

"I'm pretty sure that means I don't have to wait for you to grow up anymore," he said. And then looking unexpectedly vulnerable, he added, "but I do need to wait to hear whether or not you'd be willing to let me officially court you."

"Yes," Gwen whispered. "Please don't wait any longer, Lewis. I don't think my heart can stand it."

Pure joy filled his eyes, and he pulled on her hand, forcing her to bend nearer. "I love you so much, Gwen Humphreys," he said, placing a gentle kiss on her forehead. "And when I'm no longer covered in spots or coughing or feverish, I'm going to kiss you again, and it won't be like that."

"Can you start getting better faster?" Gwen said, and for the first time since Lewis had arrived home with the measles, he laughed.

◆

From then on, Lewis improved rapidly, and each family member credited his remarkable turnaround to something different.

"I just knew he'd sleep better and that awful cough would go away once he started eating again," Mair told Gwen as she handed her a large bowl of vegetable soup for Lewis's dinner. "Good home cooking works wonders."

"It's that strong Morgan constitution," Owen announced proudly when he arrived home from the smithy to find Lewis walking laps around the front room. "It fights back every time."

Rowland waited until his parents were out of earshot before he shared his opinion. "Amazing what winning the heart of the woman you're in love with will do for a man's health, isn't it?" he said, and as color flooded Gwen's cheeks, Rowland didn't bother to hide his grin.

All Gwen knew for sure was that Lewis's recovery was a direct answer to many prayers, and for that she was truly grateful.

She spent every day at the Morgan's home, conveying meals to and from the front room doorway, helping with any chores that needed to be done in the front room, and simply spending time with Lewis. They started reading Robert's book, *Treasure Island*, together, and Gwen brought over her sketchbook so Lewis could see the drawings she'd done at the dam site. When Gwen told him about meeting Mabel and her new beau, the look of utter relief on Lewis's face was all the reassurance Gwen needed that Mabel's feelings for Lewis had not been reciprocated.

Most of the time, however, they shared the experiences they'd had while they'd been apart. Gwen told him about her time in Llanfyllin and Liverpool, and he, in turn, told her about life in Pen-y-Bont Fawr. He described some of the people he'd met, the river that ran through the village, and the walks he'd taken on the nearby hills. Then he told her of his uncle and aunt.

"My Uncle Griff is ten years older than Dad," he said. "And even though his arm's a lot better, I think he still appreciates the help at the smithy. His daughters are all married and on their own, and he doesn't have any boys, so he's asked if I'd be willing stay on and eventually take over for him."

Gwen was sitting beside him on the sofa and turned so she could see his face. "So you plan to go back?"

"I'd like to know how you feel about it," he said, lacing his fingers between hers. "I hate the thought of being away from you again, but it's my best opportunity to save enough money to get married, and I'd have a secure job when the smithy in Llanwddyn is underwater."

This was the first time Gwen had heard Lewis talk of marriage, but she could tell by his earnest expression that it was far from the first time he'd thought about it. For a few seconds, she allowed herself to ponder on the possibility of being married to the man at her side. A feeling of warmth and happiness filled her, and she found that she didn't have to think about his question at all. "It sounds like it's my turn to wait," she said. Then she gave him a playful glance. "Will you write to me?"

Lewis groaned and wrapped his arms around her, drawing her close. "Every day, or every other?" he asked.

"It all depends on how long we'll be separated," she said.

"Remember when I told you I'm not a patient patient?" he asked, resting his cheek on her head.

"Yes," she said, loving the feel of his arms around her.

"I can guarantee I'm not going to be patient with a long-distance courtship either." He kissed the top of her head. "I promise I won't make you wait too long, Gwennie."

Chapter 35

TEN DAYS LATER, GWEN DID not get out of bed with the joyful anticipation she'd experienced since Lewis had declared his love for her. She'd spent so much time at the Morgans's home and had been so consumed with helping Lewis through his illness that the everyday occurrences and the ongoing changes in the village had passed by virtually unnoticed. But this was a day she could not ignore.

Gwen had received word two days before that her parents' coffins were to be disinterred today, so rather than going to see Lewis, she would be joining her aunt at the cemetery.

Her thoughts were on her parents as she slowly dressed in her navy-blue skirt and light-gray shirt. She missed her father's contagious smile and ready laugh and her mother's warmth and enthusiasm. She was confident that they would have liked Lewis, and when she experienced a pang of regret that they would not know one another in this life, she held fast to her faith that sometime in the future, they would meet each other.

When she went downstairs, Aunty Jane, dressed in a somber black dress, was waiting for her. Gwen could not help but be impressed by how well her aunt had faced the challenges brought on by her stroke months before. Although she now moved slowly and with the aid of a cane, she was able to get around by herself. She'd worked hard to reclaim self-sufficiency in dressing, preparing meals, and working at the post office, and only when she was very tired did her speech become slightly slurred and she favor her left side over her right.

Aunty Jane did recognize her limitations, however, and even though she was accompanying Gwen to the current cemetery, she'd already determined that the two-mile walk to the new cemetery would be too far for her. After the coffins were raised, she planned to leave so she could open the post office while Gwen followed the cart to her parents' new resting place.

The sky was appropriately overcast as the two women walked to the chapel. They said very little, each keeping their thoughts to themselves, and when they arrived, neither one mentioned the horse and cart waiting at the cemetery gate. They followed the well-worn path that led behind the chapel and found two men waiting for them, each holding a shovel. Already the cemetery bore witness to the Liverpool Corporation's work. Like new brown patches on an old green blanket, rectangles of freshly turned soil lay scattered amongst the grave sites. The turf above Gwen's parents' graves had already been removed and stacked to one side, but the ground beneath lay untouched.

"Miss Humphreys?" the older of the two men asked.

"Yes," Gwen said. "And this is my aunt Jane Jones."

Both men pulled on the brims of their hats in greeting.

"I'm glad you could be here," the man said. "We know this is difficult for the families, but we'll be as respectful as we can, given what has to be done."

"Thank you," Gwen said, grateful that the Liverpool Corporation had given this assignment to men who spoke their language and shared their religious values.

"Right then," the man said. "If you're ready, we'll get started. We've already moved the headstones onto the cart. We'll keep them with the coffins. The minister is planning to meet us at the other cemetery to help with the reinterment."

Gwen gave a nod of assent, and the men started to dig. The steady grate of metal against moist earth continued for a few minutes until the younger man's shovel hit something hard. The clunking sound jarred Gwen, and suddenly it wasn't as easy to stand and watch. She looked off into the distance, focusing on a bird sailing effortlessly in the sky above the river.

The memories came easily, tumbling over each other as though waiting for release: Quiet times spent curled up on her father's knee as he read aloud from her book of fairy tales. Her father pushing her on the rope swing that hung from the apple tree in their back garden, his laughter echoing hers as she flew higher and higher. Her mother sitting under the shade of that same apple tree, teaching her to make daisy chains and crowning her with a wilted daisy coronet before they went inside for tea.

One of the shovels scraped across the top of a casket, and Gwen felt a single tear roll down her cheek. This physical reminder that her parents were gone brought with it a renewed sense of grief, but so too came the feeling that her mother and father were not far away and that they still cared deeply for her. Gwen closed her eyes, clinging to that thought.

At the sound of movement to her right, Gwen turned her head, unable to prevent a gasp as Lewis appeared at her side.

"What are you doing here?" she whispered.

"I didn't want you to follow the caskets alone," he said.

"But your quarantine . . ."

He smiled. "Dr. Edwards stopped by first thing this morning. He's given me the all clear."

Unbidden, another tear fell, and Lewis reached out to gently wipe it away before moving to stand beside her. Then he took her hand and held it tightly as the men continued to dig until they had exposed two coffins lying beside each other. Running thick rope beneath the coffins, the workmen slowly eased the caskets upward, setting them gently on the ground before carrying them one at a time to the waiting cart.

While Gwen watched the two men lift the coffins onto the back of the cart and drape them with black fabric, Lewis walked Aunty Jane to the cemetery gate. By the time he returned, the two men had climbed onto the cart and Gwen had taken her place behind it. Lewis stepped up to her and took her arm.

"I spoke to your aunt," he said softly. "It seems that working at the smithy in Pen-y-Bont Fawr has improved my eligibility. In case you had any doubts, you and I are officially courting."

Gwen gave him a shy smile. "I'm glad she's come around. I'm sure I gave away my feelings for you the day you arrived back in Llanwddyn with the measles." She leaned her head against Lewis's shoulder and looked over at the shrouded coffins. "I think my mam and dad would be pleased."

He smiled at her tenderly. "I think mine will be too."

They followed the slow-moving cart all the way to the new cemetery. The minister was there to meet them, and after expressing his pleasure over Lewis's recovery, he rededicated Gwen's parents' graves and watched with Gwen and Lewis as the men covered the coffins with earth once more.

Even though they no longer had a funeral cart to follow, Lewis and Gwen took their time walking back to the village. Gwen was concerned that Lewis not overexert himself on his first day out after two weeks of illness, and Lewis wanted to prolong every moment outside after having been cooped up indoors for so long.

"Will you promise me you'll go straight home and rest?" Gwen asked when they arrived outside her house.

"Yes, nurse," he said, feigning deference.

Gwen shook her finger at him. "I *was* your nurse, and I don't want to see you that poorly ever again," she said.

"I'll lie down," he promised. "What are you going to do this afternoon?"

Gwen looked over at the nearby mountain. "I think I'll spend a little time sitting on my boulder in the clearing," she said.

He gave her an understanding look. "That sounds like a good idea."

She nodded. "Today was harder than I'd anticipated, but having you with me helped make it bearable."

Lewis leaned closer and kissed her cheek. "I'm glad," he said simply.

She smiled and opened the gate that led to the back door. "Good-bye, Lewis."

He gave her an answering smile. "Good-bye, Gwennie."

························ ◆ ························

There was something about the Vyrnwy valley that spoke to Gwen's soul. Its untamed beauty brought her peace, and the timeless hills brought her security. As she sat on the boulder in the clearing and looked down on the scene below, she marveled that despite all that had occurred over the last few years, her personal connection with this special place had never diminished.

The dam's retaining wall had risen considerably since she'd last seen it, but thanks to Robert, Thomas, and Harry, she no longer looked on it with anger and resentment but rather with poignant acceptance. Growing up in this valley, she'd been blessed with the kind of childhood the poor children of Liverpool could only dream of, but because of the dam, those children would eventually taste of its pure, clean water.

She did not believe that anyone could deny that the sacrifice the Liverpool Corporation had forced upon the people of Llanwddyn was monumental—she'd just participated in the reinterment of her parents' graves, and within a few short years, her entire village would be gone—but at least now she understood that Liverpool's need was just as great. For the first time, she recognized that over the last few years she had changed perhaps as much as her beloved valley.

A bird flew past, interrupting her quiet contemplation. It landed on a nearby branch, cocked its head, and trilled a bright song. Gwen glanced down at the sketchbook on her knee, wondering if the little robin would stay long enough for her to capture his cheeky personality on paper. Her question was answered almost immediately as another whistle filled the air, one she hadn't heard in over a year. With a flurry of feathers, the robin took off, and Gwen was on her feet before the last notes of "Dau Gi Bach" faded.

"You came," she said as Lewis entered the clearing.

"I did lie down for a little while because I knew you needed some time alone," he said, "but I couldn't stay away for long." He moved closer and wrapped his arms around her. "How are you feeling?" he asked with genuine concern.

"Grateful," she said.

A slow smile replaced his anxious expression. "So am I," he said.

She leaned into him, resting her cheek against his chest. With one hand, he tightened his hold around her waist. With the other, he gently fingered the ringlets framing her face.

"I've always loved your curls," he said softly.

Without a word, Gwen reached for the ribbon at the bottom of her braid and pulled it off. In a matter of seconds, she'd run her fingers through her hair so it was flowing in gentle waves halfway down her back. Then she looked up at Lewis, her trusting green eyes meeting his adoring blue ones.

"Oh, Gwennie," he whispered, and then at last he lowered his lips to hers.

Epilogue

Vyrnwy Dam, May 1891

Gwen leaned against the low stone wall and stifled a giggle. "Catch him, Lewis," she called.

She watched as her husband's long stride quickly caught up with the escaping two-year-old, whose chubby, short legs were pumping as fast as they could. She heard the little boy squeal with delight as Lewis grabbed him, swung him into the air, and planted him firmly on his broad shoulders.

"Come here, you little scamp," Lewis said, turning and walking back toward Gwen.

"Mam! Mam!" The little boy clapped his hands with glee.

"Robert Lewis Morgan, you're getting too fast for your own good," Gwen said.

Lewis groaned. "I thought it was bad enough that he was as mischievous as his namesake, but now he'll stop at nothing to get to the water."

Gwen laughed. "Look, Robert, you can see the water from Dadi's shoulders." She pointed to the vast lake that filled the valley behind them, and as Lewis slowly turned, Robert's eyes widened, and his little mouth formed a perfect *O* as he caught sight of the water cascading like an enormous waterfall through the arched overflows and down the outer wall of the dam.

"Even after living here when the dam went up, it's still a miraculous sight," Lewis said.

Beside him, Gwen nodded. The Liverpool Corporation had done their job well. The road on which they now stood traversed the dam and was lined on either side with a low stone wall decorated with pillars and ornamental pieces of stone.

They couldn't see the far end of the long reservoir, but off to one side, the straining tower that Gwen had seen in diagram form so many years before stood sentinel, adding a hint of fairy-tale magic to an already picturesque scene. On the hillsides all around the lake, conifers grew tall and proud, and rhododendron bushes thrived along the lakeside.

"I sent Thomas and Edith a few drawings of the dam as a wedding gift, but I hope Thomas brings her back here to see it," Gwen said. "He should be proud of his work."

Lewis put his arm around her. "We'll bring our children back often too," he said. "Pen-y-Bont Fawr will be their home, but they need to know what lies beneath the water here and understand the sacrifices their family made for others."

Gwen rested her hand on her swollen abdomen and smiled. "They may not ever be able to see the village we knew, but they're part of a wonderful legacy."

On Lewis's shoulders, Robert started bouncing up and down. "Water! Water!" he cried.

Lewis lifted him down and placed him on his feet. "All right, lad, we'll take you down to the water."

Gwen and Lewis each took one of their son's hands, and together they followed the road across the dam and around the edge of the lake to a narrow footpath that led to the water's edge. Lewis crouched down, picked up a handful of tiny pebbles, and handed them to Robert. With a chortle, the little boy started tossing them one at a time into the water.

"When Dadi, Uncle Robert, and Mami were young, there used to be a river here," he told his son. "We'd come here to go fishing." He winked at Gwen. "Actually, Uncle Robert and I fished. We only let your Mami come because she was so pretty."

"Lewis!"

Lewis laughed. "Well, all right," he admitted. "Dadi and Uncle Robert fished, and Mami was here because she wouldn't let us go without her."

"That sounds a little more like it," Gwen said with a smile.

"Maybe," Lewis said as he got to his feet. "But she really was beautiful." His eyes never left Gwen's as he gently pulled her into his arms. "Which only goes to show," he continued softly, "that no matter what else has happened since then, there *are* a few things that truly never change."

Then, with their young son standing beside them, he lowered his head and kissed her.

Mair's Bara Brith

2 C. dried fruit (raisins, sultanas, golden raisins, Craisins, etc.)
3 oz butter
1 C. brown sugar
10 oz water
1 tsp mixed spice*
2½ C. flour
4 tsp baking powder
1¼ tsp salt
1 egg

In a saucepan, heat the first five ingredients. Simmer for 10 minutes. Pour into a covered bowl and allow to cool overnight.

In a separate bowl, mix flour, baking powder, and salt. Add egg and fruit mixture, and mix until well blended.

Pour into a greased 8 x 4-inch bread pan. Bake at 300 for 1¼–1½ hours. Cool on a baking rack.

Serve sliced and spread with butter.

*If mixed spice is unavailable, a similar blend can be made by mixing together:

    1 tbsp cinnamon
    1 tsp coriander
    1 tsp nutmeg
    ½ tsp ginger
    ¼ tsp allspice
    ¼ tsp cloves

Author's Note

SEVERAL YEARS AGO, MY FATHER pulled me aside to tell me a true story from his family's past. It was a tale of a small Welsh village forever lost, of a community displaced, and of the resilience of simple country people who gave up virtually everything they owned for the good of those living in a faraway English city. It was, in fact, the material novels are made of.

Few people outside Wales are familiar with the sacrifice the people of Llanwddyn made when the Vyrnwy Dam was built, but after months of research, visiting the area myself, and knowing that my own ancestors lived through this experience, I feel as though I've come to know some of those villagers personally. They were real. Their loss was real. And their story deserves to be told.

In this novel, I've striven to maintain historical accuracy with regard to the building of the Vyrnwy Dam, St. John's Day, and the response of those who experienced these events firsthand, and although Gwen's story is fictitious, many of the characters in this book are based on real people who lived in Llanwddyn in the 1880s. The blacksmith, Erasmus Owen, really did help secure leases for the villagers so they could be compensated for the loss of their homes. As hard as it is to believe, the postman, Robert Jones, walked the roads between Llanfyllin and Llanwddyn every other day for twenty years. The seventy-five-pound stone said to be thrown by Sion Fawr at the St. John's Day festival still sits in the new churchyard, and the village cripple, Jack Llanwddyn, was cared for by his friends and neighbors because he had no home of his own.

The Vyrnwy Dam project was completed almost a decade after the villagers first learned of it, and when valves at the dam were finally closed, it took 361 days for the lake to reach its almost 13-billion-gallon capacity. As water started flowing down the village streets, the last of the villagers reluctantly abandoned Llanwddyn, and the buildings were razed. On November 23,1889, water poured through the dam's overflow for the first time, and on July 14, 1892, it finally flowed all the way through the newly built aqueduct to arrive in Liverpool.

The Liverpool Corporation planted trees on the hillsides around the reservoir and built a new hotel beside the lake. The area is now a popular vacation spot, particularly for fishermen and ornithologists, but if ever a drought hits the area long enough to impact the lake's water level, many more people flock to the reservoir to catch a glimpse of the shadowy remains of the original village of Llanwddyn lying beneath its rippling surface.

About the Author

SIAN ANN BESSEY WAS BORN in Cambridge, England, and grew up on the island of Anglesey off the north coast of Wales. She left Wales to attend Brigham Young University, Provo and graduated with a bachelor's degree in communications.

The author of several LDS novels and children's books, Sian has also written articles for the *New Era*, *Ensign*, and *Liahona* magazines.

Sian and her husband, Kent, are the parents of five children and the grandparents of two beautiful little girls and two handsome little boys. They currently live in Rexburg, Idaho, and although Sian has few opportunities to speak Welsh anymore, *Llanfairpwllgwyngyllgogerychwyrndrobwllllantysiliogogogoch* still rolls off her tongue.

Traveling, reading, cooking, and being with her grandchildren are some of Sian's favorite activities. Trying to do them all usually ends in chaos and laughter—which makes for the best days of all.